To Sara!
May your... in the garden... of Beauty!

TIME
IN A GARDEN

Mary A. Agria

NATURALS™ Editions
www.northforknaturals.com

Aug. 27, 2020

Copyright © 2006 by Mary A. Agria
ISBN-10: 1-4116-8702-7
ISBN-13: 978-1-4116-8702-8

Additional copies of this book may be purchased through
Lulu Publishing at www.lulu.com

To John, the love of my life who has put up with both my gardening and writing through good times and tougher ones, and without whose selfless and unfailing love and support this novel would be unthinkable.

To Rebecca my long-time writing buddy, to Jean and the Bay View, Michigan, Memorial Garden crew who contributed so much to shaping this book, and especially to Karen W. whose loving gift was the inspiration for TIAG in the first place and whose friendship and sage advice nurtured that seed of an idea at every step of the way. To Ada, Karen J. and Shirley in New York for invaluable tough "reads" of the final manuscript. To Sheila for her incredible creativity in helping shape the cover design.

To my daughters who for so many years were patient with a mom who "zoned out" to keep writing and who continue to enrich my life and work with their insights and wisdom. To my mother, Lydia, who read the manuscript far too many times when I needed it—and whose loving vision of life well-lived inspired, challenged and taught me the power of growing. To my delightfully spirited mother-in-law Rose. This book belongs to all of you.

The berm

Off ramp to Xenaphon, Michigan

Life began in a garden. We spend our lives trying to return.
Unknown

We all do battle with stony ground and unseasonable dry spells over the years. At sixty-two, I've had my share. To survive—even grow—beyond those difficult droughts of the soul, we learn to root out our share of quack grass, turn over spadefuls of spent or decimated ground and plant again. Though we may not call ourselves gardeners, it is the human experience.

And so, even as I begin my account of the past year—the strange flowering of love and friendship that changed my life beyond recognition, I am still out there on the berm alongside the interstate every Saturday morning, down on my knees in the Michigan mud. The months have come full circle. It is Spring again, at least by the calendar—April and perfect weather for staying home hiding out under the covers, sleeping in. I choose instead to risk, to get out there and cultivate hope in the form of those ephemeral wisps of green shooting up from the ground.

It's not always easy for new life or the future to force its way through the decaying stubble of the past. In my seventh decade I have run up hard against the reality of winter—that watershed season where newly turned earth can conjure up as many images of death as life. Dead-heading daffodils sets off ominous twinges in my lower back. But then at least I am not counted among the missing-presumed-deceased in the latest high school reunion face-finder.

I wasn't thinking about either gardens or headstones when I moved back to my rural roots in Xenaphon. Like many urban transplants in Chicago, I was tired of the pace and the stacked-crate logistics of apartment living, all the more so with the ominous palette of orange and yellow terrorist warning codes flashing night after night on the news networks. Early retirement offered the possibility of a simpler life, with green and open spaces around me.

Renters had been doing their best to trash the Victorian homestead on Third Street in Xenaphon that had been in my mother's family for three generations. I decided to reclaim that inheritance—moved in, went to work part-time for the *Xenaphon Weekly Gazette* and rarely looked back. My parents were deceased and my two daughters grown and settled. Between the corporate pension, a small salary instead of pay by the column-inch, and my single lifestyle, it was enough.

When a colleague in a neighboring office twisted my arm about the Saturday community garden project in nearby Aurelius, I didn't really resist. My expectations were simple. The garden promised to fill the blank spaces between press deadlines on Friday and the blank pages of Monday morning. I became one of a pitifully small crew of volunteers, ranging in age from our fifties to near nineties, strung out over that barren hillside. Each of us was caught up in our separate tasks. A crude, hand-lettered sign was a manifesto—a unifier—of sorts. *Welcome to Aurelius and Xenaphon*, it read. *Michigan's Garden Spot.*

The intentions on that signboard may have seemed clear enough for any passing motorist on the highway. Up close things seemed a whole lot fuzzier. It had begun to dawn on me that our so-called community garden was not really as advertised—a *garden* or a *community*. We volunteers really knew very little about each other. That patch we were tilling? An unpretentious 15 by 50-foot crescent of bare earth set just below the crest of a hillside of nondescript weeds and sandy clay overlooking the off-ramp of one of the state's major north-south tourist routes.

True, the *Garden Spot* itself had much older, more auspicious beginnings. But then that was a century ago. Aging has not been kind to this once thriving rural crossroads. By today's census demographics

Aurelius—technically where that little berm was located—hangs on as an unincorporated collection of a half dozen houses and a lone gas station on the outskirts of the county seat, Xenaphon.

A truck was braking hard on the off-ramp behind me. I straightened—suddenly light-headed. It was time to get my focus. The ground felt warm, alive under my hands. I breathed in the potent smell of it—the promise of rain, heavy like the thickening overcast.

As I looked around me, I expected the reassuring sight of our leader Bea Duiksma as she positioned string and wooden stakes, laying out the future, oblivious to the shredded tire fragments and tin cans still to be cleared from the site. Instead, she was talking animatedly with what appeared to be a new recruit.

My world was changing. I had no idea how much.

 # Chapter One

When it is evening, you say, 'It will be fair weather, for the sky is red.' And in the morning, 'It will be stormy today, for the sky is red and threatening.' You know how to interpret the appearance of the sky, but you cannot interpret the signs of the times. Matthew 16:2

I hadn't seen or heard it. But apparently sometime in the last 10 minutes, a newcomer had pulled a sleek late-model SUV into line behind the unimpressive collection of vehicles belonging to the garden crew. The very fact of the stranger's presence—and maleness, was intriguing enough to prompt curious glances from my fellow gardeners and an immediate go-get-him response from our crew chief Bea Duiksma.

Judging by the guy's shock of silver white hair and conspicuous furrows around the eyes, I would have guessed late-sixties. The net result was more time-worn than handsome. *Used,* my grandmother would have described him.

As to what had brought him here? I couldn't even pretend to speculate. To a casual passerby on the highway, none of this would qualify as very promising—either as a show garden or tourism magnet. Neither, on closer inspection, would our ragtag band of volunteer gardeners.

Last fall we had broken sod and dug in a bushel of daffs and a lesser assemblage of tulips, along with a few half-dead perennials that we had scrounged from the Xenaphon farm store. Even at the peak of the bulb season, the results looked rather forlorn: a meager dotting of reds and yellows against the muddy Rembrandt palette of the berm.

Undaunted, our fearless leader Bea had taken charge and was steering the newcomer over to my particular clump of bloomed-out daffodils. Whatever he thought of our operation, it was too late to back out gracefully now.

"I'm sure she'll be happy to show you the ropes," Bea said. "While I figure out how to put you to work."

So much for civilities. Bea turned and headed briskly toward her portable library, stashed on a rusty child's coaster wagon. Picking up a taped-together roll of graph paper, she studied the latest garden plan intently. Goodness knows, it didn't take a formal blueprint to conclude we needed whatever help we could get.

His back to me, the stranger watched her go. *Half intending*, I suspected, *to make a run for it*. Instead, he turned and made eye contact. Those blue-gray eyes were steel—*wary*. *Nobody's fool, this one*.

"Quite a…project you've got going here."

I laughed. "Cheer up…this'll be over before you know it," I told him. "We never work past noon."

"I seriously doubt that those two…over there—"

"Margo and Howard…."

"—will make it. They look ready to pack it in and it's barely—ten o'clock…."

So help me, the guy was wearing a Rolex. I fought a smile.

"Trust me…those two will be at it long after the rest of us call it quits. Pushing ninety and hard as nails, both of 'em."

Our newest volunteer did not look convinced. Still, after a split-second hesitation, he thrust out a hand. *A gentleman of the old school*, I chuckled to myself—someone accustomed to waiting for the woman to initiate contact. So much for chivalry. I work without gloves—obvious to us both as his hand closed around mine in greeting. Chlorophyll stains and mud make for an interesting patina.

"Adam," he said.

"Evie…well, really Eve."

I could read his reaction. *Is she putting me on?* Adam and Eve? Tentative laughter warmed the grey morning.

"You're kidding."

"No…German. Named after my grandmother, Eva."

9

"Makes sense. We *are* out here in a garden. Right?"

Just when I thought the man had little or no sense of humor, he smiled. It was one of those mega-watt flashes that signaled he got it—the bizarre incongruity of our whole situation. Maybe there was hope for the guy after all.

"So, Adam…you've gardened before?"

That was a wild guess on my part, based on nothing at all. Adam appeared to give the question more thought than it merited. After a conspicuous pause, he shrugged.

"Used to help my grandfather," he said. "More recently? Just herbs in a window box. Not anything…on this…scale."

"Local?"

I suspected the answer to that one before I threw it out there. Judging by the watch and the cut of those jeans, our newest volunteer was not a connoisseur of the local thrift shop.

"Cottager."

He rattled off the name of a familiar and upscale road on one of the nearby small sand-bottomed lakes. "Saw a sign about the community garden at the General Store on Route 131. Figured here's as good a chance as any to learn something about the local flora and fauna."

Not much value, I thought, in starting with bloomed-out daffodils. Snip and another petal-less green flower pod hits the ground. Then on to the next. I gestured toward the stands of slender fettuccine-shaped foliage around us.

"Deadheading," I told him, "isn't really rocket science. Bea says we've got to clip off these green pods on the daffs to make sure all the nutrients go to the bulb. In a week or two, we'll do the same to the tulips."

He frowned. "And the leaves…? you don't pull them up, twist or weave them together? I've seen that done—"

"It would look better, I'll admit. But Bea says it's best to leave the total leaf surface exposed. Eventually they'll yellow and dry out on their own. See that feathery foliage stretching out to fill in the gaps? Astilbe. And those strange red shoots? Peonies. In a week or two you won't even notice the old leaves are still there."

"You seem to…know what you're doing, then—"

"Bea anyway. She spent summers in her teens doing grunt work on the payroll of a bulb farm near Holland, Michigan—plus a lifetime putting together a spectacular reference collection on Midwestern plants."

"Impressive."

"Overkill maybe. Fortunately…for the rest of us, most of the tasks at hand demand more patience than skill. My claim to fame was inheriting a dog-eared copy of *Ten Thousand Garden Questions Answered* from my grandmother—and a habit of trying to rescue of half-price reject house plants from the local IGA. Mostly…in my case anyway, a failing proposition."

"Well, with the two of us, this…deadheading business won't take long," Adam said.

Another quick glance at the Rolex seemed to confirm that assessment. His eyes, grey and inscrutable like the darkening cloud cover, had taken on that faraway look again—as if already plotting his escape.

Bea's timing was perfect. From her no-nonsense stride, she obviously was prepared to enlighten us both. The shovels she was toting our way suggested that she had revised her battle plan—radically. Under an arm, she also had tucked that new garden layout, prepared to unroll it for us to study, if need be…to get our bearings.

"Can't do a lot without a tiller," Bea said. "But at least we can get started breaking sod."

Aiming a shovel at each of us, she gestured at a patch of weeds and mud adjacent to the main bed that she had laid out with stakes the previous September, then abandoned three feet into the project when the roto-tiller gave up the ghost.

"You mean work it…by hand?" The look on Adam's face was priceless.

This was not a job for Ralph Lauren. Spring was rainier than usual, and we were battling a primal ooze that once it hardens, clings like cement from the abandoned plant north of us. A casing of mud had already dulled the sheen on our new recruit's straight-out-of-the-box work boots.

"We used a tiller to shape that first bed last fall," Bea explained. "But it gave out before we could finish the second one. Vivian…that volunteer working over there with Margo and Howard, is trying to find us another one. In the meantime…."

In the meantime, Bea had an extra pair of hands and wasn't about to let that opportunity slip away. *You go, girl.* Stifling a grin, I silently cheered her on as I leaned on the shovel handle watching Adam poke around skeptically at the dense sod with the tip of his spade.

"Work from your knees," Bea suggested, "so you don't throw out your back."

Jaw set, Adam forced the steel edge into the ground. I heard his muffled out-rush of breath, sensed the explosive energy that single cut had taken.

"It's like...reinforced concrete down there—"

Bea nodded. "Now try a cut at right angles to that one."

For a split-second, I thought he might deck her with the business end of the spade. Instead, he maneuvered the steel edge to take advantage of that first thrust. With a minimum of false starts, he settled into a steady rhythm of slicing out manageable squares of sod.

"We've got a couple of extra pairs of gloves," Bea interrupted. "If you need 'em."

"Thanks...this is fine—"

Jaw set, Adam drove the spade into the ground yet again. I hated to admit it. Experienced or not—and whatever his pedigree, the man had a flair for sod removal. Once he had outlined a patch of weeds with strategic cuts, he would shim under the section and lift it off, roots and all. A periodic audible grimace underscored the sheer effort it took.

It was my turn. Setting the tip of the spade next to the ragged edge where the tiller had stopped, I experimented with a square of my own.

Planting a booted foot on the steel edge as I bore down, I took a leaf from my co-worker's book and did my best not to hunch. *That was great in theory.* Compared to his, my cuts were ragged and shallow. It took every bit of muscle power I could manage to drive the blade through the unruly mat of quack grass and stones into the clay mass below.

"Good grief, Bea...!"

Bea just smiled serenely. "You'll get the hang of it...! Have fun, kids."

With that she headed off toward the original bed again. From the look of it, our fellow-volunteers were embroiled in some sort of dispute over whether or not to divide one of the clumps of perennials.

"Yeah, right...!" I grumbled.

Planting the tip of the spade in what looked like a likely spot, I attempted to imitate Adam's technique. It wasn't working. My mood was growing blacker by the minute. After only a dozen or so spade thrusts, I was already feeling the sting of what were promising to be blisters.

At least, I consoled myself, *I wasn't the only one struggling.*

Although his exertions displayed considerably more strength, even a kind of easy grace, a rivulet of sweat had begun to trail down Adam's temple. He paused to catch his breath. When he picked up again, he flashed a wan smile and flexed his hands—gingerly—before tightening his grip on his spade handle.

"Rough going."

"Don't say it…," I told him. "I'm awful at this."

"It's about relaxing…going with the flow."

"Tough to do, when every slice half wrenches your arms out of their sockets."

"Look, Eve…." He hesitated—stopped. "I've been…watching you. At the last minute you keep anticipating the resistance and lock your knees. Not a good idea—"

"Show me, then…!"

I heard the challenge in my voice, as surprised by it as he seemed to be. *Why did this guy make me feel perpetually like I was about to fail a quiz?* Eyes narrowed and his brows contracted into a dark, puzzled line, Adam just looked at me—as if only now seeing…*really seeing*, who it was working alongside him in that barren mud-hole.

"All right," he said slowly. "I will."

Aligning his spade parallel to mine, in slow motion he positioned the blade and bore down. I heard the muffled thud of the knife-sharp edge plunge down through the matted grasses—a clean, deep cut. Working the blade free again, Adam repeated the series of movements. He made it look as easy as slicing butter in a dish.

"Now you try it."

Gritting my teeth, I did—but this time even more awkward and self-conscious. The results were disastrous. My foot slipped off the slick metal edge of the spade and when I tried to keep the sharp blade from slicing my ankle, the momentum inadvertently carried me down and sideways. I lurched against Adam more than fell—still, it was hard and out-of-control enough conceivably to knock us both down in the process.

"What . .the—?"

"Oh, m'gosh…!"

The Times-Crossword-and-cappuccino wardrobe notwithstanding, this guy was physical…even athletic. Sudden as the unexpected contact was, he was quicker. Dropping his spade, Adam shifted his body weight to steady himself and with both hands, drew me tight against him to try to regain not just his but my balance.

At least I had the sense to cooperate. I clutched at the fabric of his shirt for support—connecting eventually with the taut muscles of his back. Between that and Adam's broad shoulders braking my fall, the downward momentum stopped.

"You're going to hack off a foot at that rate…!"

Breathing hard, he suppressed an oath. It was no easy matter to disentangle ourselves. First he had to coax me out of that death grip I was using.

I glared at him, verbally prepared to give him both barrels. But after what I saw mirrored back at me in his face, my mouth didn't want to seem to move. I hadn't sensed a member of the opposite sex look at me like that in ages…and the very fact I noticed now, made me feel extremely uncomfortable.

For crying out loud, you're a grandmother, I told myself, *light-years beyond flirting with some stranger like a giddy schoolgirl. Get a grip!*

With the few rational brain cells still functioning, I opted for distance and dropped my hands as if making contact with a hot stove. For a split-second, my head swam—more disorienting even than that near-miss with that spade.

"So much," I said, "for…going with the flow—"

Adam didn't say a word.

"Are you two…all right over there…?"

From her tone, it was pretty clear Bea had caught the whole episode. Half amused, I sensed—half wondering what on earth we were doing.

"Just fine…," I lied.

"You're nuts, you know…!" Adam muttered. "The whole bunch of you. What in the…name of all that's holy do you…do *any of you* think you're doing out here? No tools…for crying out loud, a decent tiller or garden tractor would make short work of this."

14

I had to admit the comment wasn't patronizing. Just common sense. If Bea had in mind working the entire outline of the plot by hand, we'd be at it for a month. None of which changed my instinct to put some distance between me and my co-worker…in more ways than one.

"Look…," I snapped. "Our budget is…zip…! And we are …*volunteers*, for better or worse. If you want to call it quits… nobody's stopping you…!"

The words were barely out of my mouth when I knew I had no business sounding that testy. Truth was, without those lightning reflexes of his, I could have really hurt myself, or him—or the both of us.

"Point taken…," he said quietly.

Whatever reaction I was expecting, it wasn't that. The only clue to my co-worker's emotional state was that muscle working its way along the ridge of his jaw. Retrieving his shovel, he showed no sign of going anywhere.

"Adam, I…shouldn't have…jumped down your throat like—"

"Apology accepted."

We dug away in silence, while I tried to figure out just what about this guy bothered me so much. Or why I even cared? The mere fact of the questions surfacing was disturbing. Outside the ingrained vicissitudes of office politics, it had been years since a man's physical presence, starting with his motives—the "why" of him—had been high on my agenda.

It was unfair, but understandable, the source of my budding aversion. For nearly thirty years of marriage I had been coping up-close-and-personal with his brand of effortless urbanity, and more to the point, the damage it can do.

Make nice, I told myself. *If he quits, you could get stuck doing this alone.*

"Anyway…for what it's worth," I told him, "It's great finally to have another pair of hands going at it out here."

At that he looked up, his expression unreadable. "You actually do this every week?" he said.

"Me…personally? A couple of months last fall…and lately, whenever the rains let us get in here at all. Bea's office at the community action agency in Xenaphon is right next door to mine. She's been beating the bushes for help. I had the time."

"Family here?"

15

"At one time," I said. "My grandmother lived in the old homestead in Xenaphon until she died a number of years ago. I kept it as a rental until I retired."

Way too much information, a little voice in my head told me. Adam persisted.

"Married…kids…?"

"A daughter in Tucson and one outside of Chicago. College grads, grown and married. My husband Joel died five years ago."

"I'm sorry."

I let that one pass. Widowhood was a strange quirk of fate that I still found awkward to handle. After going on three decades of marriage based on very different notions of what constitutes fidelity, enough was finally enough—even given my over-developed sense of loyalty and faith in the redemptive powers of love. Before I was forced to confront the obvious, Joel's accident intervened.

Thankfully, my daughters continue to skirt the circumstances of their father's death—including my status as a not-all-that-grief-stricken widow, with the instinctive diplomacy of a toddler steering clear of an electrical outlet. Some things are just too dangerous to touch.

But then those weren't the kind of tidbits that wound up in my weekly news-about-town column—any more than guys like Adam just pop up digging sod on a Saturday morning. Why choose blisters out here on the berm? When he obviously could be steering a very different kind of tiller on that coke-bottle-green glacial lake of his.

Without my quite knowing how, he had drawn me out quickly enough. Time, I resolved, to turn the tables.

"And you?" I heard myself ask. "Wife…family?"

"None of the above. I'm in town settling my dad's estate—more complicated than I thought."

"And so, I suppose for some hard-earned…R&R you wind up out here…?"

Adam winced. "More a case of some very low…sales resistance on my part. I guess it was Bea's crazy garden poster that sucked me in. Tough to miss it. She seems to have plastered the thing all over the county."

Another embarrassment of sorts left me temporarily speechless. That "crazy poster" to which he was referring was—in fact—one of *my* more shameless pieces of hype. Whatever possessed me to bill the

16

community garden as "a venture in building our own little Eden" and a "hands-on way to jump-start community revitalization"?

Given the mud and the blisters, I could think of far more accurate appeals. For starters, *Risk life and limb…with a back-breaking, desperation move to lure traffic into town to tank up at the pumps and mini-mart of Fred's Stop 'n Save.* Well, anyway—apparently at least in the case of this one unlikely volunteer, the darn thing worked.

"*Caveat emptor*…buyer beware. Aren't computers wonderful?" I told him, trying not to sound defensive. "Truth is? That…*somewhat overzealous* sales pitch is my doing. So if you're having second thoughts about what you've gotten yourself into, don't blame Bea."

He looked straight at me, chuckled. I'd surprised him, that's for sure.

"You're in public relations?" he said. It wasn't really a question.

I was expecting the raised-eyebrow distaste that often goes with that revelation. Instead, what I read in Adam's tone and quirk of a smile was clearly intended as appreciation, even respect.

"Was," I told him. "Chicago. I got sick of the grind and moved back here—just over a year ago. Right now, I'm writing the community news columns part-time for the county weekly. The *weds-'n-deads*, as my boss likes to call it."

Adam laughed. "Quite a switch. You ever miss it?"

"Chicago, yes. Sometimes. The corporate rat race? Never. Not that I was high on the totem pole…just one of the little guys down the line. I loved copy writing, but still—"

"Still…there comes a time just to…hang it up."

Something in his reaction signaled this was getting way too personal. Only this time, it was his comfort zone that was being invaded.

"Do I detect a note of deja vu here, all over again?" I said.

His laughter had a brittle edge. "Got me. Thirty years in corporate sales. When the gate personnel at O'Hare and I started making a habit of greeting each other on a first-name basis, I decided it was time to take a breather."

"Leaping the turnstiles like that infamous TV commercial—?"

"Something like that."

"And now?"

He hesitated. "Clipping coupons, for the moment," he shrugged.

I was smart enough to know when I'd hit a wall. It was time to back off.

"Well, if it's a third age career you're contemplating, take heart. We late bloomers seem to be in the majority."

"So I hear."

Straightening from the latest lunge and thrust maneuver with the spade, I couldn't help notice the furrows that had settled in between his brows. That, and the ferocity with which he was going at a stubborn square of sod at his feet.

A low rumble of thunder spelled relief. But to everyone's credit, nobody bailed. We all just stood there like those tentatively rooted perennials of ours, faces turned toward…the roiling cauldron overhead. The brief respite from the monsoons was about to end.

"We'd better pack it in," Bea said.

We were not going to argue with her. After all that work, Adam and I had cleared barely a side-and-a-half of the rectangle. He took my shovel and started grabbing whatever else he found lying around while I ran to help Margot and Howard haul themselves up the berm to their car.

The chill edge to the wind gave us precious little time to stash the tools in the shed before the heavy curtain of rain descended. In the confusion, I didn't even have a chance to tell my co-worker so much as good-bye.

"See you next week," Bea shouted as we scrambled for our separate vehicles. At the entrance to the interstate, I noticed Adam's SUV ahead of me blink left toward the northbound on-ramp. The rest of us queued at the stop sign, headed home to Xenaphon.

Chapter Two

The real voyage of discovery consists of not in seeking new landscapes but in having new eyes. Marcel Proust.

What in the heck do you think you're doing out here? All the way home, that casual question from the new guy, Adam, kept running through my head. Truth was, I never really thought about it—not just the fact of the garden, the why or how or my modest role in creating it, but a lot of things.

Ever since my husband's accident, since I moved here to Xenaphon, there was a lingering aura of marking time, waiting for something to jerk me up short and make me figure out, *Where next?*

I had spent thirty years of my life working on a set of assumptions, most of which proved shaky at best. That love by definition lasts forever. That if you use people up the way they are, it is enough to get you through just about anything.

And now? The eyes that caught mine in the rear view mirror as I shut off the ignition in the driveway had that deer-in-the-headlights quality of those women in their burkas on the covers of the weekly news magazines: wise and wary, searching with peripheral vision for the nearest escape route. They were my eyes—yet taken out of context like this, they were strangely unfamiliar.

At least when I was writing, hidden behind the tortoise shell rims of my reading glasses, those crow's feet seemed less ominous. Living with Joel, I quickly learned there was a futility about the whole business

19

of aging anyway. After all, how young is young enough for a woman to save her marriage?

One thing no amount of rationalizing would alter or disguise. When it came to love and relationships, time was my enemy—or at least all the baggage that came with where my hard-won life lessons had taken me.

After Joel died, I had gone out on a blind date or two engineered by friends from work. They were decent enough guys who with a modicum of encouragement might have become a steady companion or even bed buddy. Something in my head and heart said, no.

Here in Xenaphon, not only age but every conceivable demographic was working against even that. Casual brushes with guys like that Preppie out on the berm—unnerving as it might have been after my long-standing monastic existence—were becoming fewer and further between. I had more or less made my peace with missing my daughters, though holding out the hope that with time, we would discover a closeness that had eluded us.

Was I willing to concede the rest as well? That adult love, mutual and passionate, in all likelihood had passed me by?

It was not premeditated, but I spent the rest of the weekend in a quiet frenzy cleaning out my closets. As domestic chores go, that annual Spring ritual has a vague Big Question, meaning-of-life quality about it, one of the few times we force ourselves to come to grips with the things in life we outgrow.

Judging by what was left on the hangers after my brutal weeding-out of the faded, outdated or woefully undersized, it is fortunate not to have to be concerned about fashion statements working for the *Xenaphon Weekly Gazette.* Casual pretty much does it.

When I limped into the office on Monday, my boss, George Herberg, was in rare form. He landed a few bunker-busters of his own. Someone, I concluded, must be slipping clandestine doses of truth serum into the village water supply.

"I'd ask, 'How's your love life?'" he called out from behind his disaster of a desk. "But from the shape you've been in after the last couple of weekends, I'm not sure I want to know."

"That's harassment, George."

I should be so lucky. George was an inveterate flirt, but reading between the lines, I sensed his taste ran in other directions. "Coming out" in Xenaphon was *not* the best idea in the world.

At least he noticed I was female and still breathing. Sometimes I wasn't so sure myself.

"Well, then, how about I offer to take you over to the emergency room instead?"

Humor was a dangerous commodity after the kind of manual labor I had been indulging in. "You know what they say about only hurting when you laugh, George."

With a groan, I eased myself onto the hard oak swivel chair in front of the clutter that passed for my work area. It wasn't much neater than George's.

"Sorry about that, Evie," he said. "I've got the coffee on. How about I bring ya some? Peace offering."

"You don't have to, George. The smell hit me the minute I walked in the door—heavenly. I'll crawl over there eventually."

George was already on his way. "I suggest you move as little as possible until you've washed down a handful of aspirin. Something stronger, if you've got it."

He handed me the steaming cup, grinned as I took a cautious sip. George's coffee would peel the paint off a barn. Momentarily anyway, the jolt took my mind off my aches and pains.

"I assume it's that pathetic looking berm that's got you hobbling around like this," he said. "What the heck are you guys doing out in that garden anyway?"

I told him a little about Bea's plan—to stir up some civic pride, however modest. A potential tourist had to drive through Aurelius before hitting Xenaphon. With unemployment in the county seat around twelve percent, it made sense if the route were a little more appetizing.

"You know, Bea...she gets these causes," George reminded me. "Two years ago it was that patch of veggies out behind the Presbyterian church. God's Little Acre. Who'd she sucker into this one, besides you?"

"Vivian Mortis, that retired school counselor. Howard and Margo Freelander...I think he used to work for the county...some kind of number cruncher. They actually live over in Aurelius."

"Is that the elderly couple you see on a regular basis poking around downtown together, holding each other up? She always wears her hair in strange pillbox-shaped mounds on top of her head. Gotta be eighty, at least."

"More like ninety."

I didn't add to Vivian's credentials that the poor woman was obviously so shell-shocked after nearly thirty years in the school district that she ducked and covered every time a truck backfired on the off-ramp behind her. Or that Margo was so sight-challenged, she routinely pulled up the few legitimate patches of perennials with the omnipresent Creeping Charlie.

While not part of the official garden crew, Margo's husband joins us more often than he ought to. If ever I saw a candidate for a Pacemaker, it's Howard. Since none of us are certified in CPR, that gives his exertions on the berm an unsettling sense of drama.

Then there was our resident control freak, obsessed with imposing some sort of order in this improbable Eden. Roger Van Nuyl—one of Bea's colleagues from Social Services—offers his expertise as Master Gardener, churning out rolls of garden plans in his microscopic block printing.

What George would make of that? I could only imagine. No one would accuse George of being a neat-nik.

Then, of course, there was our newest recruit, Adam. I knew better than to go there—on many levels a bad idea, and not just for the reaction it would get from my boss.

"They're really an interesting bunch," I told George, brusquely. "And you gotta admit, the off-ramp's really starting to look a lot better, considering. At least we're getting rid of the shredded truck tires and beer cans."

George had that look on his face that usually signaled more work for me. I tried ignoring it.

"So, why don't you write about it?" he said finally. "Torturing perennials is big these days with the weekend set and those syndicated columns on gardening cost an arm and a leg. The stuff from the cooperative extension is way too techy. No Martha Stewart either. Just practical, earthy. You could slip in little digs about civic cleanup in general. Might just take off."

"And we could call it, *Doing Time in a Garden*," I suggested. "Now that could really increase readership with the inmates over at the county lockup. Especially if I include stuff about grow lights and pot plants."

George ignored the sarcasm. And resisted cracks about felons as a potential readership base.

"I like that," he said. *"Time in a Garden.* Put together a couple of columns to see how it goes, and I'll start running it."

"Sounds like that old Jim Croce song. Except right now the only thing in a bottle I'm interested in, is liniment—that, or a good, stiff drink!"

George didn't have time for a comeback. The phone was ringing. But from that scowl he shot in my direction, I could tell he was dead serious about the column, at least as serious as George ever got.

Just what I needed, another project. The caffeine was finally kicking in which made the prospect somewhat more palatable.

While George chatted with the sheriff, I started sorting through the piles of junk mail on my desk. In spite of myself, the weed-out was grounded on a whole new set of priorities. Pitching most, I set aside the stuff from the farm bureau that would seem to fit: soils, growing conditions, weather projections for the summer.

Truth was, I wasn't as clueless about perennials as I pretended. My grandmother, Eva, had done her best to hook me on the hobby. But then that was a long time ago. I had put an awful lot of space and cold urban steel and concrete between myself and those memories.

"Evella," she used to call me as I tagged along behind her in the arrow-straight rows of bush beans and bell peppers with the feathery carrot tops tickling at my ankles. Gramma Eva was tireless. After a while, my hands aching and green with chlorophyll from pulling weeds, I would look for a place to sit down or an excuse to call it quits.

"When is it gonna be done, Gramma?" I would complain in that world-weary, high-pitched pre-adolescent voice.

Her answer was always the same. Or at least it was a variation on a theme.

"A garden is never done, Evella. It grows. It changes. It becomes tired and rests for a while and then it starts over again."

"And if you just…quit…? The garden dies—?"

"You can do that," she would say in that deliberate Germanic way of hers. "You can neglect it…let a garden go to seed and let the weeds take over. But it's not really…dead. Under those broken stalks it's still there—still a garden, just waiting for someone to wake it up, to love it, to help it be what it was meant to be."

"Well, then maybe you can just let it stay…*grass…in the first place*!"

Gramma Eva would laugh. "See that lawn out there, Evella? If you look hard…*really hard*? Even under that plain old patch of green—there's a garden. Just waiting for you to see it, with all its amazing colors and smells and tastes. Waiting, Evella. Beautiful."

Wise woman, my grandmother—planting in my childhood memories the seeds of what she hoped would be my future. It had taken my boss, George, with his poking and prodding to make me fully appreciate it. After all, wasn't he asking the same thing of me? That column was just another not so subtle challenge for me to risk and grow and find the words to capture my love for this place, for this unlikely Eden to which I had returned.

I had a lot of catching up to do if I was going to come up with any kind of a credible column week after week. My colleague Bea's running tutorial out on the berm every weekend would help. I was becoming a fan of the home improvement channel on TV, one of the few diversions of any note that comes with the basic package. It would be easy enough systematically to begin journaling on the subject.

Then too, until now—from whatever motives—I had resisted trying to revive Gramma Eva's garden. It still wasn't too late in the season to salvage a flat or two of vegetables from the local co-op and dig them in. Potential failure or not, at the very least my hands-on digging around in the backyard could lead to some interesting panicked Q&A calls to the Ag Extension office.

By one o'clock, quitting time, my desk at the *Gazette* was more organized than it had been in ages. And despite some lingering misgivings, I was beginning to make mental notes about possible column topics. I had to admit, the idea had a certain ring to it. More to the point, I hadn't been as excited about anything in a long, long time.

When I got home, the message light on my answering machine was blinking. A quick replay netted a rough column-inch for my community news column. Baptist Church organist Edwina Fremont had broken her hip and would be moving to a nursing home in South Carolina

24

near her oldest daughter. The daughter, I reminded readers, was the homecoming queen and runner-up to Miss Xenaphon her senior year in high school. Fascinating the trivia you come up with snooping around in the old newspaper morgue.

Stopping long enough for a quick yogurt lunch, I sketched out the Edwina Fremont story on my laptop. It was a tough business, since my hands were still curled taut as if still clutching a shovel handle. Then on a whim, I called up the latest entry in my electronic journal, and read:

> We *keep calling ourselves a team, a crew, always in the plural. Truth is, if gardening is about community, our little Saturday berm squad doesn't qualify.*
>
> *Our collective lack of skill is obvious enough. But what brings us together in the first place? Now that's a lot subtler. About all we share, as I see it, is that each of us out there seems to be carrying some private pain shut up inside us. Like an undiagnosed angina wrapping itself around our hearts, that cuts us off from really getting close to one another.*
>
> *And so, it took this newcomer to our ranks to hit the nail on the head. Maybe we need to ask why we are there, before we can decide where we're going. If you're going to garden successfully, it helps to know where you are, what was there before. In rural America, we are never far from that history.*

Intuitively, my brain went into the edit mode. Picking up the last paragraph, I started a new file for Garden Columns, cut and paste.

```
If   you   are   going   to   garden
successfully, it helps to know where
you are.  That means keeping track of
soil  conditions,   weather,   plants
selected,   and   possible   footed  or
winged  intruders.    It   may   be
impossible to control the variables,
but  at  least  keeping  a  journal  or
diary helps sort out what you, the
```

gardener, are up against.

Then uncurling my aching hands, I just let the words flow—taking me where they wanted to go:

Right now there's a team gardening out east of town near the interstate off-ramp: trying to make it look a little better. The leader came up with idea from another thriving community north of here. "The Beautiful", that town calls itself. And to prove it, they have got foot-wide ribbons of petunias flowering along the curb from one end of town to the other.

It is hard to cultivate a climate of hope if the main source of income for the few remaining residents under the age of forty is rebuilding junkers abandoned in the Park 'n Ride lot. Or worse, growing suspiciously-leafed flora in abandoned garages with tar paper over the windows. It didn't start out that way.

Peculiar thing about towns settled around the 1850s in this part of the country. Not only from the architecture but the town names themselves, you would think the place had been settled by refugees from ancient Empires of the Mediterranean or overly optimistic graduates of Eastern classical academies. Names like Pompeii [pronounced Pom-pay-eye], Ithaca and Remus are all over the map around here.

In fact, the early settlers were not all that glamorous. A lot of them were just malcontent East Coast folk trying to upgrade their fortunes on the frontier. Still, when they came, they brought with them aspirations for

civilization as lofty as brick-clad
emporiums, opera houses over the
hardware store, and school houses
built to last.

We all know what happened. A
century-and-a-half later? Many of
those storefronts and classrooms are
abandoned, done in by population
drains, consolidation and mega-chains.
Except for government, and you know
how most rural folk feel about that.

Now, this does not mean we all
should run out and buy a bunch of
perennials or seed packets. But maybe
we ought to think about planting the
notion around town that we are a great
place to live or even cultivate some
new ideas to help outsiders feel that
way about us, too.

Great gardens don't just grow.
Folks make it happen.

A quick word count confirmed it was a little long for a column. But it could be worse. For a first try anyway.

I was on a roll. With the home improvement channel blaring in the background, I started churning out notes in my electronic journals, including a lot of technical stuff I had been learning about spring gardens crawling around out there on the berm. Dinner was unpretentious—cold soup out of the can while I started cutting and pasting files by topic so I stood a reasonable chance of finding the references later.

By the time I ran out of steam, it was close to nine o'clock. The lights in the neighborhood were beginning to flicker out. I took one last quick read through the file of my journal I was working on, then tapped in a final paragraph before shutting the computer down for the night.

Nice, too, about gardening, I wrote. *When the head hits the pillow, I'm ready.*

Chapter Three

One of the first signs of civilization is the presence of a garden. When plants take root, so do people. Planting a garden says: here is a community...here are people willing to commit to a place and to one another. Human survival depends on it. Notes from a gardener's journal.

The entry today in my journal read:

Saturday, May 29. Unseasonably hot, humid. But at least it's stopped raining. Out on the berm, our numbers had grown. There were the regulars Bea and Vivian, Margo and Howard, plus a burly unemployed Teamster client of Bea's.

Artie the Teamster loaned us not only his killer sod-buster, but the muscle to go with it. Fortuitous, since by now last week's swamp hardened from the unexpected heat wave into a brick-hard surface that would have made our previous attempts at hand-spading impossible.

I could not decide whether I was disappointed or vaguely relieved that the newcomer Adam was conspicuously absent. Bea noted that fact with a disinterested shrug.

"Easy come, easy go," she sniffed. "Gardening's a distance event...a marathon not a sprint."

For my part, I couldn't suppress a lingering twinge of curiosity about our defector. Volunteering for a garden project in Aurelius was hardly a mainstream choice of upscale charities—not with a regional hospital and a dozen other aggressive non-profits out beating the bushes for help on a regular basis. Unless, of course, a guy really had a thing for flora and fauna.

The speculation was short-lived. I drew the assignment of following Artie the Teamster and his tiller with a hard-tined rake. The ideas was to toss back into play any sod clumps that would have evaded a second pass by the tiller.

Two hours later my forearms were stiff and aching. Pools of sweat had soaked through the back of my olive drab tee and threadbare jeans. A far cry, I found myself thinking, from my day-to-day of tracking down the local birthdays, engagements and Golden Wedding celebrations that otherwise evaded the public notice.

```
The O'Connor farm is up for auction
and St. Rosalie's Rosary Society is
holding a bake sale to help the family
relocate.   The sheriff speculates
that three recent break-ins on Carver
Lake cottages are the work of local
teens looking for booze.  Despite
local custom,   folks are being
encouraged to lock their houses until
the perpetrators are caught.
```

My partner Artie had settled into a curious stream-of-consciousness social commentary of his own. Part profanity at the performance of the tiller and part editorial on the state of the local economy that led to his current layoff from the milk bottling plant. As was, the bottling job was a far cry from his once-lucrative stint hauling stone for the cement plant. Just how many times can one human being survive a major career transplant? We rural folk were writing the book on the subject in the past two decades.

On the third pass with the tiller, the newly turned earth began a subtle rebellion of its own, releasing microscopic dust clouds that gave a serious workout to my daily regime of antihistamines. Still, around noon our dusty and over-heated crew gathered in an impromptu bonding ritual. We laid the gardener's cloth across the newly turned bed.

Margo, Howard and I held the corners. Vivian and Artie the Teamster fretted over tucking the dark mesh in place with stakes and fieldstones.

Artie's take on the results? "If that doesn't stop the [expletive] weeds, nothing will."

We picked up the tools, and headed for our cars. I didn't quite make it to the Taurus before Bea flagged me down. In a moment of weakness, I agreed to hit up two or three of the local nurseries during the week for hardy perennial stock. Ideal would be drought resistant plants that would blossom into the summer or even the fall with the minimum of care.

I tucked the sheet of addresses Bea gave me in my Day Planner around mid-week, then shoved the whole thing in my briefcase. Forgot all about it.

Momentarily, my writing had hit a mini-drought. A week of journal entries had deteriorated to a banal series of weather forecasts:

Saturday, second week in May - Dry and high eighties. Anyone who waxes lyrical in song or rhyme about the glories of Spring in Michigan never experienced a swarm of no-see-ums.

It seems my week at the newspaper had evolved into an endless series of crises. Worst were a cranky hard drive on the main office computer and unanticipated labor pains on the part of the classified ad sales rep. In the excitement of the moment, the woman deleted the entire week's gleanings with a single keystroke, then left us with the mess while she went off to give birth.

Finally by about 4 o'clock Friday it occurred to me that it would be tough gardening this weekend on the berm without plants. My intentions were good when I volunteered last Saturday to be responsible for soliciting some more plant stock. As so much in my life, the details simply got lost in the shuffle.

There was still time to make amends. The most likely nursery was Groft's, usually a ten-minute trip. But this was Friday afternoon, the county's equivalent of a rush hour. In just a matter of hours, a fair share of the state's population migrates south to north. Add to that the omnipresent road construction and a trickle of locals on the final legs of their homeward commute, and the result? Bumper pool. Thanks to my procrastination, I was in the middle of it.

 Chapter Four

Definition of a weed: a perfectly good plant that winds up where it doesn't really belong.   Overheard in a garden, Bay View, Michigan, summer 2004.

I tried staying on secondary roads on the way to Groft's, but it wasn't much of an improvement over the interstate. Funny how we gravitate toward what we try hardest to avoid. The irony of the situation occurred to me as I sat sweating through multiple light-changes at a crossroads about a mile from the nursery.

How had I gotten myself into this in the first place? Successful ad copy writer or not, direct sales per se had never been my long suit. My late husband, Joel—the absolute master of cold calls—used to tweak me on the subject every time I was tempted to take the routinely offered chances to move up along the food chain into major account management at the ad agency.

"On paper, Kiddo? You sizzle. One-on-one? A day-old campfire. Sales means larger than life, my girl. Either ya got it…or ya don't!"

It used to make my blood boil. But in my heart, I knew he was right. If I were a novelist, even I would consider my persona "flat". More to the point, so did Joel.

Joel's flings of choice, as near as I could tell, tended to be young, leggy, chatty fashion dolls with enough *sizzle* to spare. Judging by the turnover, he also must have bored easily—my way of rationalizing the aroma-copia of scents that mysteriously came and went on his clothes. My dubious consolation, as I gritted my teeth through his snow-jobs aimed in my direction? At the end of the day, he was still there at home and hearth, even if only to recharge his batteries.

Pathetic, in retrospect. All of it. But then life doesn't come equipped with instant-replay or quick fixes to reconcile one daughter chiseling a pedestal for her father with another pleading with me to leave and take her with me.

Well, *sizzle* or not, it was time to suck it up and steel myself for the pitch. My fellow gardeners were depending on me, and realistically, I had barely a ten minutes before close of business at Groft's to mount a successful appeal to the owner and load up whatever loot I could scrounge.

At least I had started out dressed for success. Instead of jeans, for some reason I had gone up-scale this morning with a tan short-sleeve tee and pleated black linen dress pants. On a whim, I topped them off with a cameo and matching earrings that had belonged to my grandmother. My boss liked to tease me about my 1910-classic look. Unfortunately, by the time I turned into the Groft parking lot, I was feeling rumpled and out of sorts.

This was not going well. Only three vehicles were left in the lot—obviously, the staff's. The lone clerk was already at the door, keys in hand, ready to close up. With a pointed frown at her watch, the young woman scowled and wandered off to track down the nursery owner.

Perennials, she told me, were out back. An open greenhouse door appeared a likely shortcut, so I headed through it. I promptly stopped dead in my tracks.

Jungle. If ever the word had application, it was here. Vines snaked along the girders and cut-leaf tropical floor plants that normally would have long since been shipped off to some retailer, trailed into the aisles.

All things pointed here to spectacular neglect. Grasses sprouted up in the cement pipework at my feet. Trays of black starter pots were set out haphazardly along the potting tables. The seedlings they contained sprawled like adolescents after a growth spurt, elbowing one another for room.

"I understand you're looking for me."

I was not alone in Paradise, and I had heard that voice somewhere

33

before. Steeling myself for an even more major sell job than anticipated, I swung around—dumbfounded. In the doorway through which I had just come stood none other than our erstwhile volunteer from the berm. *Adam.*

The paper had run an ad months ago announcing a change in management in this, the area's oldest nursery and greenhouse operation. That fact only now began to register.

"Adam Groft…," he said. "And you're Eve…?"

"Brennerman."

Groft—as in Groft Nurseries? Obviously that name could *not* be a coincidence. For the life of me, I didn't know how to react. I bought time as I wiped my sweating palm on my slacks, then took the initiative and stretched out my hand in greeting.

Those smoke-gray eyes of his didn't reveal much. Still, he clearly was not expecting this any more than I was. My mouth didn't seem to want to function, but I forced the words all the same.

"So, then you're the…you must have—"

"Inherited the place, six months ago." He chuckled, but there was no humor in it. "Go figure. After a lifetime of evading anything green—except a regular paycheck and an occasional margarita? The prodigal son winds up with the farm."

"Well, you've already got the…*sales job* down pat," I told him. "*Learning about the flora and fauna…*I think you said?"

That was a cheap shot, one I instantly regretted. Adam just shrugged it off.

"Either that," he said, "or look for a buyer. Fast."

All my finely honed arguments about a long-time company reputation for civic responsibility migrated at least two climate zones south. The nursery was in extremis and this man knew far more about tulips and daffs than he was willing to admit out there on that berm two weeks ago. There was no sense in being politic.

"You saw what we're up against in Aurelius."

"True."

Thank God, that knowing quirk of his eyebrow didn't smack of condescension. I was prepared to grovel, even suspend judgment about that aw-shucks demeanor he had been feeding me out on the berm, but not put up with that.

"We laid the gardener's cloth last weekend," I told him. "That

34

sort of shot the budget for the time being."

"And you're looking for cheap...?"

"Free," I amended. "Easy grow, prolific bloomers, drought tolerant."

"Suggestions...?"

Surely, the guy could sense how nervous I was? By now I was paranoid enough to believe him capable of deliberately making my pitch as difficult as possible.

Earlier in the day, I had been making a point of memorizing the Latin genus and species names of everything likely to wind up on the business end of my trowel—tough, when I was still trying to imprint a new cell phone number in my memory banks. Through gritted teeth, I rattled off as much as I could remember from the list Bea gave me.

"Rudbeckia, Monarda, Erigeron...."

I hesitated. He was looking at me as if I had just returned from the moon.

"Or maybe...if you think that's too much, just throw in some...*Digitalis*...?" I stammered. "In case I decide to brew up some *hemlock*...for later...if I don't come back with some plants...?"

As in Sophocles downing the poisoned cup? What on earth was wrong with me? Zinging one-liners had never been my style. I didn't deserve it but fortunately, although Adam look pained, he ignored the sarcasm.

"I assume you mean Deadly Nightshade? You...*are* talking about classic prairie plants, here. *Simple English would help*...!"

"Okay, then...Brown-eyed Susans, cone flowers, bee balm. Or maybe Fleabane...I think it's sometimes called wild aster."

All the while, I could see him mentally calculating acreage and the tab. Prolific bloomers that were likely to survive our minus twenty Fahrenheit ski season don't come cheap—you buy them in pots by the inch, not the flat. After his close encounter with that empty bed, Adam knew exactly what a skimpy planting would accomplish. It didn't take a degree from Cornell in horticulture to figure out we would need one heck of a lot.

"Fair enough. I'll make sure Dutch gives you what you need," he said curtly. "And helps you load up. A couple of everything you don't have out there already should do it."

Nobody had to tell me this nursery couldn't afford even half of what I—or he—was proposing. The peeling white paint filtering the greenhouse glass did that all by itself. It took a minute to process the enormity of what Adam intended.

"We weren't expecting that…you don't have to—"

He waved me off before the words were even half out of my mouth. "Take it."

"Well, then…we can bring the pots back. They're probably reusable."

"Not necessary."

"At least we…you…*won't* have to dig 'em in."

Finally, a genuine hint of a smile. But before I could even pull myself together enough to blurt out even a simple, *Thank you*, Adam had already turned and was walking back toward the office.

While I waited for Dutch to make an appearance, my thoughts were churning and murky like the throwback of a winter sky outside. That ruler-sharp line of clouds low on the horizon that trailed me all the way from Xenaphon was a dead-giveaway. A front was moving out—with the promise of clear, cooler weather beyond.

Not so down here on terra firma. Totally out of character, I hurl some pretty outrageous slings and arrows in Adam Groft's direction. And in response? He practically turns over the keys to the proverbial store.

My instinct was to cut and run. But by now this wiry wisp of a guy, as seasoned as an old leather glove, was headed my way with two pots in each hand. Obviously, Dutch.

"Ya got somewhere to stash these?"

"H-here…."

Fortunately, Dutch was the silent take-charge type. While I stood there trying not to drop the plants, he popped the hatchback on the wagon and crawled inside, maneuvering down the back seat in the process.

"It's gonna be tight," he muttered.

An understatement. My rising anxiety level translated quickly into wildly inept handling of the foliage, as load after load, I followed the ancient nursery employee back behind the greenhouse to where the perennials were being acclimatized to the spring temperatures.

From time to time as we worked, I caught him looking my way with this odd expression on his face. But whatever he thought of the windfall or my bizarre behavior, he kept his opinion to himself.

"Mr. Groft—Adam...he helped us work on the community garden a couple of weeks ago," I volunteered finally. "We do appreciate this...."

"Got your hands full with that one."

True enough. Although from his tone, I couldn't be sure whether he was talking about the berm or his boss. Or both.

"You've worked here a long time...for the Grofts?"

"Too long."

I laughed—apparently the intended result. Based on the knowing wink Dutch aimed in my direction, I seem to have passed some kind of test.

"Seventy-some years ago I started," he drawled. "This dumb gangly kid...with a gosh almighty crush on the first owner's wife. Just kind of hung around after that. Wound up in love after all—just not quite like I thought...!"

He grinned, hefted two pots in each of his huge hands for emphasis. Then giving up on the cargo area, carefully tucked them in next to the gear shift on the passenger side, leaving room for more.

"A little like running an adoption agency," he said. "Plants. You never know when you grow 'em where they're gonna wind up. Heck of a lot happier startin' here, though, than their just popping up in a piece of ground someplace. When they walk out this door? Usually its 'cause somebody wants 'em—"

I sensed I was about to hit on a touchy subject. Adam had hinted as much. Still, I couldn't resist poking around the edges.

"Must be hard for you...new owner and all. Probably a lot of changes—?"

"Always a good kid, that young Adam." Dutch said abruptly. "Used to follow his Grandad Jakob around this place like a shadow. Heck of a homecoming for a man...after all these years. Hard to sort out your options, when the ground is heaving under you. Just cut and run until you're clear of it? Or do you hang on to the plow, keep it as steady as you can—?"

Any way you played it, life would never be the same. I'd been there, done that. And the choices weren't pretty.

"Before that...you worked for his father?"

Dutch looked thoughtfully in my direction before tackling that one. I got the feeling it was more me—my reasons for asking, than the answer itself that was the source of his hesitation.

"It's a funny thing," he said slowly. "Most garden folk are pretty good with people. Takes a whole lot of patience to grow a plant. You set 'em in, give 'em room to grow, fertilize, watch out for the stuff that's gonna choke 'em out, water 'em—mostly though…and some say this is the hardest part, be prepared to hunker down and wait."

"Tough thing to learn sometimes."

Dutch's smile was kind, maybe even a little sad. "Some folks, Miss?" he shrugged, shook his head. "They never do."

The sun was heading on the downward run, and hard as we had been working, I felt a sudden chill. Jaw clamped tight, Dutch was hell bent on maneuvering the last half dozen pots into the front seat without damaging the fragile stalks and stems.

I couldn't shake the lingering picture he had left me with of a sun-tanned boy of six or so clambering over the potting benches. The boy's face and hands were streaked with mud, loving every minute of it.

"So…Dutch is giving you what you need…?"

Startled, I instinctively turned toward the sound. How long had Adam Groft been leaning in that greenhouse doorway watching us? That was anyone's guess. Dutch didn't even flinch, just kept loading the last of the pots into the front seat of the Taurus

"Yes…," I stammered. "Thank you, again. They're beautiful."

Dutch looked over at his boss then back at me. I couldn't read the older man's smile, except to sense there was no malice in it.

"Like I said, Miss…," Dutch said gruffly, "these plants here are a lot like people. Wind up in some pretty interesting places—not necessarily a bad thing, mind you. Just interesting."

It took a while to fish around in the bottom of my purse for the car keys. By the time I felt the familiar key-chain tag in my hand and looked up again, the two men had disappeared from sight. For the longest time afterward I just sat in Taurus in the nursery parking lot, hands stiff and awkward on the wheel. The words began to jell in my mind:

```
     We rural folk are the absolute
masters of suffering in silence. Our
struggling weekly papers are full of
the stories of loss, mainly glossed
over by the euphemisms we create to go
```

    with it. We learn quickly to read
    between the lines.
         Another family is about to lose
    the farm? The obituary runs on page
    20 and the "gossip" column talks about
    your kids traveling to get to the
    funeral. Auction ads are buried in the
    classifieds a couple of months later.
    The survivors move into town? We read
    neighbors are planning an open house.

Not a promising beginning for one of those motivational columns George was expecting of me.

But then there was nothing nice or printable either about what Adam Groft was facing, or what he appeared tempted to do with that nursery he had inherited. Truth was? It was getting a whole lot tougher to dislike this man. Dig down beneath the surface—the clothes and the superficial aura of self-confidence that smacked so much of Joel—and I could sense intuitively where Adam was coming from.

I had a lot of practice—knew desperation when I saw it. Though in Adam's case, the source remained a mystery, my own sorry history was transparent enough. Try living decade after decade with someone whose definition of love leaves out the part about fidelity. Try coping with a daughter who despises you for sticking with the relationship and another who blames you for its failure. My choices or lack of them had contributed mightily to that hell…but a hell it was, for all that.

Just stuff it…suck it up. Never verbalize your private agony to anyone. Meanwhile all that pain eats away at you from within, until you are nothing but a hollow, empty shell, no longer asking what matters or caring what it would take to turn your life around. I had acclimatized myself very well to these particular realities, knew all the symptoms.

The counter girl from the nursery cast a curious glance my way as she crossed the gravel lot to her car. Moved on. So, eventually, did I. But I took my time and a lot of back roads before I hit the village of Xenaphon limits.

As I pulled in front of my Victorian fixer-upper, the living room light snapped on, set on auto-timer. It was a banal bit of fiction to create that illusion of warm bread just out of the oven and the sound of voices in the kitchen. Right now, I needed that.

 Chapter Five

What is a weed? A plant whose virtues have not yet been discovered. Ralph Waldo Emerson

Even spending the night crammed in my eighty-nine Taurus wagon, the future Aurelius perennial garden was none the worse for wear. I couldn't say the same for my own state of mind. Sleep hadn't come easy—leaving me tired and more than a little depressed.

Fortunately, the reception the haul got from my coworkers at the berm was enough to revive anybody's sagging spirits. When the atta-girls and hugs subsided, Vivian, Artie the Teamster, Margo, Howard and I began to unload the treasure trove of pots.

We left to Bea the problem of making order out of the stash. By now she had done a three-sixty from incredulous to elated to positively shell-shocked. Clutching her sketchbook for dear life, she nervously stood by the open hatch, jotting down the plant species as fast as she could.

"You got all this...*where*—?"

I had told Bea the source already. Twice. This time—reluctantly, I elaborated.

"Adam Groft. You know...the guy who showed up that Saturday to help and never came back."

"You're kidding. As in, Groft Nurseries?"

"He owns the place now. The...senior Groft died a while back."

"Well, Junior must have cleaned out the greenhouse. Where on earth are we going to plant all this? We *really are* going to have break more sod—"

A universal groan greeted that proposal. Bea quickly reconsidered.

"Okay. Short-term? We'll pack them in where we are...then worry about crowding later. We're going to need more box cutters, though—some of those pots are rootbound. I only brought one for slicing through the ground-cloth."

Artie the Teamster offered to make a run to the hardware for a half dozen of the blades. Bea, meanwhile, would stand sentinel at the bed pointing out the perfect spot for the contents of each of those ten and twelve-inch pots. Vivian, Margo, Howard and I would step and fetch.

"You told him we'd give him...Groft, a receipt—right? For taxes," Bea fretted.

"He didn't seem particularly worried about that. We aren't really officially tax-exempt—"

"Look at the prices on this stuff. Of course it matters."

"Bea, stop feeling so guilty. I only asked for a dozen pots—max. I don't know what got into the guy."

That wasn't quite true. I didn't tell Bea about the over-the-cliff look on Adam Groft's face or what I concluded about the financial shape of Groft Nurseries. There didn't seem to be any point enlightening her. It would only stir her up all over again. Our octogenarian Margo wasn't mincing words, though.

"Don't look a gift horse in the mouth, Bea!" she said. "You want a garden here anytime in our lifetimes? Howard is ninety. I say—take the stuff and run."

She also pronounced our benefactor a "hunk". Time, I decided, to change the subject.

"Look, Bea," I said. "I'll draft a nice model thank-you letter. We can leave it on my computer for future donors. Margo's right—we really need this stuff."

Vivian hadn't said much. When she finally spoke up, her reaction was typical caution.

"How on earth will we know where to put it?"

Bea had brought her sketchbook with a few likely possibilities, but then she hadn't expected this windfall. Flipping to a blank sheet, she quickly sketched out the long and relatively narrow kidney-shaped berms.

Separating them from each other was the small grassy strip we had left intact.

"Okay…read the plant tags before you set them down somewhere. The tall stuff—three feet or more, goes at the top of the beds and toward the ends closest to that central green space." Bea pointed to the spot on her drawing. "All along the lower borders? Set in the chunky six-inch or less creepers that can hold their own against encroaching weeds. Everything else goes somewhere in between."

I watched the shaded patches taking shape on her sketch pad. The configuration would draw attention straight to the center, then pull the eye outward along the natural slope of the berm. Bea held the sketch at arm's length and squinted to test the results for herself.

"Okay…good. It'll work," she said. But her frown stayed. "Then, too, we've got to worry about color. I sure wish Roger was here."

I can't say I was sorry our master gardener had other commitments. True, Roger had an amazing eye for the end results. Downside? We all would have stood around for hours waiting for the muse to strike. To her credit, Bea was far more pragmatic. Get the plants in and worry about the problems later.

I had given the glossy photos on the plant tags a perfunctory look while Dutch and I were loading the pots in the first place. The shades ranged from purples, blues and burgundies to yellows, hot pinks and whites. If there was a unifying color scheme here, I didn't see it.

"This is like designing a wardrobe around a bag of M-n-M's, Bea."

"Normally," she admitted, "a designer would limit the palette a little more than this. Roger will probably have a fit. But I think we can make it work."

Bea fished several stubby colored wooden pencils out of her shirt pocket and began filling in the main blocks of color. The darker blooms—purples, burgundies and blues—would be massed along the top and inner edges where the two long and narrow beds came closest together. Yellow would dominate toward the center and outsides of the bed.

"We'll use whites and hot pinks as accents randomly through the bed to tie the scheme together. It'll be tough on the fly like this to make sure we've got a rhythm to the blooming dates. I'll keep double checking before we commit. We don't want to wind up with a lot of bare spots anywhere."

"Complicated. Hard to visualize."

Bea shrugged. "The yellows and oranges confuse things a bit. But then everybody does the red-white-blue thing nowadays. I am *not* about to turn down a perfectly good plant because it doesn't fit some plan or other. It'll be lively—that's for sure."

By the time we got the pots positioned around the beds, Artie was back with the box cutters. On hands and knees, Vivian and I began slitting openings into the gardener's cloth wide enough to house an individual plant while Bea fussed her way through the bed, checking tags for height and color to make sure they were ready to plant.

Margo hunkered on her ancient canvas garden stool, lovingly performing surgery that would allow the rootbound plants to grow. Sweating profusely, Artie single-handedly took charge of digging them in while Howard drew on his World War bunk-making expertise to tuck the flaps of the gardener's cloth in place again.

It was an unlikely blitz operation, but in the end it worked. Just when the first mosquitos of the season began to notice our presence, we finished the job and stood back to admire our handiwork. I had to admit, we were collectively awestruck at the transformation.

"Well, who'd a guessed?" Artie said after a while.

That pretty much summed it up. Even Bea seemed relieved at the results.

When planning a garden, I wrote later in the monastic calm of my living room, it helps to think in terms of manageable chunks:

What do you want to accomplish? How much are you prepared to maintain? Even if you dream big, start small.

Think perennials. Planting these hardy bloomers is like cultivating a whole new circle of friends. They're with you, year after year. And if you treat them right, they'll spread.

By the time you're ready to break more sod again, there will be enough of them to spread around in the new bed so it will not look so bare and

empty. Call up a gardener friend with
a roto-tiller and throw a party, if
you need help to get started.

Get the word out to your friends
that you are gardening. Perennial
gardeners love to share. It is the
mark of a successful gardener to have
so much excess plant stock, you do not
know what to do with it.

Never throw anything out. If
somebody new moves in to the
neighborhood, show up with a couple of
thinned-out iris bulbs in a pot as a
housewarming gift. And encourage them
in turn to pass along their largesse.

Be flexible. Plants figure out
where they grow best. Give them a
chance. They are tougher than you
think.

There was a lot of Artie the Teamster in there before it was done,
and doses of folk wisdom from cautious, officious Bea. I thought of
Vivian, Margo and Howard…even control freak, Roger.

Monday morning I took the first two columns into the office and
showed them to my boss. It is now running weekly in the *Gazette* on
page twelve, right hand top. The name stuck—we're calling it, *Time In
a Garden*. Who would have thought it!

Chapter Six

Each flower is a soul opening out to nature. Gerard De Nerval.

The donor acknowledgment letter to the Groft Nursery went out on Tuesday, over my hastily concocted official letterhead and Roger Van Nuyl's signature as Master Gardener of the Aurelius Community Parkland project.

Despite the stiff legal-ese, there was a poignance about the moment. For the first time in the ten months we had been at this, our enterprise assumed a sense of legitimacy that went beyond the handful of us scratching away in the dirt alongside the interstate.

We had received donations before, most notably that post-season collection of scraggly bulbs from the manager of a hardware chain just before the snows set in and a few tools scrounged here and there. This was different, and every one of us on the berm that Saturday felt it. Although no one but I even suspected the real cost those dozens of black plastic pots represented, somehow Adam Groft's gift took on a sacrificial quality that transcended the mere dollar value.

We suddenly felt like gardeners. With a care akin to reverence we held those plants entrusted to us, rooted them in the earth. We dug in the nutrients around each one. Our labor rose like incense into the still, heavy summer air, calling down a blessing from forces outside our control or ken.   But then that is not something you can easily put into bottom lines acceptable to the IRS.

If scientists eventually discover that there is a benevolence virus, I for one will not dispute it. Adam Groft—probably without his even realizing or appreciating the truth of it—was the carrier. I was the last person to predict how quickly it would spread.

It all started with a phone call. Although faithful enough with her time, Vivian Mortis, the retired school counselor, kept pretty much to herself on the team, expending just enough energy to get her allotted task in the garden done...eventually.

Fear hovered over her presence, like those dialogue balloons over cartoon characters. Unwritten or spoken, it was a kind of emptiness, a pregnant pause that separated her from us, from her work, maybe even her self.

Which explains why her whisper of a voice on the phone Thursday morning was so surprising. But there it was.

"I've got this trellis. For the garden. You know...that weedy green space in between the beds...."

"Hey, Viv, that's great," I said. I was waiting for the 'but'.

"Thing is...I can't lift it."

Visions of dollar-store flimsy gave way to visions of a full-blown pergola of inch-thick arsenic treated pine. Heavier than hell.

"No problem, I'll help."

"Bea and Roger probably won't like it."

Typical Vivian. She was already fully prepared to fold without firing a single shot.

"I'll be right over," I said.

"Over" turned out to be a pale lime bungalow with peeling white window trim and forties-vintage yew bushes masking the cement block basement. A curtain in the living room moved slightly as I started up the walk. Vivian had been watching for me.

"It's out in the garage," she said by way of greeting as she joined me on the front stoop.

Dodging a rusty fifties-vintage bike, several cobweb streaked tires, and cardboard boxes labeled in an indecipherable scrawl with black oversize marker pen, we picked our way to the back wall. The photo on the enormous carton had faded almost to gray, but was still legible enough to make out elegant double redwood arches with bench seats and lattice screening around it. It even showed several short sections of fencing on either side.

Complete in one box, the stenciling said. I quickly saw that any tentative attempt to move the thing would be foolhardy. The carton was the size of a large double refrigerator. Once assembled, even with a nasty front blustering through on that exposed berm along the interstate, this sucker was going nowhere.

"Holy Smokes, Viv, where d'ya find this thing?"

"At a yard sale fifteen years ago. The people brought it over here for me, unloaded it. But it was so heavy, I never even got it out of the box."

"Well, we're going to have to, if we're going to move it. No way in Hades are we going to carry it. Even the two of us. Getting the box open will be bad enough."

"I've got a box cutter. Artie gave it to me last week after we finished cutting the gardener's cloth for all those new plants out on the berm."

Vivian produced a menacing looking blade and tentatively began slicing at the cardboard. I quickly took over. The box was so water-logged after more than a decade of Michigan winters that the blade chewed more than cut through to the wood of the trellis beneath—darkened from age and the damp storage conditions, but otherwise as good as new.

"We can load the pieces in my trunk," Vivian offered.

"Not without bottoming out on that driveway. At least we can tie the lattice on the top of my wagon."

Divide and conquer. Over the next half hour we worked at coaxing the fetally compacted contents out of the carton, careful to save the plastic bagged hardware and assembly instructions. The parts were rapidly assuming far more imposing proportions than the whole.

Sweating in the dry and musty air of the garage, we shuffled awkwardly out into the noon sun with load after oversized load of lumber. Finally, we tucked the last of the smaller pieces into Vivian's Chevy, then secured as best we could with twine the by now overflowing trunk.

My aging Taurus too strained under its cargo. The stack of lattice screening hung well beyond doors and windshields, front and back. For all the world, it gave the impression of a wide-decked yacht, mast-less and languishing in dry dock at the Carver Lake boatyard.

"I'll make us some tea," Vivian said. "Iced. There's mint."

Funny how little you know about people from just an on-the-surface point of view. Vivian's back yard was anything but the sterile and nondescript facade that had greeted me on my arrival. Delicately contoured around her back stoop was an herb garden that would have done Martha Stewart proud.

Chives flowered next to lush and fragrant lemon balm. Ornamental sage branched up like coppery-hued peacock feathers. There were basils–burgundy and green, at least four varieties of mint, French tarragon and rosemary. As complete an herba-copia as I've ever seen. And not a weed in sight.

"Wow. You've got a chef's heaven back here."

It was an amazing experience to watch Vivian blush. Her paper pale skin and liberal dusting of freckles caught fire not unlike a match flame eating its way along the roadside in the summer heat. For a moment she seemed positively radiant.

"I'll just snip off some of this mint," she said. "Chocolate, they called it."

The leaves were a pale green and creamy white. But the scent, as I crushed the distinctive puckered leaves between my fingers, subtle Godiva.

"How about you?" Vivian said. "Do you garden, too?"

A smile of understanding flickered between us. I knew what she meant. For Margo and Howard, even Artie the Teamster, our little berm was their one and only foray into the world of horticulture. But mainly that was a lifestyle issue—both the older couple's health and Artie's long-time road warrior habits had made sustaining a garden impractical. Circumstances permitting? Any true gardener will tell you, tilling the soil can become an addictive business.

"A little…though nothing as exotic as this," I said. "Vegetables mostly. I'm still feeling my way…."

Vivian nodded. "It takes time. You need to let the space speak to you. The more I thought about it? Herbs made the most sense."

It also took a while for my eyes to adjust to the shadowy light in Vivian's kitchen. As I settled down at the Formica and chrome table, the whole scene had a Tennessee Williams palette about it. Lots of dark woodwork and a wallpaper pattern in gray with mauve cabbage roses.

Vivian was bustling between sink and refrigerator, organizing

48

glasses, ice cubes. A long-handled spoon to stir in the tea granules tinkled like a wind chime against the mismatched crystal.

"Good," I told her, sipping at the amber brew. "Great. I needed that."

Vivian was now caught up in arranging cookies on a plate. Homemade, no margarine here, I noticed…biting into a chocolate chip with some difficulty. Straight out the freezer–solid as sheet ice on a pond in mid-January.

"You like to bake?"

She nodded. "It's hard, though, for just one…and even when mother was still alive. She always liked my chocolate chips best. Taste the macadamia nuts? She liked that. So, I figured out that if I baked a big batch and kept them in the freezer, they'd always stay fresh. Got to like them that way."

It was the most sentences Vivian had ever put together at one time in my presence. Surprisingly, the words just flowed out in that quiet voice of hers—cool and quieting, like the tea.

"You think they'll like it? The others?"

For a bit there, I'd actually forgotten what had brought me here in the first place. The trellis.

"No question about it."

"It wasn't in Roger's plan."

Some things you just can't anticipate. Like the hug I gave her as she walked me to my car. Vivian stiffened for a moment, like she always did when Artie the Teamster fired up his tiller or a driver honked impatiently at the guy in front of him slowing down too soon for the exit ramp.

Then she hugged back. Shy, beaming. Like a third grader who just got her first and only A-plus, and still didn't know quite what to make of it.

"I've been thinking," she said. "I go walking mornings at six—Mondays through Fridays. Just forty minutes or so and not when it rains hard or anything. I thought maybe you'd like to join me."

"Why, Viv," I told her. "I'd love to."

We started our regime the next morning. In the most unlikely of quarters, I had just gained a walking buddy. It was largesse of another kind entirely.

49

 Chapter Seven

More grows in a garden than the gardener sows. Old Spanish Proverb

By the time Saturday rolled around, the whole county was rife with rumors that Bea's nutty green thumb gang was about to build a hundred-seat terraced band shell on that hill over by the interstate. News seems to expand to fill the context in which it surfaces. This was a small town. The supply of interesting conversation was equally limited. I couldn't even imagine what the gossip mill would be doing in another week.

In fact, it took only two hours to assemble the edifice, mainly thanks to Artie the Teamster's impressive tool box. Partly, too, because out of the blue, Adam Groft dropped in to see what we had done with the prairie plants he unloaded on us.

No one commented either on his absence, or unexpected reappearance. He fended off an awkward round of thanks, then just grabbed a wrench as if he had never been gone. With Artie the Teamster providing the muscle and Adam the know-how, the two made short work of bolting the pile of two-by-twos in place. The rest of us held and fetched and speculated wildly out loud about what the finished product would look like.

The prognosis was that Vivian's trellis was a definite asset: neither too grand or flimsy for the new bed. Unplanned, but perfect. Even Roger—always the skeptic about garden structures—showed up toward the end and approved of the change.

The central eight-foot high double arches were impressive in themselves. On either side, the delicate wings of fencing gave the whole structure the impression of impending flight. Vivian was urged to christen the sheltered bench seat. The Queen of England could not have conveyed a more dignified pride of place.

As for me, at first I tried to avoid Adam Groft as much as possible. Tough, when you are rubbing shoulders hefting an eight-foot trellis into place with a crew where the median age was pushing seventy.

My better instincts won out when I realized the others were holding back as well. I sensed it wasn't out of spite because Adam had deserted us once before. Mainly, like me, the other volunteers could not quite decide what to make of him.

Adam had dressed down. The gray polo shirt was sans logo and his jeans showed wear at the cuffs. Still, the patrician elegance about the man was not something a person shed with a change in wardrobe. Clearly at loose ends, he wandered over to the fringes of the berm where I had been gauging the impact of our work from a motorist's perspective.

The traffic behind us actually slowed. People were rubber-necking.

"It works," Adam said, half surprise and half caution in his assessment. "That new bed is coming along well."

"We dug in a lot of peat moss and organic stuff before we set in those plants you gave us. Artie trucked a load of leaf mold from the county landfill. Heinous to work with, but effective."

"I've learned an awful lot about fertilizer myself in the last couple of weeks," he said. "We've got a potent brew in that hothouse. Black gold. Unless you create your own mulch, build up the soil over time like that, the stuff can cost a fortune."

"Up to your knees in manure…not your style, I'd think…."

It didn't come out the way I intended. I sensed it the minute the words flew out of my mouth. Whatever the man's lifestyle or plans for his family's business, he had made a huge investment in this berm—had been incredibly generous, and against all odds, he was out here again, helping us. I noticed the beginning of a frown settle in between his brows.

"Have I…offended you, somehow?" he said slowly. "If so…it wasn't intentional."

"Nothing personal. I just…."

But it *was—personal.* And from the way his eyebrow arched, I knew Adam sensed it.

"Just...*what*, Eve?" he said quietly.

"We're out here, rain or shine...up to our elbows in mud. I find it hard to figure out why...someone—"

"Someone like me...as in, a *Groft...*? Or a *weekender* playing at being a *local*?"

"I didn't...say that."

"But you were thinking it."

True enough. That—and how much this guy reminded me of my late husband, except by now Joel would have been looking for the exit. I may have been feeling increasingly uncomfortable, but rare as it was, Adam's laugh was disarming. I had to admit, it suited him.

"To put the crassest possible spin on it?" he said. Why am I out here? A retailer can't afford to ignore the potential customer base...."

I shot him a puzzled look. "You've...decided not to sell, then?"

"Not a lot of choice with the economy in the cellar. In the meantime, deferred maintenance only works for so long. If we don't do something...?" Adam shrugged. "There won't be anything left to sell."

"That guy who loaded up the plants for me—"

"Dutch."

"Dutch seems to know what he's doing."

"He worked for my grandfather, then my dad. Seventy years, at least. Thank God, he isn't the kind who retires."

"You never thought about going into the business? When you were younger, I mean."

Not that the man was ancient now. The question popped out, even suspecting—knowing—the reaction it would trigger. Adam's face stiffened, like the arbor frame forced into shape, all planes and angles.

"Back in the dark ages?" His laugh had no humor in it. "That nursery was the last thing that would have occurred to me at eighteen. Fathers and sons and a business to run can be a...deadly combination."

"I didn't intend to pry."

It was a bald-faced lie, as disclaimers went. Adam didn't seem put off by it.

"Go ahead, pry away," he said. "At least I can talk about it now. That's something, I guess."

"When did your dad—?"

"Died six months ago. Cancer."

Blunt, I concluded, even emotionless. But the shadow across his features spoke otherwise.

"I'm sorry," I told him.

"Don't be. Nobody should have to go through that."

"So, then, you came up here to take care of him?"

"Yes and no. By then he pretty much needed a round-the-clock professional. Most of the time Dad was so whacked out on morphine, I could have been a total stranger getting him to sign off on payroll, power of attorney, you name it."

"Your job in Chicago—the company gave you a leave of absence?"

His twitch of a smile spoke volumes. In the corporate circles he came from, family leave was reserved for the ranks of the secretarial pool.

"Was I burning bridges?" he said. "Believe it or not, it wasn't hard to walk away from it. I was ready to get out. Something had to be done about the nursery...and fast. The stack of bills Dutch dug out for me could have floated a battleship."

"You seem to be good at it...all the nuts and bolts stuff."

"A Northwestern MBA's got to be good for something." He paused. "How did you put it—? Like deadheading, its not exactly rocket science to tell red ink from black. Then too, I'd put in my time out there in the greenhouse as a kid. All good in theory. Except faced with a stack of empty starter pots? Most mornings I'm not even sure where the hell to start."

"One day at a time," I said softly. "Isn't that ultimately what all of us are doing out here?"

I was thinking of Margo and Howard over there—doggedly enjoying their senior years together, flat out pedal-to-the-metal, and of Vivian pursuing her secret yen for herbs. Until *Time in a Garden* intervened, I was prepared to spend the rest of my days chasing down all the news fit to print or otherwise. Life doesn't always stick to the blueprint any of us, even well-meaning folk like Bea, carefully lay out for ourselves.

Adam must have been reading my mind. "These are good people out here," he said. "I can see why you stick with it."

"Not a mix you'd expect."

"True."

He chuckled, thinking about it. The sound flashed through my memory banks like a flash of sunlight off a passing windshield. I was thinking of that childhood rhyme about silver bells and cockle shells. *How does your garden grow?* Our berm was a very strange place for the poetry of childhood. But it worked.

One summer in her garden Gramma Eva had let me have my own bed, a tiny little plot in full sun, all mine to plant as I pleased. I wasn't there to water it every weekend, so she advised me to plant something hardy, drought-resistant. Six and stubborn, I settled on lupines. By mid-July I had nothing left but scorched and withered roots and stems.

"Gramma," I sobbed, "they d-d-died…!"

"They did the minute you set those little guys in the ground," she said quietly. "If you want things to grow, you gotta know what they need and what you can give 'em. Some folks do better with vegetables. Some with annuals. Perennials are sturdy but it can take 'em a while to get going."

"But how do you know—?"

"Seed packets don't lie, sweetie. If it says partial shade? You better pay attention."

My nose was running and I was ready to give up. "I'm no g-g-good at this, Gramma. I w-w-wrecked it."

"Gardens aren't about winning and losing." Gently she wiped at my face with her well-worn square of a handkerchief. "They're about learning. Now…let's see what we can find to fill that hole out there."

It was an odd time to remember my Voltaire. But if anything at sixty-plus, like that French writer's youthful and fictional Candide on his precarious life journey, I was discovering the value of staying power.

The words for a column began to shape themselves in my head. They would have to keep. I sensed Adam had picked up on what—to an outsider unfamiliar with my writing habits—must have seemed like my drifting off into a semi-catatonic state. My laugh had an oops-you-caught-me quality about it.

"Sorry. I must have been…zoning out again," I said. "Not senility…just an occupational hazard. I was starting to obsess about a column…."

He chuckled. "Good thing you told me. I was about to hit 9-1-1 on my cell. I'll consider myself warned."

"And…thanked, I hope. We would still be ankle-deep in mud with barely a plant in sight if it hadn't been for you."

"My pleasure."

His voice was gruff. But his smile was genuine enough.

This time when we finished for the day, I made a point of seeking him out—hand extended. Dirt, calluses and all.

"You're welcome out here any time, you know," I told him.

He frowned. "Saturdays are…potentially the…busiest days of the week for us—"

From his expression, I could sense it wasn't an excuse. Unless I misread him, he seemed almost disappointed to have to put me off like that.

"Well, then just…come…whenever, Adam. The rest of the gang will understand."

I didn't add the footnote—that by now, so did I. It didn't matter on some level why Adam Groft had decided to join us. He was here, apparently wanted…even needed to be. And much as I was still loathe to admit it, we needed him.

It was a lot less threatening to write, than think about it. Back home, the computer was waiting. As I slid in front of the darkened monitor, for a split-second I caught my face staring back at me.

Flushed with anticipation, the bodice-rippers would have described it. Looking down at the keys, I began to write:

> There are as many reasons for gardening as there are gardeners. The what and the how of our garden say a lot about what makes us tick as people
>
> For some, gardening is practical. Ever since Eden, folks have been cutting food bills by cranking out bushels of vegetables or herbs to spice up their culinary creations. But vegetable gardening also appeals to sports fans—obsessed with who can grow the biggest, most or heaviest. History buffs can cultivate plants by century or culture. Literati can specialize in species named in books or a single author, like the Bible or Shakespeare.

Flower gardeners favor style over substance. Neat-niks gravitate toward French and Italian formal gardens, where plants are laid out in rows and patterns. An English informal garden becomes a collector's excuse to fill every square inch of the front yard with plants.

Are you into quick and dirty? Go with annuals. Plants like impatiens and petunias bloom like crazy from the get-go. Water, fertilizer and an occasional pinching back of dead blooms will keep annuals going until the first frost. Next season just buy a whole new batch and start over.

Myself? I am a perennial gardener. Some of that is laziness. Once a perennial bed gets going, it is hard to kill it. The biggest chore becomes deadheading or cutting back bloomed-out flower heads. Perennial gardening also takes a certain ruthless ability to prioritize: to thin out the beds every couple of years so the plants do not suffer from lack of space.

In his novel *Candide*, the French philosopher Voltaire writes of a teacher who talks for pages about how since Eden, human beings were destined to work. Thoroughly bored with that philosophizing, the student replies: *Great idea. Only forget all the chatter. Let's just make our garden grow.*

So, then, why do **you** garden? Even if it is just an excuse to play in the mud—we would like to know. Or send us your favorite gardening quote and we will share with our readers.

At the bottom of the column, I key-stroked in my name and email address, along with the newspaper's post office box. Then I sat back and waited to see what kind of a response I would get.

Who would have thought it? Within twenty-four hours of the column's publication, my e-mail box was clogged to overflowing. It seems our little garden gang has an awful lot of company.

 # Chapter Eight

If gardeners will forget a little the phrase, "watering the plants" and think of watering as a matter of "watering the earth" under the plants, keeping up its moisture content and gauging its need, the garden will get on very well. Henry Beston, *Herbs and the Earth*, 1935.

I ran into Adam Groft in Harold & Daughters' Hardware on Wednesday. His arms were loaded with sections of plastic plumbing pipe. I had come on my lunch hour to pick up a rain gauge for the garden—maybe inject a bit of hands-on science into my weekly garden journaling.

In fact, there had been no rain in weeks. Major worry for the crew was no longer weeds or sudden wind squalls, but merciless unrelenting heat.

"Artie stopped by the nursery," Adam said, by way of greeting. "Located a beat up old watering trough…thought we could use some pipe and hose to rig up a drip irrigation system. Old Harold here was willing to part with some."

"Sounds complicated."

"Not really…except for the water supply. Dutch—the guy who loaded all those perennials into your Taurus—rigged up a jerry-built system years ago, long before that new sophisticated stuff. In the greenhouse, we can tap into the well, though."

"That's where the trough comes in?"

"Crude and uglier than sin. But if we hide the trough in that stand of trees, there wouldn't be a hunk of corrugated metal just sitting out there in the open. Artie's made some kind of arrangements with the volunteer fire department to haul their tanker truck out here for a fill-up. Thankfully, once there, water does flow down hill."

"Don't you have to regulate it somehow."

Adam grinned. "Haven't quite figured out that part, yet. Next stop is the Extension Office."

By Saturday, he and Dutch had assembled a maze of thin black tubes and tiny clamps. Together all eight of us—counting Dutch who was not going to entrust his handiwork to a bunch of amateurs—sweated and dug a trench to bury the main pipework.

Bea took in her growing army of gardeners with the proprietary air of a Patton inspecting the troops. Eventually Adam drilled random holes into the feeder sections of pipe running down through the beds themselves, while Dutch and Howard patiently threaded in the thinner black feeder tubes and snaked them over to the roots.

Except for an alarming leak that Adam quickly tackled with a hunk of duct tape, the water flowed as intended. Drop by drop it fell on the thirsty roots.

We were too tired, and from past experience a tad too cautious to cheer. With blistered palms, we joined Bea's tentative applause—still half expecting a geyser to send the entire contents of the feeder trough into a spectacular arc over the intended target. It was good old Margo who started the round of hugs. Although stiff and awkward, I managed to beat down my anxiety level when it was Adam's and my turn.

Ever the grass roots philosopher of the bunch, Artie the Teamster, pretty much gave the benediction. "Well, it works. But it sure as hell ain't the village water department!"

Amen to that. But bottom line was, the thing worked.

I had not given thought to the rest of the weekend, but after yet another stand-up lunch cold out of the refrigerator, I found myself spending it bent over my laptop, the words pouring out on to the blank screen like seed strewn along a furrow.

Gardening is as much about people, as plants, I wrote:

You learn and reveal a lot about yourself in the process. Take me, for instance.   I am learning that I am not good with chaos or change.

Gardeners' cloth was made for people like me. Once that sheeting is on the ground and plants are snugged inside the slits cut for them, they can grow relatively undisturbed by weeds.

Problem is, nature is not always that tidy.   Most perennials want to spread out, and unless a gardener is careful, they rot when held back by that rigid plastic.

It would be nice to have it both ways: to shut out the difficult and still be able to grow. Life in the plant world rarely works that way.

Time never stands still in a garden.   Just when I seem to have created the perfect balance, something comes along to spoil or at least unsettle it all.   A rainstorm wipes out the tulips. Bare earth starts to show where just a couple of weeks before the snowdrops were in their prime. Summer ends and then fall, and before I know it, my garden is nothing but bare stalks drying in the wind.

Good gardeners learn not just to live with change and loss, but to reshape those painful passages into something better. They plan but also risk.   The   unexpected   becomes opportunity.

Gardeners accept what they can control and what they cannot. They ask the right questions, ones that

look ahead not just to the past or the
way things have always been. When the
daffodils are finished—what next?
After the gale force winds, then what?
       A gardener I know sums it up this
way: "Takes a whole lot of patience to
grow a plant." It takes humility,
too. Wise man, that gardener.

There was something different about what I had written, though
it took several read-throughs to figure it out. Scrupulously I had
avoided the first person in columns before, alternating between the royal
"We" and the directive "You"—a consistency in voice that engages the
reader without letting the veil slip.

This giving in to the first-person, creating an in-print persona was
far riskier. I was not so much worried what my boss George would think
of the approach, but what I thought about it. If allowed to run its course,
I sensed that over time, this change in voice would lay bare my own
experience, ultimately the essence of what I thought or felt or believed.

My style, it seems, was changing—along with my work habits.
And it made me anxious, maybe even a little afraid.

I had written in short bursts most of my professional life,
sketching out paragraphs of advertising copy that had more to do with
the reader than myself and more recently the weekly terse, chatty but
impersonal tidbits for George's local news column. All of it was finite
stuff that I could put down and take up again like a change of socks or
hairstyle: shaping sound bytes like some stream-of-consciousness
crossword puzzle into cohesive wholes designed to persuade or inform
or titillate.

Although the garden column was longer, it was still constrained
by that 350-word limit, readable while waiting for the water to boil or the
toast to eject. Tough—any or all of that, I realized, to do justice to the
cast of characters that had wandered into my life. I was thinking of Bea
and George, unlikely visionaries as different from one another as two
people could be, of Adam Groft with his love-hate relationship to
greenery and the growing of it, of the gruff yet romantic Dutch with his
calloused palms cradling his children about to venture forth into the
world.

I, too, was part of the equation now, not just an anonymous

61

omniscient voice hiding behind a curtain issuing pronouncements in the *Weekly Gazette* to a bewildered Oz. I had stopped being an outsider, and was becoming part of this strange microcosm of humanity struggling to become a community around a tiny plot of earth alongside a rural interstate.

My style as a writer was changing, and with it my life—my sense of self and sense of my connectedness. It was not, I am sure, what George had anticipated when he first proposed that gigantic leap from the garden of my life to the garden of the column. Subtly but inexorably, my roots in this place, as writer and woman, were beginning to spread quietly into the unknown, carrying me with them.

Apparently I wasn't the only one who noticed. Out on the berm that weekend, Adam and I wound up together on a work team again—a habit, I had to admit, I was beginning to welcome, even if it meant also handling some pretty nasty chores. If his volunteering was causing problems at the nursery, he gave no sign of it.

This time the two of us and Artie were slogging away redefining the boundaries where grass met bed. It was another no-brainer of a job, one that required more brute force than finesse to slice through the invading root structures. Artie had wandered off to get a blade sharpener out of his truck while Adam and I hacked away as best we could with our increasingly blunt edgers.

I hadn't noticed Adam was watching me, until I came up for air. My arms aching from the effort it took to move just a couple of feet along the border, I stood there propping myself up with the handle of the edger, trying to catch my breath.

"Amazing—by the way, your column last week," he said quietly. "I've been meaning to tell you. Gutsy, creative stuff."

I shivered, partly at the soft tug of the breeze ruffling my sweat-drenched hair. More, I sensed, at something I heard in his voice.

"Thanks...." My laugh sounded nervous, even to me. "Easy to write...harder to do."

"Tell me about it—"

For the life of me, I couldn't figure out his expression. Still, anybody on the business end of that intense, thoughtful scrutiny would have felt compelled to try.

"It's rough going out there I gather...at the nursery?"

"True enough...but red ink isn't necessarily the kind of bottom line that keeps a guy up at night." Adam paused. "Though after…reading between the lines in that column of yours? I think you already…*know* that."

It wasn't a question. From the look that went with it? I sensed Adam had a sub-text of his own going on here. This was proving to be neither the time nor the place to deal with it. Over the crest of the berm, I saw Artie headed our way with a whetstone significantly larger than the proverbial breadbox. My words came tumbling out in a rush.

"I'm not…sure…what—where…you're—?"

"Headed with all this? After all that great prose of yours about risk and age…and blooming where we're planted?. A guy could get… just a tad…*curious* how much of that is…hypothetical and how much you're *really* prepared to…practice what you preach."

Face flushed, I dropped my gaze. So he caught it…my thinly disguised soul-baring? He not only caught it—unless I had badly misjudged the edge to his words, Adam Groft was intentionally…flirting with me.

My jaw clamped shut and I just stood there, looking at him. Fighting a smile, Adam gestured toward my edger.

"Ladies first…!"

Artie had set up the whetstone alongside the bed and was waiting for customers. Face flushed, I scrambled to hand him the unwieldy tool—a frightening cross between a medieval pike and a whaler's blubber spade. By the time it was Adam's turn, I had made up my mind to stay as clear of him the rest of the morning as possible.

Long-term, though, *avoidance* wasn't exactly an option. Not when the garden crew voted at the close of business to add a mid-week weeding night as a blitz-krieg tactic to root out the worst of the Creeping Jenny and wild mustard snaking into the beds from all directions. Still, I relaxed a little when Adam Groft begged off. Apparently a potential client had asked him to pitch some kind of major landscape deal.

Margo and Howard didn't drive evenings so that left just Bea, Artie, Vivian and I out there after work on Wednesday. We had our work cut out for us. For all its lacy and delicate leaf-structure, wild mustard is one tenacious plant to keep under control. *So much for appearances.*

A reward was catching our lone peony bush at its peak. An overblown mass of enormous blooms that call out to motorists clear across the southbound and passing lanes to the northbound traffic beyond.

We were having so much fun making peony jokes that I started to flesh out a column on it in my head, a kind of tongue-in-cheek ode to peonies. The peony is the poor man's cabbage rose, I began:

> This is a perennial that all but shouts, Look at me. I'm alive.
>
> Even in the dead hot sun, peonies radiate a defiant blaze of whites, hot pinks and wines. Their burst of color and scent is so bold, it stops you dead in your tracks. Still, those same flower heads are so fragile that the slightest rain or burst of wind, the act of transplanting them to the tame confines of a summer bouquet can explode all those gaudy blossoms like fireworks, all frazzled tatters of petals.
>
> That old saw, *bloom where you're planted*, appears to be written just for them. They may take a while to hit their stride. But once they do, they flower away, season after growing season in those stormy weeks as the garden changes from spring to summer.

Working on the opposite side of the bed from me, our Teamster was far less poetic about his experience with the flower.

"Holy Shit...," he roared, as he started flicking at his arm like a sixth grader shooting spit wads. "There are ants all over the damn things. Keep crawling down my arms any time I get near 'em."

In between gales of laughter, I was taking mental notes. I would have to clean up the language. But to be fair to my column readers, I had better point out that interesting downside, too.

Even working with a greatly reduced crew, our extra evening work session was pronounced a success. We got the job done in record time and at least we weren't fighting the usual heat or bugs. Except, of course, Artie's ants.

My laptop was waiting on the dining room table when I got home, daring me to finish what mentally I had started:

> No need for fall "lifting" of bulbs with these old standbys. Living here in rural Michigan, I can identify with peonies. Our America is a mobile society. Pride of place does not rate high automatically on the scale of cultural values.
>
> Gardeners know better. Plants bloom every day in the most unlikely of circumstances. So do people. The median age in rural America may be inching upward, but it does not follow that we, as a community, are past our prime or anything like it. The need to flower luxuriously and extravagantly does not automatically stop as arteries begin to harden and knees begin to stiffen.
>
> Staying put is not necessarily a bad thing. It all depends on whether we keep on growing, flowering in the soil that holds us.

Case in point? I concluded. *Consider the lowly peony.*

And then I reread the draft again—harder, the way I now knew Adam would. Reading between the lines, as he put it, what would he make of all that budding and blossoming?

My instinct was to cut the juice out of the imagery, but something in me rebelled. If a little flirting with some guy over the petunias was cause for alarm, I was really in trouble.

I ran a quick word count. It was close. Let Adam Groft think what he might, with a steady hand I maneuvered the cursor to the Send button. George would have this week's column before I had time to reconsider.

65

 Chapter Nine

The horticulturalist Henry Mitchell once said that magnificent gardening and magnificent heartbreaks go hand in hand. I believe it. Eve Brenneman's journal

It never occurred to me when I didn't show up in the garden the next Saturday—felled by a vicious summer cold and fever of a hundred-one—that I hadn't missed a weekend in the garden for two months. Not until Adam Groft showed up on my doorstep, grim-faced and leaning on the doorbell. Expecting what, I'm not sure, but probably not the reddened nose and terry towel bath robe in the middle of a late-June heat wave.

"Get dressed," he said.

I bristled. Then it dawned on me that the edge in his voice was alarm not hubris and it had nothing to do with me.

"It's Howard," Adam said. "Collapsed while deadheading those damn peonies. I used the cell phone to call 9-1-1. Told Margo I'd meet her at the hospital. Thought you'd want to know."

"Will they even let me in the place?"

I meant my cold. He obviously never got beyond the bathrobe.

"Try jeans," he said tersely.

"Give me five minutes."

Three would have been a better offer, judging by what I read in those usually cool and contained gray eyes of his. No time for major couture decisions.

The bedroom was dark and reeked of menthol. Scooping yesterday's tank top from the floor next to the laundry basket and grabbing my khakis off the footboard, I tore into my clothes, ran a perfunctory brush through my salt-and-pepper mop of hair and slid into a pair of Birkenstocks.

Good enough, under the circumstances. Back turned, Adam had stopped pacing in front of my collection of mismatched frames sitting on the fireplace mantle in the living room. Children, dogs, a wedding portrait in sepia—parents, judging by the forties wardrobe. A reminder of my own nuptials, of course, was conspicuously absent.

"Ready," I said.

"Let's go."

He beat me to the door though I was closer. Letting it slam shut behind me, I followed him down the steps to the SUV. He had left the motor running.

Every pickup in the county seemed to be in town, provoking a subdued rumble of profanity at every stop sign from Adam. I rarely heard him swear, not even when deploying that duct tape on the irrigation system.

"It's bad, then?"

His knuckles tightened on the wheel. Shifting in his seat, he gunned the SUV enough to pass a rusted-out junker of a pickup immobilized mid-block for no apparent reason.

"I said it before, I'll say it again. You're all crazy, you know," he said. "Slogging away in the god-awful heat week after week. Margo's blind as a bat. She's going to lose a finger one of these days—or worse. If Artie doesn't stop lacing his coffee with brandy, he's going to keel over out there of sunstroke. Vivian sprays on the Deet like Chanel invented the stuff—can't image what it's doing to her lungs."

"And you...? I suppose you're...*above* all that...?"

"Okay. I've got issues. Who doesn't?" His gaze jerked my way, zeroed in again on the road. "Very interesting, by the way—that collection of photos on your mantel."

"My daughters. They've finished college, married. Both of them."

"Happily?" he insisted. "Still speaking to you?"

"Who ever knows? But yes, I'd say the girls are happy enough. And we usually phone a couple times a month. More or less."

It was true, all of it, but not the whole truth. But then he hadn't asked me why, conspicuously, there were no pictures of my husband Joel in that rogue's gallery. Or of myself for that matter.

"Well, good for you," he said slowly. "More than I can say for me and my old man."

"And I thought we mothers and daughters had the monopoly on—"

"Dysfunctional."

Adam laughed but there was no humor in it. I sensed I wasn't the only one holding back.

"You never…married?" I said.

"Not high on the priority list. My older sister moved to Anchorage the day she graduated from high school—haven't heard Word One from her since. After that, homecomings turned into a perpetual guilt trip. By sixty, mom was a heart attack waiting to happen—one way to get out from behind the sales counter at the nursery. To the end, dad was clueless. Why him? Not exactly the kind of role model that inspires confidence in one's life choices."

"Families all have their problems, Adam."

That would have sounded a heck of lot more convincing if I hadn't started out fudging that bit about my own familial history. Whatever the reason, Adam softened his tone.

"Right now Margo and Howard sure have their share. Thank God, her eyesight is so bad, she couldn't tell how white Howard was."

"Heart attack?"

"If we're lucky, it's heat stroke or dehydration. God, the guy wasn't even wearing that old Milwaukee Braves ball hat of his out there. You could have fried an egg on that metal watering trough, even in the shade."

The hospital lobby was fraught with the kind of disasters you'd expect in a resort town. Sunburned kids squirming over bug bites and sprains while their shell-shocked parents fished around for insurance cards. A red-and-gray bearded guy clutched an elbow encased in a skin of black leather tattooed in places with rusty-orange sew-on Harley

Davidson patches.

Alone in one corner, oblivious to it all, Margo sat upright as a dowager empress, her usually impeccable up-do wispy and slipping off to one side. A portrait of bewildered grief.

"Margo, I'm so sorry," I said, sliding into the seat next to her.

Her hands were like paper in mine, thin and brittle. She was trembling. Over at the desk, Adam gestured over in our direction, deep in conversation with a harried-looking young woman in surgical blues.

When he rejoined us, he dropped to one knee on the carpet so he could make eye contact. Margo looked right through him.

"Listen to me," he told her. "They're doing blood work to make sure. But so far, they don't think it's his heart."

At that, her hand fluttered like an moth caught under netting. Stilled again.

"So, you're saying—?"

"It looks like he's going to be okay."

"I don't suppose…will they let me see him?"

Adam shook his head. "It's pretty hectic in there. We'd just be in the way."

At that, she sagged against me, her weight a mere nothing. I put an arm around her. The tears that had been stinging against my eyelids just let go in a slow, steady rhythm. I let them fall.

Adam's face swam into focus. Watching me.

"Do you…did the doctor have any idea when—?" I started to ask him.

"Could be an hour before we know anything," he said. "Most likely longer."

He looked back at Margo. A muscle worked along his jaw line.

"I suggest we wait in the coffee shop next door," he said.

He was right, of course. The hospital was too small to have a cafeteria of its own. An aura of crisis permeating the lobby was enough to traumatize any one who wasn't that way already.

 # Chapter Ten

Where flowers bloom so does hope. Lady Bird Johnson,
Public Roads: Where Flowers Bloom

Margo let herself be led without complaint. Adam stopped at a booth near the door, slid into a seat as if all the tension of the world had just eased from his shoulders. I steered Margo into the opposite bench and took up residence alongside her.

The café obviously once had been a soda shop, complete with well preserved tin ceiling and mirrored counter. The upholstery on the booths must have been replaced somewhere along the line and the vintage fifties-era mini table-top juke boxes still glowed with life.

A mechanical bell device on the door—also probably authentic—set the lone waitress in motion. She'd been perched on a stool at the end of the counter, absorbed in a magazine. From the kitchen we could hear the mechanical rumbling of a dishwasher. We were the only customers.

"What'ja like?"

Not hostile, just preoccupied. Impatient for a response.

"Coffee," Adam told her. "Black and hot."

"Make that two," I said.

Margo looked up, confusion stamped on her fragile features. "Iced tea?"

"We got it. How d'ja want it?"

When Margo didn't immediately clarify, the waitress slipped into

70

that dealing-with-a-five-year-old voice that younger people sometimes use when talking to the elderly. At least the woman didn't use the royal, We.

"D'ja want lemon or sugar?"

"Just plain," Margo said. "Maybe a little mint."

"Don't have that."

"Then skip it," I broke in, trying not to sound as annoyed as I felt. "Just plain is fine."

As Adam caught my eye, I saw a smile curl faintly at the corner of his mouth. Then he leaned back against the faux leather seat and closed his eyes. He looked as whipped as I felt right about then.

"We had our first date, here, you know," Margo said. "Howard and I. BLTs and a soda. Nineteen thirty two. I was...," she ticked off the decades in her head. Gave up. "Just kids. And we've been together ever since."

What do you say to something like that? Especially after that tense dance-around-the-subject True Confession conversation between Adam and me on the way over here. The comparisons to Margo's simple profession of enduring love were worse than invidious. Silent, not making eye contact, the two of us just sat there drinking in her story, along with deep, harsh droughts of coffee that had sat way too long to pass the quality control test at a Starbucks.

A part of my brain kept coming back to what he had said, last week in the garden. That maybe the two of us were more alike than I had been prepared to admit. *Damaged, both of us*—disconnected from relationships by that very same passage of the seconds and days and years that somehow had forged together lives like Margo's and Howard's into a powerful bond of love and shared memory.

Like so many of that Greatest Generation, they struggled against wars and the rumors of wars, depressions and recessions, scandals in high places and the lowly day-to-day of raising a family on the meager pay of a rural accountant in the county clerk's office. Margo took in alteration and custom sewing jobs to help put their two sons through college. One was lost in the jungles of southeast Asia, the other killed in a freak accident years after on the commute into Los Angeles one morning—leaving behind a widow and three small children.

So Margo and Howard face their end as they began. They had each other. Their love was comfortable as only couples can be that have spent over six decades together.

I had watched them out on the berm every Saturday gently poking at each other's foibles, holding on in the dark. But that was then. This was now.

"I don't know what I'd...," Margo began.

Stopped. Began again. Stopped.

"Margo, we aren't going to let you struggle with this all alone," I told her quietly. "Remember, you've got Bea and Artie, Vivian, Adam and me to—"

At that she started to cry. An inaudible outpouring of fear and emotions too powerful to name shook her frail shoulders like a spray of astilbe when a front is passing through.

Adam's jaw tightened. I sensed him start to respond, hesitate.

It was all there in his eyes—his unshed tears over his father, the sad ambiguity of it, a grief still newer than my own. My own dad had died in a boating accident when I was very young. Mom passed away suddenly my senior year in college. Grandmother Eva lived into her nineties, alone and independent until she went to sleep one summer night and never woke up. The intervening time had brought a kind of peace with their absence, or so I thought.

Goodbyes matter. In all the greatest losses of my life, there had been no time to say them—not even that gut-wrenching dawn when the police showed up on my front stoop in Chicago with word that I had been widowed.

Margo's tears and the aching truths behind them had caught me by surprise. They were my own as I held his tiny woman cradled in my arms. I let them fall—unchecked.

Adam's voice startled us both. "We need to...go back there."

Disoriented, I looked at my watch. An hour had passed without any sense of it. Margo was calmer now, steeling herself to face whatever came next. So was I.

Slipping a sizeable bill on to the table top, Adam stood and waited as I helped Margo maneuver her way out of the booth. After what we'd just experienced, the hospital lobby seemed strangely empty, for all the barely controlled pandemonium that once again greeted us there. Nothing had changed, and everything.

Adam sought out the most likely scrubs-clad person and came back to report that Howard, in fact, was suffering from an onset of the same virus that had so effectively felled me.   He was tired and dehydrated, needed one heck of a lot of rest and fluids, but could go home.

Margo had left their tank of a mid-eighties Town Car back at the garden. So Adam drove the two of them home to Aurelius while I rode shotgun in the front seat. Utterly exhausted, none of us said much, and when we pulled into Howard and Margo's driveway, both of them needed a lot of help making it on to the porch.

"Thank you…we can take it from here," Margo quavered as she fumbled with the latch.

Adam started to protest. Then he caught my eye, and thought the better of it.

"You'll call us if you need anything?" he insisted.

The elderly couple was already maneuvering together through the front door, seeking out their own parallel universe behind that solid oak and beveled glass barrier. Adam cracked the SUV door for me, waited until I was inside. A long time, I thought, since anybody had bothered to do that.

"You were wonderful," I told him as he backed out into the street again.

A muscle worked along the edge of his jaw, the only sign he had even heard me. Deft, the way the man dodged compliments.

"Ditto," he said brusquely. "They're a great couple."

"I had a friend in Chicago who made a career of catering to that age and mindset," I told him. "OFT Inc., he called it–Over Fifty Travel. Friends used to tease him it meant Old Fart Tours. He loved his work. Adventurous but not crazy. Wouldn't have swapped for the Botox crowd for all the money in the world."

Adam chuckled, shook his head, remembering. "Sounds like my grandfather. He took off alone on one of those packaged deals to Holland at ninety. When my father complained he was too old, Gramps just told him not to worry: 'If I croak over there? They can bury me. At least I'd have seen the Old Country once before I died!'"

Our laughter felt good, cleansing—that same strange rush that comes when a fever breaks and every nerve ending is on hyper-alert. Conversation was demanding more energy, I realized, than I could sustain right now.

The truth was I was exhausted, drained, and my cold symptoms were reasserting themselves. I wasn't even sure I could manage to brew myself a cup of Echinacea tea before I crawled back into bed. All the more reason why I sat up and took notice when Adam negotiated a cautious U-turn, heading us back in the direction of Aurelius.

"Problems…?"

"Unfinished business back at the berm," he shrugged. "Margo and Howard's car."

"Keys…?"

Adam chuckled. "Knowing those two? Right there in the ignition."

The berm was deserted except for the Town Car. Sure enough, the keys hung there as advertised, a whole corroded wad of them, including at least two-thirds from what had to be long-discarded padlocks or luggage.

"Forget which of these is the right key," I muttered, as Adam thrust the fistful in my direction. "My driving at all right now is not necessarily a good idea. I've got enough cold medicine in me to qualify as a junkie."

Adam laughed. "This isn't the Dan Ryan Expressway. Throw on your flashers and I'll stay close behind you in the SUV. That boat of a Lincoln practically drives itself."

Twitchy and chewing on my lower lip the whole way, I tried to avoid curbs, parked cars and telephone poles. Fortunately for all concerned, the streets themselves were largely empty of pedestrians or oncoming traffic. Once safely in Margo and Howard's driveway, I awkwardly cut the engine. Margo had seen us and was already on the porch.

By the time I succeeded in opening the driver-side door, Adam had sprinted over to escort me back to his SUV. Until I stood up, I didn't realize how unsteady on my feet I had become. His hand was already cradling my elbow.

"Just brought your car back…," Adam called out to Margo over his shoulder as he steered me toward the SUV. "I'm going to drive Eve home before she runs out of steam."

Margo waved to signal she understood. We left her keys in the ignition where Adam had found them. No sense in complicating things.

"You handled that battleship of theirs like a pro," Adam teased as he slid the vehicle into gear.

"Yeah…well, if the gendarmes had stopped us, I'd have let *you* do the explaining."

This time on the road to Xenaphon, we let silence do the talking. It was the kind of uneasy calm that comes after an earthquake when the commentators are still warning about the possibility of aftershocks.

There was so much I wanted to say. That I had lied about my life…not by what I said, but what I left unsaid. That I had misjudged him. Badly. But exhausted from the emotional stress and the lingering effects of the antihistamines, the words swam in and out of my head like the mailboxes zipping past along the shoulder of the roadway.

As we pulled into my driveway, Adam left the engine running. I struggled with the door latch for a while before he noticed and reached down to pop the lock button.

"You really ought to let me help you—"

I shook my head. "Thanks…but I'm fine. Really."

We both knew that wasn't what was going on here. Even in my head-cold-ravaged condition—about as unattractive as a person could be short of hospitalization, I didn't trust myself to let the guy in my house. Still, it was tough to muster up the energy to go, when what I really wanted was for somebody to hunt down my jammies wherever I had thrown them, brew me some tea laced with brandy and talk to me until I fell asleep.

"Next Saturday is the Fourth of July," he said.

Yet another thing I'd totally forgotten. But then living alone, holidays tended to blur after a while into just one more day lost among the perpetual march of weeks around them.

"At the garden this morning," he added, "Bea said that since we wouldn't be working on the berm, maybe we'd be willing to help put together some kind of float for the Xenaphon parade. Drum up a little visibility for the project."

"Great idea…maybe we'd even shake out some more recruits."

Margo and Howard were probably going to be out of commission for a while. The garden was expanding, and none of the rest of us were getting any younger either to keep up that kind of maintenance regimen.

"We're meeting over at Bea's the night before to work on it," Adam said. "Artie's borrowing a flat bed and tractor from a friend of his."

I nodded. "Sounds good."

"And I thought maybe—afterward, on the Fourth…the two of us could drive up to Little Traverse and watch the fireworks over the Bay."

He threw it out there as if he were talking about a new set of valves for the irrigation system. I couldn't read a thing in either his face or his voice, any more than I could have anticipated the sheer panic that simple suggestion triggered.

"I don't know…with this crazy cold—"

"Best darn home remedy I know," he said.

Adam's smile glinted like a sudden flash of sunlight on the water just after a summer storm. He wasn't giving me a chance to say, No.

"A friend sails his 32-footer out to the mouth of Little Traverse, Eve. So we can catch the fireworks over the water fronts all the way from Bay Harbor and Petoskey to Harbor Springs. Somebody brings a hamper with wine and cheese—"

The memories he was conjuring up were fresh as yesterday. "Every summer when I was a kid," I told him quietly. "The whole family would camp out for hours along the shore road to hold on to the best spot."

Adam smiled. "I suspected as much."

Michigan is at the far edge of the eastern time zone, and by the time the sun had set enough to set off the first volley, we kids were hyper with anticipation. With all the others huddled around us in the darkness, we oooh-ed and aaah-ed as we watched the shimmering fire in the moonlight. The sound came later, muffled by distance and the vast expanse of water, waves of thunder echoing off the sleeping hillsides of Boyne and beyond.

I hadn't realized I had drifted off again until Adam called me on it.

"You're tired…I know," he said quietly. "You can think about it. Tell me later—"

"Bombs bursting in air."

"Say again…?"

"I was remembering the fireworks…and then Margo, telling us about Howard coming of age at Normandy. All that shelling…."

There was more, though that I didn't say. I could still see that wisp of a woman sitting alongside me in that narrow booth of the café—devastated. But not from those war memories of Howard's, life-changing as they were. *It was the terrible prospect of facing life alone…without the love of her life at her side.*

Adam was looking at me strangely. *What the heck was I thinking of? I wasn't a kid anymore, looking for some long-lost childhood flame over BLTs and cherry coke.* And still I heard myself saying it.

"Sounds like fun. We can make a day of it."

At least I had the presence of mind not to say, "It's a date."

 Chapter Eleven

Gardens are not made by sitting in the shade. Rudyard
Kipling

The air in the house was hot and stuffy after all that running
around outside, the hall mirror inescapable.   It wasn't the lingering
evidence of my summer cold, either, that got my attention.   Whatever
prompted Adam Groft to issue that invitation for a Fourth of July junket
on Little Traverse, I didn't see it staring back at me from that unforgiving
sheet of silvered glass.

Buyer beware. But then, I reminded myself, Adam Groft wasn't
some poor clueless soul out there waiting for his blind date. He had seen
me covered with sweat and mud, hands blistered and nose running. And
yes, the recent sighting of me in my bathrobe just a couple of hours ago
was enough to scare anybody. If it was glitz and youth Adam Groft was
looking for, I didn't qualify.

My husband Joel always said my eyes were my best feature, green
or hazel depending on the light. That hadn't changed—about the only
thing. Even thirty pounds lighter and as many years younger, those
shoulders and cheekbones were always more at home illustrating a Willa
Cather novel than selling resort togs.

My current wardrobe didn't help. All but a few items from my ad
agency days wound up at the thrift shop before I relocated to Xenaphon.
For a year now, I'd been living in slacks and tees.   My recent

housekeeping frenzy had made the lack of dressier options all too apparent. A goodly share of my makeup had melted from the heat in the moving truck en route.

I'd been so caught up in making over the berm, it never occurred to me that maybe more than that overgrown hillside was crying out for some major rehabilitation. Question was, where on earth to start?

All those glossy covered women's magazines at the grocery checkout didn't promise much help. Even the ones touting overnight tone-em-up regimens showed a conspicuous lack of interest in handling gray hair and age spots. For a split-second, I imagined myself sneaking out of the local drug store with a plain brown paper wrapper full of products designed to conceal and firm and tone. Scary thought.

About some things a gal just had to draw a line. Adam Groft or no Adam Groft, I was not about to pretend I wasn't graying. That was non-negotiable.

Still, one thing our mutual friend Margo had managed to communicate. Despite her somewhat eccentric notion of style, at eighty-six the woman was living proof that you didn't have to just throw in the towel either. I decided I owed it to myself to drag my aching body out to that outlet mall north of here tomorrow. The pamper-yourself boutique might at least offer some emergency triage.

When I got up the energy to write, my local community news column this week also included a brief entry:

> On the sick list this week over in Aurelius, Howard Jorgensen. If you think about it, send Margo and Howard a card. He's on the mend and should be back on the community garden crew again soon.

Adam called me up as soon as the paper hit the mail boxes. He wanted to thank me for the bit about Margo and Howard.

After we hung up, I found myself staring at the phone in my hand like some rare artifact that just surfaced while turning over a spadeful of earth on that berm of ours. Even if I was still wrestling with grave doubts about Adam's motives and character, I had to admit—when I least expected it and even at my most cynical, the guy had class.

As planned, the night before Fourth of July parade, all of the crew but Margo and Howard hung out in Bea's driveway. Our mission? To stuff yellow, white and assorted green crepe paper wads in a six-foot chicken wire daisy that Artie and Roger had constructed earlier in the day in the middle of a borrowed flatbed trailer.

Precarious was a kind description for what we were trying to beautify. To hold up that enormous blossom, Artie and Roger had bolted together a tower of wooden mini-cable spools from the phone company, then wound chicken wire around the outside of the spools to conceal the rough and uneven edges. When the wire mesh was stuffed with green paper wads, that massive base was supposed to look like a stem.

I tried not to let myself dwell on invidious comparisons between that scene and one decades ago—getting ready for my first high school Homecoming celebration. But then, as my Gramma Eva always said, "If you don't laugh...you die!" While Vivian and I stuffed away on the chicken wire, I decided to pour out my pitiful saga.

Dateless until the last minute, the math teacher—a friend of my mom's—took pity on me and bribed a geek whose dog had eaten his homework into taking me by promising the kid an excuse. Risk an F or take Eve to the dance. It wasn't a formula for success but it got results.

So had my retelling the story. Artie was shaking so hard with laughter, I was afraid he was going to burst a blood vessel—and I hadn't even hit the punch line.

"We finished the float the Saturday morning of the parade," I told them. "It was ninety in the shade and I got a sunburn you wouldn't believe. The float ran over my foot so I couldn't dance. I had so many cuts on my hands from working with the chicken wire that mom made me wear white gloves. The geek showed up two hours late—hammered. And you can guess what happened when he walked me home...."

I paused. At that, Adam made eye contact over the curved wire outline of a petal.

"So help me?" I said. "The kid started to kiss me and threw up on my shoes."

His explosion of laughter matched if not exceeded Artie's. Finally, gasping for breath, Adam shook his head. "Hard to top that one—"

"Yeah, well...forewarned is forearmed. Or is the other way around?"

It was barely out of my mouth when I realized how Adam could take that disclaimer. After all, he was about to head off for what could turn out to be one very long evening—with anything but prom queen material. Adam's eyebrow arched as he caught my meaning. Chivalry or not, there was still time to back out if he felt so inclined.

"Nice try," he muttered. "Just try and get out of this."

I felt my face go hot, but glancing around me, I sensed no one else had heard. Artie was engrossed in helping Vivian secure a wayward section of chicken wire to one of the support braces. Adam just laughed.

At least I had to concede it was cooler working away on the hulk of a daisy than either that fateful Homecoming or tending the real Shastas growing out there on the berm. A front had passed through during the day that must have pretty much decimated the rest of the peonies.

Let's hope that the daisy we were building wasn't headed for a similar fate. Thinking ahead, Adam had brought some wire to help anchor the mesh sculpture to some cleats along the floor of the flatbed. He also supplied random hunks of dark gardener's cloth to made the furrows and cover up the wires as much as possible.

The idea was to make the daisy look like it was out blooming on the berm. Vivian turned out to be quite a calligrapher, so Bea put her to work lettering a sign with the same text as the one in our real garden.

Once completed, Artie the Teamster hitched up his borrowed cab, cautiously tugged the float out into the road and parked it against the curb. We could see even in those few yards, that the effect was more realistic than we anticipated. That daisy bobbed and swayed like a summer storm was kicking up.

By default—the youngest and least likely of the crew to be bothered by heatstroke—Adam and I were drafted into riding with the flimsy structure the full length of the parade to make sure it didn't slide off into the road half way down the Xenaphon main drag. It was a rather steep hill for the high school drum and bugle corps to say nothing of jerry rigged floats. Artie installed some cable fencing used to keep cargo from shifting to make sure Adam and I didn't join the daisy on the asphalt.

In front of us marched a contingent from the regional library, slamming book covers open and shut in tandem: the first and only librarian marching band I'd ever experienced. Behind, a dozen multi-aged students from the local martial arts academy kicked and chopped their way along the route, garbed as everything from Lady Liberty to Robin Hood. Only in Northern Michigan.

81

By the time Adam and I finished baby-sitting that daisy, first during the hour-long mustering and then the additional hour the parade was underway, the bloom was off more than the crepe-paper perennial. "Ladies don't sweat," my grandmother always told me. But I was long past glowing when I finally took off my straw hat and changed out of the jeans and Aurelius Gang-Green tee shirt that Vivian had created for the occasion using one of those killer sewing machines that do everything but weave the fabric. The name, of course, was vintage Artie.

"If there were a lake within arm's reach, I'd jump in it," I complained out loud to Adam.

We had been waiting out in the sun on that flatbed for some time now while our intrepid Teamster eased the float into Bea's narrow driveway. And we still had the final deadheading of our erstwhile daisy ahead of us before Artie could take back the borrowed flatbed.

"Why don't we, then?" Adam said. "Pick up your suit on the way out of town. Mine's in the trunk. By the time we've helped Artie and Bea dismantle the float, it' ll be three o'clock."

Bad idea. But it would be tough to get out of it now. Fully clothed, I could delude myself that I could pass for mid-fifties. The only hope for achieving the same thing would be a chin-to-ankle wet suit—and even then, I had my doubts about its power to salvage my sagging silhouette.

Chill, I kept telling myself. This was not a date, after all—just two relative strangers getting out of the heat, watching the fireworks. Any other fireworks were about as likely as that daisy-on-steroids we had cobbled together taking root on that flatbed.

"I'll think about it." I said.

Adam just grinned.

Chapter Twelve

Time, for a garden, has a peculiar kind of rhythm.
Weeding and watering, thinning and cultivating demand
attention minute by minute...the consummate Now. But
between that minutia and the Big Picture of the season to
come, between the struggle and the blooming, are always
the memories of growing seasons Past—what the garden
was and what it can be again. Eve Brenneman's journal.

The mirage of Lake Michigan shimmered on the horizon of the windshield the entire drive from Xenaphon to the birch and pine shaded shoreline. I hadn't been there since I'd moved back to northern Michigan, and it was time.

We found a spot at a deserted little pullout west of Petoskey and parked. The usual tourists were probably grilling out at their cottages or trying to placate the kids with mini-golf waiting for dusk.

Adam went ahead to scout out the least rocky stretch of beach. For the past ten miles I had been mentally tackling the logistics of switching from my khakis and navy blue pocket tee to my swimsuit—in the car, no less. It was like wrestling an alligator into a Hefty bag, but I managed. The oatmeal summer weave cardigan I had brought along for later would work as a makeshift coverup over my suit.

Even with a plan, I took my time making my way through the beach grass to the shoreline. Adam had knelt down to test the water temperature. The prognosis was not good.

"Be prepared for the shock of your life, Eve," he said.

"Cold?"

"Antarctica. Try low sixties."

"If you're planning a heart attack…? I don't know CPR."

Laughing, he chose the get-it-over-with approach. Wade in ankle deep and then just sprint like heck and take the plunge.

I had two choices, none of them good. Either risk cardiac arrhythmia as he had done or shiver my way to shoulder depth. The latter, of course, would accentuate the deplorable state of my one and only bathing suit. I'd bought the black swim dress with an eye for practicality not style. It was supposed to "slenderize" without resorting to major surgical nips and tucks.

I didn't give either one of us time to think about it. Reluctantly, I opted for the polar bear express. Leaving the coverup behind at water's edge next to several enormous towels Adam had deposited there, I tore in and struggled back out again just as fast.

It was hard to breathe. I tried to cry out, but no sound came.

The rocks along the water's edge made it tough to keep my footing as I picked my way toward safety. An alarming red, and not entirely from sunburn acquired on the float along the parade route, I grabbed one of the oversize towels and wrapped myself in it. I was shivering so hard my teeth chattered.

Out in deeper water, Adam had been taking it all in. His laughter echoed across the deserted beach.

"A little brisk out here," he said.

"You're telling me."

Adam sliced his way through the water in my direction, confident hand-over-hand strokes that left a trail of wake churning behind him. Someone who works out, without being obsessive about it, I concluded. No washboard abs, but not in bad shape for our age either—broad shoulders and strong runner's legs. A guy does a lot of lifting and hauling in the nursery business.

By now I had toweled off and pulled on the coverup, painfully aware that even in my prime, nobody would have ever pegged me for a jock. I took faint comfort in the fact that at least I had managed to avoid the deadly ten-pounds-a-decade disease. Fortunately, too, the worst of the problems were now literally undercover. Joel always said my ankles were my best feature.

"Believe it or not," I stuttered through lips still reluctant to move, "my brother and I learned to swim in this lake. To get us to even go in, they had to convince us that the life guards plugged in heaters every day an hour before we showed up for lessons."

"And you believed them?"

A shower of icy water set me shivering again as I handed him his towel. "Dear God, I didn't think it was going to be that cold," he muttered through clenched teeth as he headed for the car to change into jeans again.

In northern Michigan, it is considered an art form to go from beach gear to resort casual in the front seat of a Chevy. And to do it without mooning the occupants of the car parked right next door.

When it was my turn, Adam discreetly chose that moment to head back to the water's edge to rinse the sand off his feet before sliding into his docksiders. I hastily got dressed, gave my close-cropped salt-and-pepper hair a brisk toweling, and then slapped on a dash of the new lipstick I had picked up earlier in the week. At least it made a dent in that blue pallor only a plunge into Lake Michigan can induce.

"What say, we find someplace in the Gaslight District?" Adam suggested. "Dinner? Antifreeze?"

I laughed. "Right now I'd kill for a plate of mid-winter comfort food—burgers, chili, anything hot and spicy." Anything to stop shaking.

Instead, Adam talked me into a leisurely two-hour round of wine and upscale northern Michigan cuisine. Smoked whitefish for an appetizer, morels on flank steak. The menu read like a familiar novel, worth re-experiencing time and again.

I still had grave misgivings about what I had gotten myself into. But for the most part as the afternoon wore on, the two of us just talked as I hadn't talked in a very long time. The waiter arrived with our salads, temporarily stemming the flow.

Closing my eyes, I savored the tart nuggets of dried Michigan cherries hidden among the baby field greens. It was in part culinary ecstacy and in part the only practical way to avoid Adam's quizzical gaze.

"There's something I've been wanting to ask for weeks now," he said finally. "You haven't offered...so I assumed maybe you didn't want to talk about it."

"Ask away."

"So, how did *you* wind up in a place like this, Eve? You know my excuse—*Groft*. It's plastered all over that greenhouse."

Laughter is an amazing growth hormone. We were learning how to use it.

"Nothing traumatic or earth-shaking. Just simple geography," I told him. "I grew up on Lake Michigan just outside of Petoskey. Since my grandmother lived in Xenaphon, as kids my brother and I went down there a lot. After dad died, mom continued to teach school outside of Petoskey and in the off-season she supervised the teens working at a custard stand here in Xenaphon. It's gone now...."

"Then, you know little Traverse Bay resort country. Not too hard to take."

"That do-it-yourselfer of mine? Originally, Gram left it to mom," I told him. "Then she passed as well. Since my brother lives in Oregon, he could have cared less about the house. That left me—"

"Sounds familiar."

"I suppose so. The place may be a bit of a wreck now—not like what you're dealing with, but there was never any question I'd live here some day. Every summer that yard of Gram's was my playground, her garden my therapist. She was the only woman I ever knew with arms so long that she could actually weed standing up. Everything seemed to thrive with that Green Thumb of hers. Solid German stock—worn and chiseled like the Niagara Escarpment."

"That same bedrock coming through in Margo." Adam chuckled. "Grandmother Groft was like that."

"Just between you and me? As a young man—I think Dutch had a crush on your grandmother."

Adam looked up from his salad, searching my face. For what? I asked myself. His own expression gave no clue.

"Most people did," he said brusquely. "Me included."

"That's kind of how I felt about Gramma Eva, too. Mom was widowed so young—preoccupied a lot of the time. Gram always had the time to tuck me in at night and hug me like there wasn't anything more important in the world."

"You must miss her."

"It hit me at the point her lawyer turned over her house keys," I told him. "My husband's estate was pretty much settled. I was still working at the ad agency but it made less sense every day. Maybe I hoped some of Gram's Prussian endurance would rub off on me.

Anyway…one Friday, I just drafted my resignation letter, pumped out a stack of resumes and wound up working for fun money at the *Xenaphon Weekly Gazette*."

It was the most spontaneous decision of my life, I realized. And for all that, the one that made the most sense.

"And her garden?"

There he touched on a nerve. Until this very moment, I didn't realize how raw the subject was. If pressed, I couldn't have come up with a reason.

"I've started to resurrect it…starting with a few vegetables," I shrugged. "But there's still a lot of square feet back there somewhere under a jungle of brush and debris!"

"Nervous you're not up to the job?"

"Maybe. Partly. More the feeling, though, that she'd want me to make it my own and not quite knowing how."

"So, you started in on that berm out there instead." It wasn't a question. "I can understand that."

The same reason, I suspect, why Adam showed up on our garden crew that first time. I took a deep breath, fired off a non-question of my own.

"I still can't quite figure out…why you gave us all those plants."

He thought about it hard, before answering. As if wanting to get it right.

"It was either that or just hand you the deed," he said. "You caught me at a low point that day. Funny what a mountain of pain can go into an insignificant piece of real estate. I'm not sure I can ever make my peace with that place."

"But you've decided to try."

"Nothing so noble. Between Dutch's pep talks and the Internal Revenue Service? I'm not sure I really have a choice."

"Are you familiar with the story of Candide?"

Adam winced. "Voltaire or Bernstein? I'm not sure the situation out there is worth a 65-piece orchestra."

He obviously knew where my thoughts were headed. The philosophical novel and opera based on it are the classic tale of the wandering son who finds redemption in hard work and literally making his garden grow. My latest column was based on it.

"Take your pick," I shrugged. "I can think of worse scenarios for making sense of our niche in the great scheme of things."

I couldn't understand why I hadn't pegged him as good looking. It was that magnetic smile and the eyes that explained the transformation. When you had his attention, you knew it.

He obviously was literate—a man with sophisticated tastes, but one who never flaunted it. As I got to know him better, I never had the feeling he was out to score points in a verbal game of Trivial Pursuit. One topic we both avoided like the plague. What all of this really meant on a you-and-me level, apart from a mutual trip down memory lane?

Around six we headed down to the breakwater and hooked up with his friends. I carried our jackets while Adam fished around in the back of the SUV and came up with a wicker picnic basket. Heavy, from the look of it.

"Rocks?" I speculated.

"Vino."

The expectations of our fellow sailors quickly became obvious. The party, it seems, had arrived. As we got ready to board, our host—a tall, muscular man in khaki shorts and a university tee-shirt—reached over and snagged the wicker basket and passed it along toward a teakwood storage bench at the side of the cockpit.

"Adam's here…let the pyrotechnics begin!"

I don't know what I had expected of anyone who actually sailed something bigger than a sunfish, but Adam's friend Jake Perry was as disingenuous as his cue-ball haircut. Whether it was a fashion statement or a way of dealing with a receding hairline, the net result was to give him the rakish air of a Barbary pirate.

The whole bunch of them were huggers. And I thought our gardening crew had the monopoly on that habit!

Jake's companion, Angie, was a garrulous blonde whose age I pegged as a good twenty years his junior. The other couple was introduced as a professor of English literature from the western part of the state and his wife, Margaret. Based on body language, I'd say Margaret and spouse were not exactly on the best of speaking terms.

One positive note. At least the other women were not the type to spend the evening bombarding me with endless questions about kids, grandkids, and domestic minutiae. A Bachelor's degree grad in general studies, Angie defined her status as putting in time as an office assistant mainly to save up for an around-the-world cruise. Margaret, I learned, recently sold a highly successful real estate office she had run for thirty years in a college town down-state.

Jake filled in the blanks.

"We grew up together…the three of us," he said. "Adam, the Prof, and I. Lost contact, then hooked up again several years ago. Adam's the only one who seems to be digging in up here. I'm shuffling back and forth between summers here and winters in Hawaii."

"Trying to sail year-round?" I teased.

Jake grinned. "Or work on my tan…take your pick. In any case, not a workaholic like our pale-as-the underside-of-fish friend, the Prof here! I made my bundle in the market, got out while the getting was good."

His blond companion snickered. The professor's wife, Margaret, was not amused.

"Our Prof, here, is not emeritus," she snapped. "Nor likely to be. Someday they'll find him slumped over the lectern, cold as a mackerel. I, for one, am not waiting that long. I've booked two tickets for a winter in the Virgin Islands, and by god I'm going to use 'em!"

The Prof—I never did learn his real name—grimaced but said nothing. Instead, he fished around in the basket Adam had brought and hauled out a bottle of merlot, corkscrew and a stash of unbreakable wine glasses.

"When in doubt, my sweet," he said, tipping his ample glass in Margaret's direction. Proceeded to drain it.

We were well beyond the Petoskey harbor light before Jake started to hoist sail and cut the engine. Adam busied himself securing hardware and hoisting lines on command as his friend maneuvered the craft into open water.

"Wanna get your sea legs back?"

Adam demurred. "Thanks but I've gotten to a point where I'd just as soon watch the hors d'oeuvres slide across the deck—than be hanging on to that tiller. Go right ahead."

He settled down with me on the front deck, but not before I caught the quizzical raised-eyebrow exchange that passed between the two men. Message sent, message received.

"Been there...done that, Lord help me," Adam muttered under his breath, as he reached around behind me to snap a line free from behind a stay where the wind had caught it.

I wasn't sure what he was trying to tell me. Still, from his tone, this much was clear. Whatever passed between the two old friends, Adam was distancing himself—for my benefit at least—from his friend's lifestyle. Goodness knows, for starters Jake's taste in women and my presence on that boat were as about as far apart on the old compass as a guy could get.

The other two women were in the process of breaking out an impressive spread of gourmet fixings. I must have looked at loose ends—wanting to help, but not knowing quite how on that narrow deck. Adam laid a hand on mine, flashed a reassuring smile. Jake must have noticed.

"Trust me, Eve," Jake said, "you don't want to get caught in the middle of that."

"Too many cooks?"

"Something like that."

He wasn't through. "So...," he ventured. "Adam tells me you're an amazing writer?"

The question caught me mid-bite. I chewed away thoughtfully on the square of melba toast and smoked brie, wondering just what else Adam might have passed along by way of a biography.

"Journalist would be more accurate at the moment," I told him. "Before that? Advertising—"

"Ever thought of taking a crack at fiction?"

At that I saw the Prof perk up. I remembered, too late, that literature was his speciality.

"Can't say I've had the urge," I admitted. "Although they used to say at the ad agency that most copy writers have at least a novella stashed away somewhere. Makes for great cocktail party conversation—"

"True enough," Margaret said grimly. "The Prof here has been at it for twenty years. A hundred-fifty pages, a fortune in toner cartridges—and a hell of a lot of cocktail parties later? There's still no end in sight."

I truly regretted inadvertently sending her down that road—communicated as much with the pained look I flashed in Adam's direction. Jake's date giggled. The Prof just shrugged, downed the last of the Merlot in his glass, then reached for the bottle, anticipating number three. It was hard not to keep score.

"Radically different styles, of course, Eve," he said, a trifle testily. "Advertising and journalism. Mastering plot structure and dialogue…now there's a challenge."

"A friend of mine," I told him, forcing my most conciliatory smile, "used to write with the soap operas or talk shows blaring away in the background. Said it helped to create a more faithful rhythm of speech."

For a second, the Prof just looked at me—then a slow smile spread across his flushed features. He had gotten the message. I wasn't letting him get my goat. More to the point, I knew a lot more about writing than he had assumed.

Score one for the little guys. As Adam leaned over to top off my glass, he gave me a subtle thumbs up.

"Actually, Jake," he said, extending the bottle in his friend's direction. "Eve is being far too modest about her story telling skills. I don't know how she does it, but even weeding a bed of peonies sounds adventurous."

"So…*that's* how you wind up on that damn berm every Saturday morning instead of out here on the Bay, hanging over the rail, crewing for me!"

Jake's girlfriend took that as a cue to assert her proprietary rights. "You don't know what you're missing, Adam," she said, snuggling alongside Jake on the narrow pilot's seat. "We came in fifth in the regatta two weeks ago. Jake says I'm great with a winch."

Right now—judging by Jake's sheepish look—her current public display of affection was playing havoc with his helmsmanship. There was hardly any breeze, and after a few failed attempts at a tack, he gave up. Firing up the engines, he aimed the bow north and west toward the setting sun. Mercifully, the steady progress of the boat calmed the tension level on board considerably. The air was cooling off and a light mist rose from the water. Halfway out into the Bay we dropped anchor next to a growing cluster of boats.

It was an interesting collection of water craft. Sleek yachts like our own hunkered next to small outboard driven putt-arounds. The queen of the fleet was an elegantly refurbished Vintage lake steamer used to transport passengers from the railway to area resort hotels in the late

1800s.   All gleaming teak and brass bright-work.

With the low cloud bank against the horizon, the sunset promised to be spectacular. It didn't disappoint. Intense red-gold rays splayed out across the water and at the very last moment, just after the sun itself disappeared, its afterglow shimmered like a fiery path stretching toward us across the still surface of the lake.

"Not much a guy can say after something like that," Adam said softly as the light dimmed, vanished. "You could bury me right here and now and I'd be a happy man."

"For a while there?" I told him in a discreet undertone. "I thought it might come to that. With all that…thrust-and-parry stuff going on? I was getting ready to get out a Tevlar vest."

"Or pass out the valium."

Our muted laughter suggested an intimacy that wasn't intentional. Still, I couldn't help notice Jake's curious glances in our direction.

Chapter Thirteen

I'm not aging, I just need to be repotted. Unknown

Some nights you just remember. This turned out to be one of them.

The sky was still tinged a faint turquoise along the horizon when the first of the salvoes went off along the south shore of the Lake. Transfixed, we spent the next half hour in a garden of exotic delight as the bombs and rockets flowered into shimmering mounds of red and blue and gold, only to have the breeze carry away the fragile blooms in a shower of metallic ash.

I felt myself shivering at each new burst of light playing itself out against the brooding sky. Adam must have noticed. Whether it was his doing or just the narrow confines of the bow, we wound up snugged against one another. His arms were warm and comfortable cradling my shoulders.   And whatever Jake and the others thought, it wasn't an embrace.

Grounding one another, if I had to put a label on it, the way people do watching forces at work they cannot explain—aware of their shared sense of finiteness.   But then none of that needed words to express.

The moment passed. Jake guided our boat safely through the shoal of humanity around us back to the break wall. Adam and I said our farewells and started for home. We still had a long road ahead of us back to Xenaphon so we fortified ourselves on the way out of town with a scalding cup of high-test at one of the burger chains.

"I'm going to need a snooze alarm 'til that caffeine kicks in," Adam told me.

"How about I talk your ear off...?"

He grinned. "The stations around here are way too mellow after midnight. Go for it...!"

After ten minutes of comments on the fireworks and Jake's boat, for some reason I found myself telling Adam about a friend years ago who had bought a 25-foot sail boat similar to Jake's at a marina out of town. The guy didn't have a license for the trailer to haul it home, so the marina owner told him to slap a sign on the back of the boat, "In Transit", and then worry about the license later. The only things required for the permit were a couple of bucks and a name for the boat.

"Three months later? That sign was still there and the guy still hadn't thought of a name. It was really getting to him...until it finally occurred to him that maybe the sign itself was trying to tell him something."

"As in...sell the thing? Bad investment...?"

I laughed. "Possible...but, No. By default, it seems, he had found the name for his boat. Carefully lettering 'In Transit' on the side of the bow, he went and bought his permit."

"That's one way to do it—"

"The idea makes a lot of sense," I said. "I believe we're all...in transit, one way or another. We plan or dodge, thinking we have life under control—"

"And then when we least expect it, things that started out one way...wind up another."

I thought about it in the comfortable silence that settled in between us. We had left the shoreline long ago, were driving through miles of dense evergreen woods, thinned back from the highway because of the deer. The road spun out like a ribbon of black ahead of us. Although the headlights were halogen, they were no match for the vastness of the night.

"I'm really glad you came." Adam said.

His voice was low, tentative, as if wanting to say something else, and not sure how to start. I shivered. It had the same feel as this

94

afternoon at the lake—standing on the edge of the unknown.

"I am, too."

I meant it. The rockier moments notwithstanding.

"Jake can be…." Adam hesitated as he shot a glance in my direction. "I was worried you might find him a bit too…hail-fellow-well-met."

"I liked him," I protested. "A lot. He's unpretentious. Knows what he wants, and just does it. No guilt trips or second-guessing there."

I thought I heard Adam's intake of breath. He hadn't expected that reaction—but then, neither had I. Adam easily could have left it at that. He didn't.

"That…could have been…*me* out there a couple of years ago," he said. "Provided you didn't dig around too far below the surface."

When an explanation wasn't forthcoming I just waited. As the mile markers flashed past, I was becoming more and more unsure where he was headed or how to react.

"But then I suspect you pretty much had me pegged from Day One out there on the berm," he said. "Dating someone at least a decade or two younger. Trying to convince myself I wasn't on the downslope of sixty. Assuming all this is forever—that if I just moved fast enough I could outrun not just my past. . .but my own mortality…."

His voice trailed off. Gaze fixed straight ahead on the white center line on the roadway, he wasn't in a position to notice me watching him. I found myself sketching in my mind's eye that strong profile outlined by the soft glow from the dash panel and the tension in his shoulders as he clutched the wheel.

"Don't misunderstand me," he said. "Jake's my oldest friend in the world. He's smarter than hell, richer than Midas…has saved my bacon more than once."

"We want different things at different points in our lives, Adam. Understandable."

When he didn't respond, I chalked it up to the car's headlights coming at us in the other lane. One look at his face caught in that harsh glare told me otherwise.

"After dad died," he said bluntly, "I hit rock bottom. If you'd have given me a nickel for the business, I'd have been tempted. Join Jake in Hawaii…? Hell, I would have talked him into that round-the-world junket he finally got around to planning—with or without his latest live-in."

"But instead you stayed. In Xenaphon—"

Adam laughed. He shook his head.

"Go figure," he said. "That crazy garden started it, I suppose. By comparison even a godforsaken greenhouse out in the middle of nowhere started to look good. Margo and Howard—now, how the heck do you just dismiss something like that? Even Vivian and her Taj-Mahal of a trellis."

And then came the punch-line. "And *you*," he said. "Something else I didn't anticipate."

Adam shifted in his seat, shot a quick glance in my direction. I'll be forever grateful that this time the lack of light was in my favor. My reaction was unreadable.

He wasn't through. "You've risked a hell of a lot more in your life than I have," he said. "You married, Eve…raised a family, handled the death of a spouse. I did none of those things. I spent sixty-five years so obsessed with what I *didn't* want to become, that I don't know if I'm even *capable* of taking that kind of chance—prepared to trust another human being that much. Myself included."

"And you seriously think to have tried…and *failed* makes it any easier?"

Adam must have wondered what the heck I was talking about. But to his eternal credit he chose not to ask.

"For the record," I volunteered, "when Joel…my husband was killed? He had been drinking. The woman in the car with him—not the first, by the way—hung on in a coma for another month. Under the circumstances, at least her husband wasn't in a good position to sue."

"None of that your fault—*none*…!"

"Tell that to my daughters. I've got one who pretty much has concluded I drove her Dad to it. The other? Pretty much blames me for not divorcing him before it ever came to that."

Adam's hands flexed, then tightened on the wheel. His mouth was clamped in a hard line. When he spoke, it was so quietly that at first I thought I had only imagined it. He repeated the question.

"How long were you—?"

"Too long. On the books? The marriage lasted twenty-nine years. Of course, all pretext of passion went out the window quick enough. Joel, it seems, wanted a mother not a wife."

96

I let that tough bit of reality sink in. Grandma Eva told me that all marriages have their rocky moments. By anyone's definition, I was describing a minefield.

"His...loss, Eve. Not yours."

"Were it only that simple. By the time I woke up...tried to get up the courage to finally pull the plug—?"

"Circumstances intervened."

"Real moral courage, huh...!"

I broke off my halting confession. No one had to tell me that loyalty was not going to wash as an explanation for why I stayed with Joel for nearly thirty years. The sound of the tires on asphalt was hypnotic, strangely comforting in the awkward silence that followed.

"Before you ask how anyone can be that...stupid? I'll tell you," I said. "Joel had been on the road so much, I felt...alone a lot of the time anyway. And much as I loved my girls, I was angry at myself—or at least the choices I had made. Good old German logic argued, I had made my bed and had to lie in it, come hell or high water. There's nothing commendable in any of that...and in the end? I'm not sure it was the best thing for the girls either."

"You lived through it, Eve. Humor intact. I'm not sure how many in your shoes can say that."

"Let's just say, I came away with one of those priceless life lessons," I told him. "Some things are worse than being alone."

"Such as...?"

His voice was gentle, but persistent all the same. I would have thought that was fairly obvious after what I had just admitted—and for a split-second I was on the verge of telling him that in no uncertain terms. But then, I figured it out...sensed what Adam was really asking. It was not the relationship or marriage I had given up on. It was something far more basic.

"The worst?" I told him softly, only now admitting it even to myself. "It's knowing you aren't loved. Not the way you need to be. Amazing what *that* can do to your self-respect."

It was so still in the car, I would not have been surprised to hear our breathing. For a long time Adam didn't react. When he did, it wasn't the way I was expecting. Not at all.

"So if...what would you say, if I said I'd like us to start...seeing each other?"

We already were, more or less on a regular basis. But that was not what he was talking about. I had to hand it to him, the guy had guts. After what I had just laid on him, most men—I suspected—would run for the hills.

The incongruity of the situation hit like a sudden flash of headlights from the road ahead. I had not even seriously considered dating since Joel died. The "why" of it had never come up. Yet here I was…alone in the middle of the night with a man who for much of his life, by his own admission, had cultivated a pattern of relationships not that different from Joel's.

There was no point in avoiding the inevitable.

"I'm…flattered, Adam. Truly I am—"

"But…?"

"I'd would be lying if I said I'm not attracted to you. But then, you're also smart enough to figure the odds. In second relationships, people tend to stick to type. And in a lot of ways? Face it, you remind me of my…of Joel…!"

"Ouch."

We had hit a particularly dark stretch of roadway so I wasn't even tempted to look in Adam's direction. Still, I had started us down this path and by gum, I had better finish it.

"Your clothes, your friends, your…ease with handling people—the very fact I *am*…attracted to you scares me witless. I've lived this one. I know how it can end."

The silence throbbed in my ears like the quiet purr of the engine. Taking us farther apart, I suspected, with every passing mile marker.

"So much for the power of redemption," Adam chuckled softly.

"You think I'm being…judgmental—?"

"Honest. I respect that. But surely you see, you've maneuvered me into an impossible position here?"

I bristled. "*Maneuvered*…?"

"*Maneuvered.* I've been dead honest with you…about where my life has been and where I want it to go. If I try to convince you that clothes don't make a man, that good manners and political horse sense are not necessarily character flaws, and that your instincts are a lot sounder than your fears? Then, I'm just ladling out more of everything you're convinced ruined your life. A classic no-win if I ever saw one."

It seemed an odd time to remember. But I kept coming back to my conversation with Dutch that afternoon in the greenhouse. I remembered what he said, about the boy this man had been—the detours along the way. How it takes a whole lot of love and patience to grow not just plants, but people.

"Do you…honestly believe people can…*change,* Adam?"

"There are two people in this car, Eve," he said slowly. "Are you talking about yourself, here? Or me—?"

He was right. The truth hit me as if that air bag coiled up in that dashboard in front of me had suddenly gone off in my face. This was not just about Adam…who he was and what his life had been. *Where was I in all this?*

After all those years with Joel, was I capable of trusting not just this relative stranger sitting alongside me but any man? Even more to the point, could I trust myself…my own heart and my own judgment? Every cell in my heart and brain was screaming out at me—*this was no Joel*, his candid autobiography notwithstanding.

Could people change? I gave him the most honest answer I could.

"I guess, I'd have to say, I'll think about it."

He straightened in his seat. That was followed by a quick glance in my direction.

"Fair enough."

This was unknown territory into which we had blundered, like that silent void beyond the reach of our headlights, deceptively endless. The Xenaphon village limits sign told us otherwise.

Once in the driveway Adam broke his usual pattern, let me manage the car door, sparing us both that awkward march across the lawn—that inevitable wondering how to end it. The expression in his eyes was telegraphing another scenario entirely.

The man was only honoring my scruples, giving me the space I had asked for. So, then why did the prospect of navigating that solitary stretch of lawn toward my front steps leave me feeling so subdued—even vaguely abandoned?

"While you do…think about it?" he said as I started to close the SUV door. "I assume we'll see each other Saturday…if not before."

Saturday? I didn't say it, but the question must have registered all the same.

"The garden," he prompted gently.

His mouth curled into a smile as I processed that familiar reference point. Yes, of course, the garden.

"See you then," I told him.

Chapter Fourteen

Operas, music critics say, are about sex and death. So are gardens. In both cases, the beauty that results? A bonus. Unknown

The phrase TMI—too much information—was made for the relationship between parents and children. As teenagers and young adults we think the keep-details-to-a-minimum system of communication was invented just for us as we stonewall the older generation on any and every occasion. At some point in life, I have discovered, the principle works just as well the other way around.

A wake-up call from my eldest wasn't unusual, but this time Leslie's voice on the line triggered alarm bells all the same. I hadn't exactly gotten a lot of sleep after Adam brought me home and this—the morning after, my head was still feeling the impact of a little too much merlot.

"Mom, you're there. Called last night to wish you a happy Fourth, but nobody answered."

Leslie had been supportive enough since her dad's accident. Still, I wondered, what would she think of her sixty-two-year-old mother spending half the night out on Little Traverse Bay on a yacht with a hunk in his late sixties? The closest thing to a date I'd had in nearly thirty years.

"Was out with friends," I told her. "Watching the fireworks. We got home really late."

Mercifully, she let that pass. Her quick intake of breath signaled a major pronouncement.

"Mom? Dan and I have something to tell you."

"Fire away."

"You're going to be a grandmother again."

The wind deserted my sails not unlike our boat last night as we rounded the Petoskey lighthouse. That would make two for Leslie. Youngest daughter Gina had a son about four, little Emma's age—although I had never seen the boy. Forget that I still wasn't totally prepared to handle the fact that I was the mother of a twenty-eight and thirty-year-old.

"Wonderful," I said. "When?"

"Christmas. We were thinking maybe you could take off from the paper and come out then for a week or two."

A lot could happen in six months. "Yes," I told her. "Great. I'd like that very much. Let's work on it."

The two of them and granddaughter Emma had been living just outside Chicago for a little over a year, in a little town along the Michigan lakeshore but on the Wisconsin side of the line. I'd been there the Christmas after they moved. After all the years living in Chicago, I still found it strange as a Michigander to adjust my frame of reference to all that water sitting due west not east of me.

Even a stranger memory elbowed that one aside. Only yesterday. It was Adam's broad shoulders and strong, muscular frame cutting through the same icy blue water toward me, that half-smile of his betraying more than a casual interest—daring me to take the plunge.

"Mom, are you okay? You sound kind of—"

"Just distracted," I told her, shook myself alert. "Making coffee. I've got a column due and it's been bothering me."

It wasn't quite the truth, but close enough That's the trouble with writing. Once you start, you can't always control the flow of either thoughts or words that come percolating up.

Leslie and I talked for a while after that, about kids and her job with a local vanity press specializing in regional art and history, about Dan's traveling too much for his sales job with a building materials manufacturer. Several times I came just inches from blurting out the truth. "Leslie, what would you think if I started dating again?" Or worse, "You see, there's this guy—"

102

Instead I kept nursing my coffee and, eventually, wound things down, promising to call again soon. Once off the phone, I headed again for the safety of my laptop journal.

*I keep thinking about that book—now a film, though I haven't seen it—*Life as a House. *My life, if it ever comes to that, would not revolve around what it means to build, but about what and how to grow. Alone and together.*

At first I thought what my boss was proposing was odd, if not impossible: to talk about gardens in one breath and then community development the next. Fact is, the two things have more than a little in common.

After all, isn't gardening about creating a community? Plants can be a community. But they don't start out that way. Separated at first in that bed, over time they grow together until it's tough to tell where one starts and the other leaves off. Some of that may be intentional; some of it, inevitably just happens.

Every once in a while a "volunteer" pops up–that's what gardeners call it when a plant self-seeds or sends out its roots and just shows up somewhere else. Usually that is where you least expect it.

Then you have to decide—are you going to root it out? Or maybe you'll decide that stranger looks good wherever it staked out its spot. After a while, you get used to it. Like a splash of red or yellow where everything around it is green or lilac.

Even if you start gardening all alone, you can't help over time to create a community of people, too. Somebody loans you something. You give someone roots from those day lilies you just dug out because you can't bear to just throw them away. Even if you set the stuff you dig out along the curb on rubbish day, somebody is bound to come along and pick it up. You may never know who or where, but a part of you—what you've helped nurture—is flowering away somewhere else. Those give-away-throw-away plants wind up impacting places and people, sometimes even without their knowing it.

I don't know where Adam Croft is in my garden these days. And it bothers me. For the first time since Joel died, I actually admitted—out loud—to someone the truth about his death, our marriage. To his eternal credit, Adam didn't go running for cover: although heaven knows, I wouldn't blame him if he had.

But then I look in that full-length mirror in the hall with a dispassionate eye, trying to reconcile the extra pounds and the laugh lines that have as much to do with sorrow as joy. There are times in the night when I don't care about them or any of the reasons I conjure up telling me it's impossible that another man could ever want me as much as I want him.

And then all I can think of is the touch of Adam's arm brushing against mine as we stake up a plant together. Or I shiver at the memory of his breath coming hard against my skin, as he looks over at me weeding alongside him in the July heat. Laughing at the sheer, wonderful foolishness of it all.

Maybe my daughter Leslie wouldn't have been shocked if I'd told her that physically I'm coming alive again to feelings I thought were long dead and buried in the wreckage of a loveless marriage. But I would. Be shocked, that is.

At sixty-plus you just don't talk about those things. How did a friend put it when an acquaintance suddenly announced she was getting married again at eighty-two. "Isn't she past all of that?"

How much simpler for the first Adam, with no one there to tell him how it "ought to be". So he just stumbled out of that first Garden and started a family that went on to build the first cities, till and sow, create the first music, and somehow managed to survive. He lived out his days in that post-Eden world until he was a couple of hundred years old. Eve, I've got to assume, did the same. Although nobody wrote about that.

Today we read through all those "begats" that follow, chapter after chapter of excruciating lists, as if it's the most natural thing in the world. And then we shut the book, strip the genealogy of all its burning, wonderful sexuality. And we pretend that we can channel all those basic human needs and hopes and dreams into safe, sedate, controllable bounds.

My book—my "time in a garden"—would be about those thousands of years after Eden. Creating a new Garden out of sweat and grief and emotions so powerful that even now scholars argue over them ad infinitum.

Did Eve ever forget the anguish of raising those two sons who hated each other? Did Cain blame those first parents for a childhood that somehow made him unsure enough of himself even to think of destroying someone with the same incredible double helix spiraling through his body? What did that first couple whisper to one another all those years in that chill and starry night over the desert?

I want to know, need to know. For their story is my story. Growing from the same soil rich with hope and despair, our shared sense of touch and taste, and our aching passion to be held and loved. To be told that some things simply are too powerful to ever die.

Like Artie's peonies, blooming away out there on the berm, even knowing the risks, I wrote. *It's who we are.*

Column inches? Zero at the moment—at least not without some pretty heavy-handed censorship. My life was changing and with it my writing, even my column. Finding a way to make the personal and the textbook—first person and third person—style fit was going to take more work than I was prepared to do at the moment.

The house was a mess and I was exhausted. I had plenty of excuses not to dwell on any of it as I worked away my Sunday in mindless, solitary domesticity. The holiday was over.

 # Chapter Fifteen

Gardening requires a precarious truce between hope and despair. Seasoned gardeners experience loss and failure with frightening regularity, a situation that can become tougher to handle, not easier with time. And yet every true gardener clings to an even more powerful reality. Gardeners know if you had a garden somewhere once? One can be there again. Eve Brenneman's journal

Margo and Howard were back on the berm this week—July 11th—outfitted with sun hat brims ample enough to shade a small porch. Their brush with mortality two weeks ago left all of us on the garden crew shaken and edgy.

Bea showed up with enough equipment to set up an Emergency Rescue Squad, starting with a clip-on beach umbrella, collapsible camp chair with arm rests and foot stool plus a cooler full of mineral water. Her first aid kit would have sufficed for a professional hockey team. Artie the Teamster actually ditched his usual brandy for a cooler of his own, packed brim full of diet soda—just in case. Vivian had brought along one of those sit-and-ride garden weeders that doubles as a toolbox. If Adam was right and she overdosed on bug spray, at least she wouldn't have far to fall.

Since our "expedition" up to Lake Michigan for the Fourth, Adam had limited his contact to daily phone calls. We drove to the garden in separate cars.

That said, I came equipped with a healthy dose of resolve to limit our public conversation out on the berm to the contents of the rain gauge. Still empty, by the way. But then the weather service was predicting storms for the coming week.

Adam, too, had picked up on the forecast and had brought along a carton of stakes and pre-cut twist tape to shore up some of the more fragile plantings. We used forked branches from the nearby woods to stake up the largest of the flower heads.

"And if that wind starts howling, we're going to lose the astilbe," Bea lamented.

There wasn't really any way to protect those tall, delicate flower stalks…especially if they actually bloomed. Adam thought if the nights stayed cool, we might get lucky and they would peak after the round of storms moved on through..

Moderate to hot clear days, intense afternoon storms to push out the humidity, and nights that let you sleep without benefit of air conditioning. It was that contrast that drew the down-staters along with fugitives from Indiana and Ohio to the Top of the Mitten well into August.

Not that I was sleeping a lot lately. Whenever I let my guard down these days, my thoughts all seemed to be straying single-mindedly in one direction. *Adam Groft.*

While I couldn't pretend any longer there wasn't an attraction, a critical look in that mirror every morning—sans foundation and enough artifice to tame at least a few of the most obvious signs of the mid-sixties slump—was enough to shake my confidence considerably. Where the heck had that thirty-eight-year-old gone? If I had to fix a "prime", that was close enough. My teenage years had been a hormonal nightmare, the twenties obsessed with college then graduate school and carving out a niche for myself professionally in the Windy City.

Adam must have gauged the silence between us for what it was—*a serious case of second thoughts.* We were working off to one side, inserting and adjusting the tubing for the drip-irrigation system. Fussy and mindless as jobs went, this one was not worth the level of concentration I was giving it.

"Where did you meet…you and Joel?" he said evenly.

I just looked at him. "Chicago."

"Work…?"

"In the park behind the Museum of Science and Industry. Joel was jogging and I was writing terse little Haiku verses in a thick, leather-bound notebook."

Adam laughed. "You're kidding....right?"

"Unfortunately? No. We went out for drinks. We were married three months later. "

So much for whirlwind courtships. Adam was too polite to ask, but I decided that needed an explanation.

"We weren't kids, either one of us. I just assumed he was ready to commit and that, for me, it was time." I shrugged. "Dangerous assumptions. At our six-month anniversary, I was pregnant and Joel took over a major Midwestern sales territory."

"The beginning of the end...?"

"In fact, our relationship never began—not if that means we saw eye to eye on what constitutes love-and-cherish-til-death-do-us-part. Sadly...it took me at least a decade to figure that out. Even longer, to admit the rest. That nothing was going to change it."

"That man was a...fool," Adam said softly. "But then, if we're doling out mea culpas? Of all people, believe me...I know how that ....road warrior game is played."

Too fraught a topic for so public a setting. We moved on—literally and figuratively, as if by mutual consent.

Anyway Bea had chosen that moment to wander over and distribute the stakes and twine for shoring up some Obedient Plant...an unfortunate name for a very invasive and unruly perennial. My back was starting to ache with all that bending. As I stood up to stretch, I caught Adam following the movement with thinly disguised interest. I just hoped Margo and the others weren't as observant or I would never hear the end of it.

"By the way, speaking of change...I read your latest column," he told me off-hand fashion. "Twice. Great stuff...the garden as a metaphor for life. One way or the other, things are changing around us, forcing us to change with it. No change? No growth."

Or maybe just a little too...off-hand...? I bit back a smile—savoring my own private little in-joke. Adam couldn't have known that column in the *Gazette* was the censored version, minus the personal bit about our biblical namesakes that wormed its way into the first draft right after our date on the yacht last weekend.

108

"Is that a critique...or a...*hint...* ?"

Adam winced. "Both maybe."

"Trouble is, people...aren't plants. And lofty as it sounds in theory, more than a tad hypocritical—? Considering who wrote it...and her current inclination to waffle."

He laughed, lowered his voice. "Whatever my faults, Eve...? I'd like to think I'm a patient man."

The storms hit with a vengeance. I had just gotten home from work Tuesday evening when the sky started to darken, that ominous green-yellow that accompanies those terse tornado warnings streaming across the bottom of the television screen.

The phone rang. It was Adam. Out of breath, he told me, from lashing thick plastic poly sheeting over the greenhouse windows.

"How's it look over there?" he said.

"Ugly."

"Do Howard and Margo have a basement?"

"I think so. Yes. I remember her saying something about storing a lot of veggies down there in the old days."

"Good."

"I hope you don't think you're going to ride out the storm with all that glass around out there?" I said.

"There's a cement block shed out in back. If it gets too bad, Dutch and I will take cover."

"You want me to help?"

"No. Just...watch it, will you? I don't like the looks of this."

An awkward silence, and the phone went still in my hands. I tucked it on my belt and went on battening down the hatches. A distant rumble of thunder, followed by a raw gust of wind, sent me scurrying inside.

I had just fastened the screen and threw the deadbolt on the heavy oak door, when the siren on the firehouse went off. A harsh, urgent wail that rose, fell, rose again. God, Adam was right. We're going to get it.

Snatching the emergency flashlight from the outlet in the kitchen,

I headed for the basement. *West, which way is west?*   And then it occurred to me. My grandmother's house had a massive old workbench on the west wall, solid maple planks with an equally thick plank underneath for a shelf.

The adrenalin was making it hard to catch my breath. Feeling very strange, above all very much alone, I shoved aside the dusty power tools and sat down on the shelf under the workbench, grateful for the two inches of hardwood between my head and the basement ceiling. I flicked the flashlight on and off, testing the charge. It worked.

Through the small rectangular windows scattered around the room, I could feel not just hear the howl of the storm. The wind was driving sideways, powerful gusts that shook the house above me. After a while, I heard the hail—heavy from the sound of it, clattering against the drain spout outside the nearest cellar window.

It seemed hours before the storm blew itself out amid long, rolling peals of thunder. The rain was still coming sideways, sending a fine mist streaming in through the caulking around the window panes. And then it was strangely still. The light outside seemed brighter.

Checking my watch, I went upstairs. A half hour. I clicked the on-switch on the phone, but there wasn't a dial tone. The lines must be down. Par for the course, my cell phone was MIA.

Out on the front porch I looked out over the neighborhood. The rain was steady, nothing out of the ordinary. Leaves and small branches were strewn everywhere, but otherwise there weren't any obvious signs of damage.

I tried the phone again, unsuccessfully, then got in the Taurus and aimed it in the direction of Groft's Nursery. Outside the immediate safe haven of my block, Xenaphon hadn't gotten off so lightly.

Golf ball size hail dented cars and even shattered a few windshields. In spots, heaps of the icy white projectiles still lay there like the remnants of a spring snowfall. North of the village, straight line winds tore the roof partially off the mini-mall and there were downed trees everywhere. Big old maples and evergreens lay on their sides, roots torn right out of the earth.

My hands tightened on the wheel as I swung past the berm. But even from a distance I could see the arbor was still standing, at a cockamamey angle, but upright at least. The turnoff to the greenhouse at Groft's was blocked by a birch tree, sheared off about two feet from the ground. I just parked the Taurus as out of the way as possible, scrambled over the limbs and branches.

Heart thudding and not entirely from the exertion, I caught sight of two figures—their backs turned, standing off to one side of the nursery parking lot, assessing the damage. I recognized Adam from the bright yellow sailor's slicker. His companion was bareheaded and pointing with a flashlight toward the roof of the greenhouse—Dutch.

They'd already stripped back the tarp, exposing a few cracked windows, but no major structural damage that I could see. With the gusting of the rain they hadn't heard my car, but Adam must have sensed movement. At any rate, he turned, and when he saw me, started my way with brisk, determined strides.

"What in the hell are you doing here?" he demanded. "It's gotta be damn dangerous out there...downed limbs, power lines—."

I stopped short, unsure of my ground. Without a word, Adam just closed the gap and pulled me in his arms. The harsh rise and fall of his breathing did the talking for him. That, and the strength of his body shielding me from the rain.

"You're all right?" I kept saying, knowing how inane it sounded. "The worst of it missed you?"

Giddy with relief, I clung to him. Not caring that we weren't alone.

When I finally levered some distance between us, I could see Dutch was still standing there where Adam had left him. Watching us—with what Artie the Teamster would have described as a "shit eating" grin on his face.

"Weathered another one, Missy!" he said.

"Dutch, I believe you've met Eve." Adam was trying to sound casual, not succeeding. "Eve Brennerman."

"Had to park out on the road, did'ja? That birch had way too much crown. Been there a long time...for a birch."

"Sad," I told him. "It must have been beautiful."

Dutch shrugged. "Time's your enemy...time's also your friend in the nursery business. Ya clean up the mess and start over."

He was right there. It was amazing what a little time can do.

Because of the storm, my boss was putting out a special edition which kept the two of us hopping. Although the damage at the greenhouse itself was relatively minor, Adam and George had their hands full trying to save some of the field-grown nursery stock. At least we knew our little garden crew was okay, thanks to a phone-athon Bea got going.

Vivian had a tree fall on her garage, but was taking it well enough under the circumstances. "Always planned on renovating it," she told Bea. "Now the insurance'll help."

Margo and Howard, it turns out, never even went to the basement as the storm roared overhead. They just sat on the sofa, away from the windows and let the elements do their worst.

"Figured at least if we go, we'll go together," Margo said.

"Shoot, Margo," was Howard's response. "We'd be more likely to do ourselves in trying to crawl down those basement stairs."

Adam and I didn't want to wait until Saturday to check out the garden. Finally on Thursday he picked me up and we drove out together, apprehensive about what we'd find. My quick drive-by after the storm was encouraging enough. But closeup, the garden looked like a war zone.

The astilbes were shredded, sprigs of leaves and flower stalks strewn across the grass all the way to the interstate off-ramp. While the arbor was still standing, a tree limb had hurtled like a missile from the woods and took out a section of the lattice. The daisies were flattened and mud-caked. It was hard to tell what was salvageable and what was not.

Adam had brought a few tools, and while I braced the leaning uprights of the arbor in place, he deftly retightened the bolts to bring the two-by-twos square again. The one hunk of lattice he removed entirely, intending to replace it by Saturday.

"I can't stand the thought of the others seeing the garden like this," he said. "After all our hard work. As is, we're going to have to chop off most of the astilbe for the rest of the season and just hope it comes back strong next year."

"It could have been worse."

"True."

But neither one of us looked forward to the wounded and discouraged faces Saturday morning as we tried to clean up the mess.

Artie the Teamster set the tone. He showed up at the garden prepared for an all-out war. After raiding Adam's nursery—and paying for every dime himself, he trucked over a half dozen peony bushes and an equal number of daisies.

Both, as it turns out, would survive with some careful pruning. Still, Artie wasn't taking any chances.

"They're the best bloomers in the garden," Artie protested. "A lot can happen by next summer. Anyway, we gotta think about making it look good now."

Trying not to laugh, Bea told him that for the time being, we'd use the new plant stock to expand that second bed. If the old ones didn't make it through the winter, we'd be sure to move some of the new ones back to fill in the gaps.

Adam and I rode over together, because with all the storm damage from the adjacent grove of trees, parking was more of a problem now close to the berm than ever. I didn't think anything of the reaction we would get.

"You and that Adam seem to be really hitting it off," Margo said pointedly as I helped her tie up a patch of daisies that still might bloom despite all the water damage. "I'll tell you, when my Howard was sick? Adam sure took charge. Good man to have around in a crisis."

I suppressed a smile. "Why, Margo," I said, "I do believe you're trying to play cupid. Don't you think we're all a little old for that sort of thing?"

"Dearie, you're never too old. And don't you forget it. If you don't snap up that guy pretty quick," she added sternly, "somebody else will. No bandy legs or spare tires around that one."

An eighty-plus-year-old pegging Adam Groft as some kind of stud muffin? So help me, I didn't know whether to laugh, blush or just ignore her.

"The line's probably around the block, Margo."

"I see the way he looks at you," she snapped. "Believe me, I'm not that blind...*not yet*, anyway!"

Across the berm, Adam heard the peal of laughter and telegraphed a quizzical look my way. I just smiled, shrugged. On the way home in the car, I gave him a censored version of Margo's grandmotherly advice, wondering how he'd react.

"That sly old fox," he said, shaking his head. "I thought she was checking us out."

Like the older generation does when they see a younger couple out together. Amused, and maybe just a little jealous. It felt odd being on the receiving end for a change.

"Well, if they're all gossiping about it anyway," Adam said, "why don't we give the natives something to really chew on?"

"As in…?"

"There's a good movie playing at the three-plex: four academy awards and it finally made it out here to the wilderness. There's also a chick flick and, behind door number three, one with tons of gratuitous sex and violence. Pick your poison."

"When?"

"Tonight."

I laughed. "You'll spring for popcorn?"

"Absolutely."

We were pulling into the driveway. My two elderly neighbors—sisters in their seventies—were sitting on their front porch. Sipping iced tea, they watched with undisguised interest who was driving me home in that SUV.

I never ceased to marvel how incredibly public small town life is. What was I waiting for? The right moment to declare itself, the courage to broach the subject with my kids, or the certainty that I wasn't about to make a colossal fool of myself?

"Ain't small town life fun?" Adam said. He too had noticed the peanut gallery and seemed vastly amused.

It was the last straw. I waved cheerily at the neighbors, opened the car door as if to leave. Then purely on impulse, I turned back to Adam and gave him a fleeting hug before I slid out of the seat and prepared to shut the door behind me.

"What time?" I said.

I wasn't in a position to see the sisters' reaction. But Adam's was another matter entirely. For a split-second he just looked over at me—grinned, shook his head.

"Give 'em hell, Eve," he said. "I'll pick you up at six-thirty."

Chapter Sixteen

Though I do not believe that a plant will spring up where no seed has been, I have great faith in a seed. Convince me that you have a seed there, and I am prepared to expect wonders. Henry David Thoreau

Ridiculous, I kept telling myself as I rummaged through my closet. *You're not thirteen—bent on convincing the neighbor boy you're not a total nerd. Even at the top of your game, all the three-inch-heels in the world couldn't save your marriage.* At 62 and 30 pounds overweight, nothing on that clothes bar was going to change that either.

Still, Adam Groft wanted us to date. *Even knowing all that.*

Starting with that premise cast a whole different light on the process. Sleeveless or a tank top? Air conditioning blowing on our necks in the dark for two hours ruled out those choices as much as the instinct to conceal my "bye-bye" arms. I winced thinking about it—the term my daughters used to describe that odd jelly-roll effect when a grandmother waves goodbye at the end of a visit. I only tended to display bare skin these days in the privacy of my own back yard.

Finally I settled on a thin gray silk blouse with long sleeves and crisp black pin-striped slacks…pleated. Both were newly acquired staples of my work-day wardrobe.

Despite the ubiquitous sun block I wore out in the garden, a light tan made it trickier to handle makeup. I didn't make a habit of foundation while at work. Still, I had to admit, the results of taking some care with it now, a hint of blush and eye shadow in strategic spots, and a deep coral lipstick amounted to a minor miracle.

The face that stared anxiously back at me in the harsh light of the bathroom mirror actually looked younger, five pounds lighter. The cheekbones were still strong and the turquoise earrings matched my eyes.

Forget the perfume. I'd sat through too many town council meetings next to women who sent the entire room into asthmatic spasms. A light scent of vanilla in my hand cream would have to suffice. Nothing, not even collagen and vitamin E, was going to conceal my habit of grubbing around in the dirt bare-handed.

C'est la vie. After all, I'd met the guy in a garden. Right?

I'd forgotten how fraught all those dating rituals are. This was a man who still opened doors and noticed whether the woman next to him was tripping over a loose hunk of flagstone sidewalk.

So, where do you meet him? On the porch? Probably looks too eager. Truth was, if I was going to let him in the living room, a quick dusting of at least the most obvious surfaces wouldn't hurt.

Disgusted with myself, I opted instead for a glass of red wine and the headline news. Nothing like wholesale slaughter on the Dark Continent to get in the mood for a hot date.

It's where he found me, deceptively calm, sitting on the sofa facing the door. I was well aware of Adam's presence long before he knocked—before that familiar smile made contact through the screen.

His wardrobe was back to north-woods chic. The navy polo shirt sported a designer logo on the pocket, and the khakis were so pressed, they could have stood alone. I noticed he'd traded those omnipresent docksiders for a pair of cordovan leather loafers. His were expensive tastes, though understated, unpretentious.

I had no reason to feel uneasy. Adam had picked me up here before...the day we sat together with Margo at the hospital. But that was then. And this was something else entirely. The sheer physicality of the man in my living room suddenly hit me like a hand cultivator taking down a patch of Creeping Jenny.

Margo was right when she stacked Adam Groft up against that world of old codgers out there teasing their last remaining hair into a cover-the-dome astroturf. This man was one good looking piece of horse flesh.

At least if he knew it, he didn't flaunt it. That much was

116

reassuring. So was the obvious approval in his eye. Fancy that—I had actually met a fan of old Katherine Hepburn movies.

"You clean up nice," he said.

"Ditto."

He seemed strangely at loose ends as I showed him around the downstairs, conspicuous for the high ceilings, lovely albeit simple wood moldings and matching 1900's oak farm furniture—all in need of some degree of renovation. Finally, I decided just to come out with it.

"Look," I said, "tonight comes with a Warning Label. I haven't done this in a heck of a long time. This is a new millennium. If I walk on the curbside am I going to freak you out? Do we split the tab? Is there likely to be some kind of awkward scene on the front porch later?"

I could get used to that straight-forward laughter. Like a quick summer shower, I let the sound settle the panic kicking up inside me.

"Am I going to jump you in the third row?" he said, picking up on my tone. "Only if you want me to. And if you'd feel more comfortable going Dutch? By all means, go for it. If I was hung up about independent women, I wouldn't be here."

"Good. I just got paid, so my movie ticket's my problem. I'll let you buy the munchies."

He laughed. "Fair enough."

That said, we still stood there and looked at each other. Clueless.

"Enough of that," he said as he held out a hand in invitation.

I hesitated, but took it. By the time we got to the SUV, my fingers felt comfortable locked in his, as if they belonged there.

We opted for the chick flick…fluff over art. The actors were half our age, the plot clever though straining audience credibility. The timing? Perfect.

I found myself laughing, a trifle envious, at the young lovers—a far cry from the saccharine Ozzie and Harriet romances of my childhood. Even more so from the sixties and my college years when love-making morphed into words that couldn't be spoken in polite company.

Romance-wise, I had skipped the eighties and nineties for all intents and purposes. Watching the cinematic machinations, trying to put myself in those shoes, made me feel as alien as a time traveler. What in the heck was I getting myself into?

"Up for a Chardonnay?" Adam suggested as we found ourselves out on the sidewalk after the movie. "I've never been to the local watering hole, but at least it stays open after nine o'clock."

He was talking about Marty's Log-Inn, an odd combination of rustic eatery, tavern and Internet café a block down from the theater. The street lights were on and the neon on Marty's sign was flashing out a welcome. Hard to believe, but only mid-July and the days were already getting perceptibly shorter.

"The Chardonnay is awful. They've got a hundred brands of bottle beer and a light import on tap, though," I said. "My boss and I've had lunch there. But thanks…yeah, Marty's sounds great!"

The bar was dark, crowded. We slid into a booth near the front. When my eyes got used to the dim light, I realized—one, that I'd forgotten my reading glasses. Worse, my boss George was holding forth with friends at a table near the back of the bar.

Great. I was never going to hear the end of this. For starters, Adam was going to have to read me the menu.

"A little problem," I told him. "Either I learn Braille or I need a translator. I left my specs at home."

He chuckled, fishing a pair of half-glasses out of his shirt pocket. Handed them my way.

"Drug store generic. That way when they disappear, my insurance agent won't worry I'll hit 'em up for replacements."

"I just buy stacks through the mail," I told him. Three bucks apiece. They're laying all over the house and all over the office. Still, it's a half hour search every time I need a pair."

From a distance, I noticed George had been trying to catch my eye, but I wasn't giving him a chance. Finally he came wandering over, obviously hell-bent on stirring up trouble.

"Big night on the town. Who's your friend, Evie?" George said.

All the while glaring daggers his way, I made the introductions. Adam stood and the two men shook hands, sizing each other up.

"Groft?" George said. "Weren't you a class or two behind me in high school? Played football or something like that? You guys regularly trashed poor Xenaphon."

"Track. We did okay."

"Your dad owned that nursery on county line road. Saw the For Sale signs out there for a while a year back."

Adam looked uncomfortable. He recognized a fishing expedition when he saw it.

118

"It's off the market," he said.

"Tell me about it," George said. "Our ad revenues dropped by a third about eight months ago. Evie here's been stuck with trying to build circulation with those columns of hers."

"The nursery just might go for some three-by-five spot ads. Midsummer promos. Who would we call?"

I noticed Adam left the question of management at the nursery vague. My boss wasn't pushing it.

"Just let Evie know where and when," George said. "We'll put something together for ya."

He couldn't resist an innuendo-tinged "Enjoy!" as he wandered back to his table. Adam sat down, shook his head.

"You're not the only one who comes with warning labels," he admitted grudgingly.

"As in?"

"Track wasn't the only running around I was known for in high school. Your boss'll probably lock you up and throw away the key."

I managed a weak smile. "It's pretty obvious what I was doing in high school. Typical band nerd. First beau? He kissed me in the cloak room in kindergarten and had a habit of eating library paste. Except for Joel, my adult love life was limited to a history grad student who dumped me for an econ major and a young socialist who had this problem with personal hygiene."

"So," Adam said quietly, "we got here by different routes. What do you propose we do about it?"

"I'm not expecting anything from you but honesty."

"By now it should be clear. If it was the flavor of the month I was looking for, I'd be out on that boat with Jake."

"I know that."

He stared thoughtfully into his Labatt's. "And you, Eve? What is it you're looking for?"

"I don't know," I told him, an understatement if I ever heard one. Since Joel died, I hadn't even let a male within ten feet of me. "I just know I don't want to 'settle' for something, or for anyone who feels that way about me. I've been there, done that...never again."

As I saw it, neither one of us were exactly prime candidates for a long term relationship. So then why on earth were we sitting across the booth from each other at Marty's? An inch away from holding hands like a couple of teenagers.

"You're an attractive woman, Eve," he said quietly, as if reading my thoughts. "Funny. Bright."

"Thanks for the reference." I think, anyway.

"And," he said, "I'd like to believe we're already friends."

"Margo and Howard pretty much cinched that," I admitted.

All of it was the truth as far as it went. But there was more.

"You can't imagine how I felt," I told him. "Listening to that tough little woman spill her guts...scared to death she'd lose someone she'd built her life around. All I had going for me in her shoes? Anger...plus a terrible sense of relief that the charade was finally over."

"People heal. People change, Eve."

"I've got to believe that." Some days it was easier than others.

We finished our beer and he drove me home, dodging the kids out cruising in their pickups and rusty four-by-fours. Just before he killed the engine, Adam turned my way. His hand still clutched the ignition key.

"Thursday," he said. "I've got the day off—am...*taking* it anyway. If George doesn't chain you up over there in the basement at the *Gazette*, how about a day-hike over at Sleeping Bear? The forecasts are sun, moderate temperatures...better than that it doesn't get."

I looked down at my hands. "I'd...need to talk to George—"

"Fair enough."

All the while I waited as Adam came around and did the chivalry bit—opening my door, escorting me to the front porch—my palms were sweating. Especially after my boss sprung his version of the Spanish Inquisition, Adam had every reason to run for the hills. And instead?

The house wasn't locked. For a long moment we just stood there in the dull gleam of the porch light, looking at each other.

"What say, we get this over with, Eve?" he said quietly.

It felt safe, letting him coax me into the circle of his arms. His mouth was gentle, the kiss just lingering enough to trigger ripples in that deep aching pool of emptiness inside me.

"Call me, or I'll call you," he said softly. "When you've talked to your boss—about Thursday?"

He was already down the steps and half-way across the lawn. I stifled the powerful urge to call him back. Instead, I just stood my ground, watching until the tail lights from his SUV turned the corner, disappeared into the night.

Chapter Seventeen

Gardens don't grow overnight. They take time. And even when a garden is established, it is folly to describe the thing as "done". Gardens—by definition—are always about growing. Unknown

Sometimes George, my boss amazes me. I was expecting the worst, and was pleasantly surprised. Except for a pointed look, I got none of his usual teasing when I showed up for work Monday morning.

Public Radio was running in the background—a special on rock stars, then and now. Some announcer was waxing poetic about Woodstock, and a new release by Melanie, *Crazy Love*. The singer had been out of the limelight for three decades: had only recently been attempting a comeback using her son as backup.

The cut the station played was poignant, hit way too close to home. Something about trying to age with grace, the woman's smoky voice intoned, with a rock and roll heart.

My boss was agonizing over a headline that just wouldn't fit. At the risk of setting him off, I had to know. It was as good a time to ask, as any.

"Exactly how well do you know Adam Groft, George?"

He just looked at me for a second. I saw him shrug.

"We didn't go to the same high schools, of course," he said. "He was at the area prep, my folks sent me to public. Still, everybody knows each other around here. Typical high school stuff. Fast cars, wild parties down by the quarry."

"That's a long time ago," I said.

"Apparently he and his old man went at it on a regular basis over the business—story was, it finally drove him out. Is he well liked around here? Hard to say. After he made it big in Chicago? Some said the guy showed up just often enough to make sure nobody forgot it."

It was a stupid question. George was the last person on earth to give anybody advice about their love life.

"George, am I totally nuts?" I said. "This is a small town. People have long memories."

"Evie, I can't tell you what to do. Are you afraid folks will think you've lost it…or are shagging every guy between here and Traverse City? You're one classy lady…nobody's going to hassle you over wanting a little male companionship in your life. The local market isn't actually booming once you get past a couple of widowed farmers."

"He's asked me to take a trip over to Sleeping Bear dunes. Except the nursery's open all weekend and—"

"You need to take time off during the week. Nice thing about our line of work? Writing is writing whenever you do it."

"Thanks, George."

His voice was strangely tentative. Was he concerned or just embarrassed? I couldn't tell. George didn't keep me in the doubt long.

"Maybe it's none of my business," he said. "But if that guy doesn't…well, let's just say, if Adam Groft gives you a hard time? I'd be the first to punch his headlights out!"

Not exactly the kind of reaction that inspires confidence. I tried to laugh it off.

"Why, George!" I told him. "I didn't know you cared."

I was carrying the phone around a good hour that night before I finally punched in Adam's number. He picked up on the second ring.

"Groft, here."

"It's Eve."

I heard a soft chuckle from the other end of the line. "Not surprising by now," he said, "that you're having second thoughts."

"Try fourths or fifths," I told him. "But I can't use my boss or work as an excuse. If you're still game for Thursday, I've got the day off."

"Seven o'clock all right? We can get a hike in before lunch. Swim in the afternoon."

"Sounds good."

He must have read something in my voice. "And Eve...?" he said. "Trust me. You aren't going to regret this."

On some level, I already did. Plugging in my laptop, I set up a new file for this week's garden column. Some of what came pouring out would need some pretty crafty editing to wind up on page twelve of the *Gazette:*

> I have a friend who moved to California and hated it. She missed the Midwestern seasons.
>
> "It's all about youth out here," she said. "And if you haven't got it, you fake it." She had a list, starting with chemical peels, blue hair and 70-year-olds dressing like kids and cultivating sun tans that turn women into alligator bags. It is all because they don't have seasons.
>
> Seasons teach what life is really all about. Stuff grows, it blooms, it dries up and eventually gets hacked off or falls over and goes back into the ground. Some of that may sound depressing, but even the weeds along the roadside after the late-October frosts have their place, a kind of wild, desperate beauty. Artists scrounge along the ditches and turn the dried-up stalks into these expensive dried wreaths or tall-pot arrangements that sit in fancy urban entrance halls.
>
> Seasons are about life renewing itself. Perennial gardening helps people notice and appreciate that

cycle. The rhythm of a garden is all about constants and changes that flow into each other, until it's hard to tell where time begins and ends at all.

Good gardeners are four-season gardeners. That means, they learn how to keep something going in their gardens every day of the year.

When one thing stops blooming, something else takes its place. In between flowering, the bare leaves themselves are interesting, spiky or feathery, mottled or different shades of green. Even the branches of bushes have a part to play: like the variegated red twig dogwood that stands out a vivid crimson against the gray backdrop of winter.

Gardening, to paraphrase my California friend, means you develop a good sense of timing. Why plant all mums? It is just as silly to stay stuck at nineteen or thirty or even fifty. Just because a bloom fades, it doesn't mean life stops.

Plants seem to know how to juggle the calendar without really trying. Wouldn't it be great if we were built that way?

About then it occurred to me, rereading what I had written. For a garden columnist, was I getting just a little *too* personal? Time to regroup.

I stared at the computer screen. Drew a blank.

All I could think of were those stupid "remember-when" lists that show up on senior citizen bulletin boards: the ones that fuss about the shock to our lifestyles from indoor plumbing and telephones. Or the bureau disease jokes...with punch lines about chests sagging into drawers.

None of that wisdom-of-old-age pop culture ever mentions the nitty gritty people stuff, the really tough stuff. Like figuring out when or *if* old is ever too old?   Or how to handle safe sex or all those crazy questions that come up on the adult channels on late night television.

Especially in rural America, a guy's love life or lack of it can get very complicated. Either way, it's bound to cause a fuss. If you get out of town?   Well then, somebody's brother who owns the gas station on State Road is bound to notice and feel obligated to get the word out. So twenty years later your discreet little liaison is still part of the folklore.

Truth must be told? It's not Adam Groft I'm worried about, it's me. After five years of living like a very hostile nun, I'm starting to feel like a rabid bat whenever he's within five yards. This is not good.

I'd feel like an idiot calling my daughter Leslie and asking her for a few handy hints. Her sister Gina would just go ballistic, then threaten to have me committed. Lord knows, George was weird enough this morning with his "keep your hands off my daughter" bluster.

My only women friends are that bunch on the garden crew. And frankly, I don't *want* to know what Margo would recommend. Vivian probably would pass out if I even mentioned the word, Sex. Meanwhile, here I was—supposed to be writing a column, and I can't think about anything but the S-word.

Tomorrow after work, I decided, I had better drive over to that strip of outlet malls and pick up the toughest looking pair of hiking boots I can find. I don't remember much about Sleeping Bear, except isolated stretches of beach and some pretty intimidating sand piles.

I am also going to dig out my grandmother's old wild flowers of Michigan book. Time for a little research if George expects me to turn into some kind of gardening guru. How much trouble can I get into if I'm crawling around tomorrow trying to tell a raceme from a bracht?

Mercifully at that impasse, the phone rang. It was Adam.

"Have you been listening to the news?" he said.

"Public Radio, earlier."

"Then you haven't heard. The state department of transportation has reshuffled its priority deck for 2004. They're proposing to redo that exit ramp at Aurelius."

There had been four accidents on that exit in the past couple of years.   Despite Reduce Speed signs and rumble strips, traffic routinely takes the off-ramp way too fast.   Once last fall a camper actually careened over the edge and landed sideways on the berm, barely fifty feet from the garden.

"George didn't get a release on it or I know he'd have told me. Did the news say what they're—?"

"No specifics.   But I can't see how they can do much without taking out the garden."

"We better call Bea."

"Already did.   Left a message."

A hard, angry knot was starting to form in my chest.   "But Adam, we got...I'm sure Bea said we had some kind of waiver from the state before we even started."

"Moot, apparently.   If the state actually has a plan on the table."

"I'd better talk to George.   Maybe he'll have some ideas."

"No mystery about it, Eve."

I'd heard that don't-mess-with-me edge in his voice once before. It was that day over at the nursery when Adam dumped all those plants on me.   Like then, this time he wasn't giving an inch.

"We're going to have to lobby like hell," he said.

Chapter Eighteen

*There is life in the ground. When it is stirred up, it
goes into the man who stirs it.* Anonymous.

Any news travels fast in a pressure cooker. George was already waiting for me, e-mail in hand, when I got to the office next morning.

"Trouble, Evie."

"I know. I assume you already heard about the MDOT off-ramp plan. The local radio scooped us again last night."

Not hard to do, of course, when a newspaper only comes out once a week. Face it, if you read the weekly *Gazette,* you've already heard the story someplace else before. George stays in business mainly because the scrapbookers in town feel good about actually seeing something in print—that, or he lets folks get in a lot of public grousing.

On a regular basis, the paper prints two solid pages of letters to the editor. These range from polite complaints over the state of the economy to pretty vicious blow-'em-off-the-front-porch fights over the placement of stop lights in town. The department of transportation just guaranteed that we would be upping that page-count to three…a volume of mail usually reserved for an act of war.

Nobody but our little garden gang really cares that the project would wipe out the berm. Eight people are hardly enough to create a ripple in local politics, to say nothing of downstate in Lansing. No, the real outrage would come from farmers who on principle were fighting for every square inch of tillable land these days and the diehard quality-of-life advocates determined to block any highway changes that would erode acreage.

Kill off a few tourists on the off-ramp? Well, then maybe it'll slow down the speed at which folks roar into Xenaphon with their Hummers. There's a logical flaw in there, someplace, but meantime George was going to sell an awful lot of newsprint.

I scratched what I'd written for my column last night, and started over:

> I found this quote on the internet, that a garden doesn't ever really "call it quits". Tell that to the planners who came up with the brilliant idea to widen the local off-ramp and in the process bulldoze the Aurelius Community Garden.
>
> Who cares if the state rips out a bunch of plants? We are just talking about a hundred perennials, give or take a few, not the Showy Lady Slipper or the Wood Orchid. Besides somebody could just dig the whole lot of them up and move them fifty yards to the right. That ought to do it.
>
> No bureaucrat is going to pay much attention to a couple of people with green thumbs or one or two landowners fussing about lost acreage. Stop development? With an unemployment rate of over ten percent, sounds like a job or two around here might be a good thing. Plus, the state actually wants to spend money on the county and stop accidents. Another good thing, right?
>
> Point is, nobody asked us. A press release shows up telling us what is going to happen and then public officials get all in a bunge because the local folk do not seem grateful.
>
> Funny thing is: nobody seems to care that the county has more

substandard housing than any other county in the state. That is a pretty sobering bit of human wreckage too when you think about it, and there's nary a health and human services bulldozer in sight. If the state is so concerned about jobs, then why write the contract requirements so that local folk do not have a snowball's chance of competing for them?

So, before the hard hats start knocking over astilbe and lattice, maybe it would be a good idea for the movers and shakers and planners to come up here and look around and listen, for a change. It could be surprising what everybody working together might come up with.

In a garden there are always those species that just elbow out the rest of the greenery. *Invasive*, gardeners call them. Smart gardeners tend to be really careful about where or even *if* they plant them.

I tossed a hard copy on George's desk before lunch. He scanned it, read it again.

"Why you sneaky little rabble-rouser, you!" he chuckled. "Whatever happened to that calm and unflappable Evie who kept turning out these nice little column-inches about the Bee Queen showing up at the Kinder Cottage day care?"

"Too bitchy, huh?"

George laughed. "Sock it to 'em. You'll probably have *everybody* yelling at you, but if it sells papers—?"

"Maybe you'll give me a raise?"

"Don't push your luck."

The sound of the office door made us both sit up and take notice. Adam Groft was standing in the doorway.

"Am I interrupting something?"

"Evie, here," George told him, "must be eating her Wheaties

129

lately. She just cranked out a gardening column with enough kick to stir up quite a hornet's nest."

Adam shrugged. "Sells papers, George."

"Told ya so," I told my boss pointedly. "I think maybe fifty bucks a column more would be satisfactory."

"Take her to lunch, Groft!" George said. "On my tab. This jawing over the fence is getting way too expensive."

Still laughing, Adam was easing me in the direction of the door. The noon sun was baking down like the infrared lamps over the entrees at the Corner Deli.

"I'd say grab a salad and sit under a tree," Adam told me, "but we'd probably fry."

"It's cooler by the creek and there are a couple of picnic tables. I'm game if you are."

The shallow rapids of the stream had the effect of a Zen mood tape on our stressed-out psyches. I wasn't the only one who had been sweating it out until noon. The greenhouse electrical system had failed. In desperation to keep down the heat, Adam had borrowed a generator from a local contracting firm to keep the exhaust fans running.

"While I was at it," he threw out in passing. "I talked to the owner—an old high school friend, about that berm business. Frank was ticked off at the state for making the bidding process so complicated that most local companies wouldn't stand a chance of landing even a piece of the contracts on the off-ramp."

"Par for the course. George told me the same thing, so I tried to hit it head-on in the column."

"Frank also is talking about getting some town meetings going to build up some opposition. So I've invited him and a few of our mutual friends over to dinner at the cottage next week to talk about it. I was hoping…thought maybe you'd come along."

"Oh, Adam…I don't know if that's such a great idea."

That just came tumbling out before I thought how he might take it. It's just that I had already learned first-hand that Adam's friends could be a bit daunting.

Obviously, he hadn't expected my refusal. From the way his expression shut down, I sensed he was putting quite a different spin on it than I intended.

"No problem," he said brusquely.

130

"Adam, I didn't—"

"You don't owe me an explanation."

It must have been obvious how uncomfortable, anxious I felt. He softened his tone.

"We *are* still on for Sleeping Bear tomorrow?" he said.

"Of course. I even bought a pair of new hiking boots."

It wasn't fair, I decided, to just blow him off like that. At least I owed him an explanation.

"Look," I said, "it wasn't the idea of a public meet-and-greet with you that was stressing me out. It's just…well, probably, most of the others know each other. I'm the new kid on the block—"

"Frank and I haven't seen each other in years either. But he's not the type to hammer you for trying to talk the state out of all that concrete. If your column this week is half as wild as George says it is? You'll be getting comments like, *and who is the Adam guy you brought along?*"

I forced a laugh. "Okay, you win. I'll come. But don't blame me if I invest in a flack jacket."

He and my boss must have been on the same wave length. When I got back from lunch, I discovered from a quick scan of the galleys that George had used my absence as an opportunity to pop my head-shot into the garden column. Another first. So much for anonymity.

Ever since college, I'd been slogging away as a very small cog in a very large advertising firm. I retire, and suddenly I find myself poised for minor celebrity status in a town where even a little visibility goes a long way. Go figure.

Constants and change. It was one thing to write about it, another to live it.

Well, at least I'd be out of town when this week's paper hit the townie mail boxes. I was about to take my first official personal leave day…ever. And the to-do list didn't even involve two or three loads of laundry or a trip to the dentist.

 Chapter Nineteen

Timing is all.   The horticulturalist Henry Mitchell once
said that even the most unlikely of gardens can seem like
Eden.   You just have to catch it at the right moment.
Eve Brenneman's journal.

Thursday dawned gray and a little cooler. A front had passed
through during the night taking with it some of the humidity.   Forecast
was for clearing later in the day and fog along the Lake Michigan
shoreline.

Wear white in the woods, I remembered the warning from one of
those evil-looking tick flyers.   Khaki slacks and a layered tee and shell
jacket in a subdued coral seemed to fit the bill.   Into a small knapsack I
tucked Gram's wildflower book, swim suit and towel, a pair of thong
sandals and an emergency kit of sun and bug stuff. Add a couple of
bottles of spring water, trail mix, fruit and paper toweling and it looked
like I was planning a small Himalayan expedition.

This time I was waiting on the porch when Adam showed up.
An amazing amount can happen on my block in fifteen minutes at seven
in the morning.

"I was on the way out the door," he apologized, "when Dutch
called about this order we've been working on for landscape plants for
a condo development north of here. I think...hope it's under control."

"No biggie. I just settled in here watching the neighborhood go
through its morning wake-up drill. Interesting sociological study. You

ought to try it. On a two-block street, I'd say we've got six commuters, three building trades employees, ten retirees—"

"The rest?"

"For Sale signs. They account for four out of twenty-five households."

"You're missing two."

"Bet the other math students hated you," I told him. "The unaccounted for? Well, I'm one. The other is probably sleeping in. The car in their driveway has a community college parking sticker in the window."

"Makes sense."

Even crossing the village limits line for me was a major event these days. It occurred to me as we headed north and west toward the dunes that all of my other excursions were Adam's doing as well—several trips out to the nursery and our Fourth of July extravaganza. Oh yes, and even my junket to the outlet mall to pick up a pair of hiking boots could be indirectly laid at his doorstep.

"Have you ever noticed how distance takes on a whole new dimension living out here?" I said. "When I lived in Chicago people routinely used to fight the expressway traffic to hear the summer symphony concerts or go to the Loop to see an exhibit at the Art Institute. Now I'm lucky if I venture out for a monthly shopping run somewhere."

Adam laughed. "Speak for yourself. You forget, among other things, I'm in the landscape business. If our driver calls in sick, guess who climbs in the truck?"

"And you like it…all that scrambling and hustling…?"

He didn't need to think about it. "Most of the time," he said, "…except for the end of the month insolvency and watching my pension evaporate. I've got a farmer's tan, am fifteen pounds lighter, and I get to listen to a lot of national public radio. It beats hanging out on the lawn outside my cottage counting cars. Not a very interesting bunch over there."

"Mainly weekenders?"

"Some. A lot of gray hair walking around, some multiple-generation cottage owners. It's hard to buy in around there, but you do find a few younger urban refugees. They mainly seem to go for the Michigan lakefront condos north of here."

I tried to picture him at home and found myself conjuring up a log cabin with a huge fieldstone fireplace, a bottle of Chardonnay and two glasses sitting on the hearth. The earth tones in a hand-braided oval rug came alive in the dull gleam of the birch logs in the grate, taking the chill off the summer evening. Smiling up at me and hand-outstretched in invitation, his face in shadows, Adam was welcoming me to share the needlepoint floor pillow with its Celtic rings and patterns.

Dangerous images—of home and love and a longing so deep that words failed to contain them. Too ethereal to last, they dissolved into the dance of sunlight on the windshield.

I shivered. When Adam noticed, I blamed it on the air conditioning.

Even Adam's enthusiastic travelogue and the weather reports that marked our progress along the route had not prepared me for the first sight of the forested inner mounds of the dunes at Sleeping Bear. Subtly at first, then like relentless and ghostly waves, the forecasted lake fog eddied toward us from the west. It lapped at the spiky outlines of the evergreens and shaded green mounds of the maples and hardwoods. Often the roiling layers of white and gray engulfed the landscape entirely. Only the dark and powerful shoulders of the great Bear itself managed to swim above the oncoming tide.

We parked near one of the trail heads and set out along the beach in a landscape of unremitting gray and silence in which water, sky, and sand became indistinguishable. From above us, a bird cry quavered, died away again. Just ahead the massive front sand wall of the Bear reared up like a brooding specter then slipped away again in the mist, daring us to follow.

All around us the air was thick and heavy, damping our voices and rendering tentative the rasp of our boot soles against the hard-packed sand near the water's edge. Our conversation was hushed, cautious in this place where existence was so tenuous and fragile. Freshwater shells, a conspicuous dearth of wildflowers and only rare tufts of sea grass—very little spoke of life abundant as we were experiencing it in the garden we were creating together in Aurelius. The occasional thinning of the fog bank only served to reveal the stark battle for survival as the ridges of the dunes crept steadily inland beyond the great Bear.

If there were other human beings in this monochromatic wilderness, we did not sense it. The only hint of civilization we had left far behind us in the trail parking lot in the form of a rusted-out Chevy of indefinable age and a park service truck with an assortment of maintenance gear in the back.

"I've never seen it like this," Adam said quietly. "Fog…yes, but not this total…blanket of white. Everywhere."

"It's like the…edge of the world out there. Water and sky and sun and all of it just beyond our reach."

Adam's eyes glittered with awareness as he smiled down at me. I sensed he felt it, too—the awe and wonder of the moment. By sheer chance, the vagaries of temperature of land and water, we had strayed into this place where we were utterly and truly alone with one another and our thoughts.

His strong, calloused hand enveloped mine—a steady point of reference where everything else was so alien and disorienting. In the silence I kept coming back to the same simple fact, miracle even—that I was sharing this space, reaching out to someone at long last, after so many years alone.

So easy on the face of it, I thought with a sudden rush of sadness. Easy—yet, something my husband Joel and I had found so very hard to do.

We walked for what had to be miles along the water's edge. By late-morning the sun finally had begun to burn its way through and we stopped to reconnoiter. Overhead, a hawk or some kind of large-winged bird was playing the air currents where water met land. We stood next to a gnarled tangle of roots thrown up on the shoreline, watching it cut graceful arcs against the blue of the sky.

"Hunting," Adam said as the magnificent creature swooped down toward the glassy surface of the lake. "For lunch…."

I laughed. "Is that a hint?"

"Suggestion," he amended. "Though our choices are limited. Keep going and forage for lunch among the contents of our knapsacks, or should we call it quits, hike back to the car and track down a restaurant—?"

"It's too beautiful to…waste all this. To sit inside in some dark, air-conditioned building."

"My thought, exactly."

Settling down with the hunk of driftwood for a makeshift bench seat, I started to break out the fruit and trail mix, the bottles of spring water I had brought. Adam, meanwhile, fished around in his day pack and came up with some high-energy bars and a slab of sinfully decadent chocolate for dessert. This wasn't the gourmet lunch we had been talking about earlier, but then the setting made up for it.

Unavoidable, our hands and bodies brushed and touched as we shared our impromptu feast. The intimacy was subtle, feeding another hunger less simple to assuage.

Time, I reluctantly concluded, *to pack it in.* On a harsh intake of breath, I leaned down and began to busy myself stashing the leftovers in my knapsack.

All that while, I sensed Adam's eyes were following my every move. Finally, his hand stopped me. His voice was low, insistent.

"Eve...leave it," he said.

He drew me closer, not hard to do where we had been sitting. Before I could react, his hands were cradling my face and his mouth had found mine. I closed my eyes.

Some things we never forget. Attraction was one of them, passion another—potent as the working of carbon dioxide in a bottle of warm champagne. Our bodies were taking on a mind of their own, intuitively fitting themselves to each other. I was suddenly young again, caught up in joyous, dizzying dance with the sun.

And then something intervened—like a shadow momentarily obscuring the light. I found myself trembling, trying to will it away, but the uncertainty was stronger now. Adam must have sensed the change. Half playful, half serious, he levered enough distance to make eye contact.

"Second thoughts...?" he said.

"N-not exactly...."

My voice quavered, but I began again. I forced a smile.

"Try adolescent jitters," I told him. "Face it...reckless abandon is a scary prospect—especially if you've spent the last 50 years trying to get your life under control."

He chuckled softly, a reassuring sound. But it was his eyes—alive with a steady, unambiguous fire—that told me that whatever else he was feeling, he understood.

"Correct me, Eve…but at our stage in life? I'd argue that the old adage…*Carpe diem* makes a certain amount of sense."

"True…and *clever*—"

"Yeah, well…I for one have had plenty of time to think about it. Ever since I saw you standing there on that blasted berm—"

"Reality check. I was covered with mud. *Totally* prepared to …dislike you."

"Fortunately that didn't seem to…last long."

"Also true."

Nothing like stating the obvious. Laughter welled up between us, quicksand bubbling up along that precarious invisible divide where dune and water meet. We had passed this way before in previous incarnations, knew where we were headed if we didn't stop this now.

"Much as I hate to admit it?" he said finally. "You're right. This deserves time."

"And maybe something more…hospitable than this hunk of driftwood?"

Cold sober. No heat of the moment. And no regrets.

Still, as we disentangled ourselves, we shared a look that didn't need any translation. He wasn't the only one having trouble letting go.

As he got to his feet, Adam extended his hand to help me do the same. That rock hard driftwood had been wreaking minor havoc with my sciatica. I stretched out my hand to meet his, steadying myself.

The fog was lifting. We could look back now over the vast stretch of sand along which we had come. The rest of the day should be clear, as promised. It was also becoming very apparent that we were overdressed for the rising temperature.

"It's quite a trek to the parking lot," I said. "Unless…judging by that map at the trail head…there might be a shortcut through the dunes a half mile back."

"Nothing like a forced march—that is, if you're still…hell bent on cooling things off…!"

Cute. But I was not going to go there. Ostensibly we had already settled that.

Adam's voice lowered a notch. "Or…we…*could* take a…quick swim—now that the sun's…warming things up a bit."

"Warming things up is…*not* the problem here."

"Come on now…we both wore our suits under our clothes. That, at least, rules out skinny dipping."

"Remember that fog…? I'll bet a month's salary that lake temperature still hasn't hit sixty-five degrees." I shot him a who-are-you-kidding look. "I don't know about you…but cold showers were never my style."

"You win. The shortcut it is." The knapsack was still lying on the ground and he snagged. it, slipped it over his shoulder. "But just for the record? That…doesn't mean I have to…like it."

Chapter Twenty

On blind faith, gardeners trust that beauty is as possible in the future as the past. If they didn't, they would never plant a seed. Unknown

The rest of the day was a cliche but a nice one. Hand in hand a lot of the time, we laughed, we talked, made adventures of the ordinary, and finally, sunburned and tired, started back to Xenaphon.

Everything around us was at the height of its summer glory. The scent of new mown hay wafted in through the SUV's ventilation system, calling up long-forgotten memories of riding alongside my grandfather in his ancient pickup on a hot August afternoon. Then as now, I felt safe, solid, needing no declarations to convince me I was loved, valued.

I had lived so many years like a sleep-walker, measuring out my life in scalding cups of black coffee, deadlines at work and hours at home that stretched out like an empty canvas. I had forgotten how draining it is to give your senses free reign. As simple a thing as reaching out to take Adam's hand crossing a creek or navigating a curb was enough to rekindle that heady shock of our connectedness.

The writer in me began to assert itself, to sift through the images to come to the heart of what I was feeling.

All lives—like gardens—have their share of dry spells. Without love, emotions become stunted and brittle. The senses shut down or become blunted. It is the difference

between surviving and living.

And then for one glorious moment, I said, No—no to the words, to the phrases. Like the photographer facing the perfect sunset, there are some experiences just meant to be lived. A camera lens or keystrokes can approximate the shape, but rarely, if ever, capture the soul.

Life was not that computer waiting for me back there in my dining room. It was here—now, alongside me in this car. I was going to live it.

Neither one of us—Adam nor I—wanted or knew how to end it. For a long time we just sat in the front seat of the SUV in my driveway, not touching, just staring out the windshield.

"Lunch...tomorrow?"

"No plans. Unless my boss—"

"I'll pick you up," Adam said.

"People are going to start...talking."

"Face it, Eve...they already are."

I memorized the way the shadows softened the planes of his face. His eyes—usually so gray and clear now, were dark as the night. Impossible to read.

The door latch was over-designed, hard to open. Adam leaned in front of me to release it, agonizingly close. If he had walked me to the door, we both knew what the outcome would be. As is, his voice was enough to get my pulse racing.

"Good night, Eve."

I managed to choke out, "Get home safe." I didn't let myself look back.

Somewhere earlier in the day, I'd slipped out of my hiking boots and into my sandals. The grass was damp around my feet, cool. By the time I hit the porch and fumbled with the key, found the entryway light, and turned to close the house door, the tail lights from Adam's SUV were half-way to the corner.

I was too exhausted to think about sleep. *You know it's summer*, the familiar constraints of my column—for starters, no contractions— began to dictate themselves as I headed for my laptop.

        You know it is summer, when the first
        butterfly lights on your sleeve as you

stake up a patch of bee balm. You look up from your garden and waves of heat shimmer all glassy and white against the noon sky. The neighbor drives by with the window open and the car radio blaring a familiar show tune about knee-high corn or lazy drifting rivers.

And without anyone telling you, you know it's time to just stop for a minute and enjoy. Because in another month all these wild yellows and hot pink perennials will be gone.

The garden has come together as it was mean to do. The tall leafy goatsbeard with its feathery white flower heads—looking all the world like oversize astilbe—towers at the back of the bed. In front of it march the spiky yellow-gold shafts of highland rocket. Trumpeting their approach are the purple bellflower, gaudy daylilies and subtle pastels of the foxglove. The succulent leaves and tiny star-like blossoms of the dwarf sedums crowd out from the border to meet you.

It is beautiful. It is enough. And yet as you stand there and watch, before you know it, you forget how beautiful summer in the garden is.

You start to agonize over the crabgrass that tries to creep beyond the edging. You fret over the bugs going after the roses. The weeding and deadheading never seem to end until all that is left of that mid-summer splendor is sprawling green foliage, lush and out of control.

Then, just when you are ready to give up and let the jungle take over, August comes along with its promise of deep golds and purple, the rusts.

141

```
Yet another flowering is upon you.
     Still,  it  is  different  in  the
garden now,  maybe even a little sad.
The  rains  are  colder,  the  aurora
borealis plays across the lengthening
night sky.  Winter is just around the
corner.
```

The phone rang, harsh and insistent. I silenced it by picking up the receiver. Then I heard the familiar voice.

"I just wanted to thank you…again," he said. "For everything."

I smiled. "Funny. I was just writing about it."

"Fit for public consumption?"

"Tell me yourself. After you read next week's column."

Chapter Twenty-One

We are all sowers of seeds...and let us never forget it.
George Matthew Adams

I was finding my voice. That was true not just as a writer, but also as a woman. Adam and the garden had a lot to do with it. But not everything.

For much of my life, I had watched life happen. When I found myself in a loveless marriage, I cultivated acceptance rather than risk the confrontation that either could have changed things for the better—or have left me utterly alone. When my daughters took sides, I let their perceptions of me stand, for fear of losing their love.

That, I sensed, was changing. On paper, I was learning to pour out my heart...in my relationships, to fight for what I believed and wanted. It didn't come easy. If I thought about it too hard, I still became frightened and unsure of myself.

But out in that garden, in front of that computer screen and in the woman I saw reflected in Adam's eyes? I knew who I was. It was a precious gift, one I was no longer prepared to relinquish.

Out on the berm, our leader Bea was mapping out an aggressive petition drive that enlisted every retailer in the county to fight the state's plans for the off-ramp. Artie the Teamster offered to spring for bumper stickers—designed by Vivian—that trumpeted, *Honk twice if you love perennials. Save the berm.* Margo and Howard had begun to get the senior crowd all riled up. Even cynical George stopped being a boss and kept the machinations front page center.

As for Adam? He did what I quickly discovered he did incredibly well. He parlayed his contacts with old guard, old wealth north-woods Michigan into a lobbying force that went after the legislature and bureaucracy downstate, big time.

I was a part of that world now, helping him organize that soiree he was planning for the first available Friday night. Together we recruited a couple of college students from his neighborhood to help. We had already scoured the groceries in the larger resorts north of us for an impressive menu of frozen goodies made for this kind of entertaining and the butcher shops for ribs. I offered to get there early just in case to help.

There were three dresses in my closet. This was one of them—a simple black tee-shirt dress that I spiced up with multiple ropes of faux coral, matching earrings and strappy sandals. For good measure, I brought along a gauzy white and black Deco-patterned long-sleeve blouse in case it cooled off later.

Adam was right about the gravel lane around the lake that led to his cottage. My Taurus kicked up enough dust and stone chips to scare off any wildlife within miles. The name on the mailbox cued me where to turn, *J. Groft.* His father? Maybe even his grandfather? In any case, Adam had never bothered to change it.

Even through the thick stand of trees, I could tell instantly that this was not the traditional lakefront home I had been expecting. A contemporary designer had used soaring glass sliced into the dark shake wood walls to bring the outdoors inside as much as possible. It was hard to separate where the rambling split-level ended and the woods around it began.

Adam must have seen the thick yellow-gray cloud that signaled my arrival. As I cut the ignition, I saw him striding toward me across the grass.

He held the car door as I shimmied out. In one hand I was clutching a large bundle of field flowers I'd picked en route. In the other, I'd grabbed my over-blouse, purse and a pair of reading glasses, just in case.

"You made it," he said, managing a makeshift hug.

"I see what you mean about the road."

The Taurus was covered from the windows down with a flour-like layer of tan dust.   Adam laughed, shook his head.

"Our solution to the Neighborhood Watch program. Nobody gets down here without our knowing it."

He was still chuckling as he relieved me of the flowers.

"For the buffet table," I said.

"You'd think…with that jungle down at the greenhouse, I'd have thought of that myself."

I laughed. "I'm told folks who live in New York City don't visit the Statue of Liberty, either."

We took the long way around to the lakeside with Adam playing tour guide.   The view was spectacular.   On the flagstone patio that stretched across the water side of the house, an outdoor brick fireplace was emitting a plume of wood smoke.   The sun was setting behind the trees on the other side of the lake, and blinding starbursts of light swam on the still surface of the water like reflections in a turquoise glass gazing ball.

"Incredible…! How can you even bring yourself to leave the house?"

I could picture myself camped out with my laptop, writing nonstop—the drowsy late afternoon sun streaming in the windows, warm and caressing against my skin. Too perfect. I shook off the image, let the critical writer's lens take over.

Curiously, I noticed, there wasn't a garden—no visible evidence of a nursery business here. The landscaping was minimalist, mainly evergreens and stands of grasses carefully designed for height and texture.   Scattered among them, boulders were placed to give the impression of a series of natural stone ledges.

As we reached the broad stairs leading into the cottage, we dodged a young man and woman carrying a chafer and a covered platter toward the long rustic wood table set up to one side of the patio. Adam had already handed off the wild flowers to a nervous looking teenager tending the barbecue grill…with patient instructions about locating oversize blue mason jars in the kitchen to show them off.

Inside, the house itself was cool and airy, a study in white and tans—with tons of open space to create a visual bridge between living-dining room areas and the kitchen. The furnishings were sparse but impeccable: some spectacular potted plants; a few marble-top antiques, obviously in the family; and a handful of museum quality wicker pieces.

Several huge oil paintings brought the missing perennial garden inside with a vengeance. They were commissioned, I suspected—especially one of them, prominently displayed on the wall above the gigantic fieldstone fireplace.

The painting's subject was ordinary enough. A woman stood backlit against a sloping field of grasses and Queen Anne's lace—around her, rows of carefully tended summer perennials. Her sunhat shielded her face and she was leaning on some kind of implement, taking in the landscape. Her presence was so intense that for a split-second I had the feeling I was being watched.

"My grandmother...Sara ," Adam said, visibly pleased I'd noticed. "It's my favorite painting in the house. Grandad commissioned it for their fiftieth anniversary. From an old photo taken a year or two after they started the nursery together."

"Beautiful. Really...*beautiful.*"

The rest, Adam must have somehow read from my tone. My reaction was not just to the painting, but to the reality that someone could and had been *loved like that*—to be part of something so powerful that two generations later, even a total stranger couldn't help but stand in awe when confronted with it.

He had moved around behind me, hands resting casually on my shoulders so that we could look at the painting together. I fought the familiar rising sense of panic, feeling very much out of place in this shrine to the Groft family legacy—wary, too, of the intimacy Adam's gesture implied.

Was this the kind of love this man was prepared to offer...? It was a love I had never experienced—not even close—in almost thirty years of marriage.

"That gray light...the darkening sky in the background?" he said quietly. "It reminds me of that first morning...out on the berm. Bea was giving her earnest little lecture on sod removal. And you...you just stood there watching us, leaning on that shovel."

I stiffened and drew a careful breath before reacting. My question began with the irrelevant, but toward the end became close enough for him to grasp where I was headed.

"*Why, Adam...?* why would somebody who grew up with all this... wind up grubbing in the mud in a ditch along an interstate with—?"

"With...*you*, Eve...?"

Adam ignored my crude attempt to lever emotional distance. Instead his hands subtly closed around my shoulders, eliminating any ready escape route.

"If you *really* want to get paranoid? Dutch was right—you look like her, you know. The same jade green eyes...the set of your cheekbones."

"Adam, get serious," I said. "This is a dynasty you've got going here. My mom was a single parent most of my childhood. My own marriage was a disaster. I can't even pretend to know what fifty years with another human being would have been—"

"Honest," he told me bluntly, "and real. With plenty of ups and downs and heartaches. Like Margo and Howard—my grandparents were like that. Jakob and Sara. The two of them together always loomed larger than either one of them alone. Funny and tragic...and—"

"Rare."

At that he chuckled, as much to himself as for my benefit. "Everybody's got something, Eve," he said softly. "We're all broken in one way or another. Question is? Do we have the guts to try to fix it?"

"Some things may just be—"

"Too tough?"

"Too late."

For starters, where was the prospect of an heir apparent in all this? Adam's biological clock might not be ticking, but mine had run out of wind years ago.

"You said it yourself once," I told him, about as blunt as I could make it. "Maybe there comes a point...willing or not, for some things in life, we just run out of time."

At that, he deliberately maneuvered so that I had to face him, then using his forefinger gently raised my chin—trying to read my mood. I tried to keep my expression a blank, but he wasn't buying. Finally, he just shook his head, smiled that funny half-smile of his.

"So that's it," he said gently. "Eve, do you really think it's a priority with me to saddle yet another generation with the...responsibility of all this?"

For the life of me, I couldn't answer. I didn't have to. The deafening silence did the talking for me.

"Groft...and...son."

I heard him weighing the phrase, as he said it, first each syllable and then the whole of it. He was calculating just how much sadness and regret a human being can pack in those three little words. Adam shook his head.

"No more," he said. "I watched my father die…still defining his life—and mine that way. I cannot…will not, let that be the last word, Eve. A *miserable damn excuse for a human being, but the kid sure could grow a tree.* I, for one, don't want that emblazoned on my tombstone!"

Once again, I had misread him. He loved this place not because of who he was—but in spite of it. It had taken him a lifetime to realize it. And for reasons totally beyond my comprehension, I seemed to be part of that equation.

"One day at a time," he said, his voice charged with emotion. "Every one of them a gift. That's all anybody can ask, Eve…or promise."

At that he coaxed me into his arms. I felt the crisp fabric of his button-down shirt, the steady ebb and flow of his breath against my face. Gradually, imperceptibly at first, the tight knot of anxiety began to unravel.

As for Sara Groft's portrait? Mercifully, this time it was safely positioned out of my line of vision.

The sound of voices coming from outside on the patio broke the mood. Adam must have heard it, too. At any rate, he pulled back—flashed a wry smile as he looked down at me.

"The natives appear to be getting restless out there," he said with obvious reluctance. "You'll find the powder room just down that hall. I'll meet you out on the patio."

There were about thirty of us on the guest list. Adam had given me a quick play-by-play on the phone several days ago. His friend Frank's circle included several environmentalists, elected representatives from area agricultural groups, a cross-section of merchants and small business owners, a lawyer, even a teacher or two.

All were about the same age—all more or less childhood

acquaintances.   Men outnumbered the women, but a few also had brought their wives. Most notable was a leggy red-head in fitted black slacks and a gunmetal tank top, early fifties if I had to guess at an age, but determined not to show it.

At the sight of Adam she moved our way. Before he had a chance to react, the woman proceeded to embroil him in a hug that was definitely more than the usual hi-there greeting of old friends.

"So it's true, then...," she said. "You finally stopped globe-trotting. Will wonders never cease?"

Her voice was all velvet and musk, the phrases turned upward in a perpetual question mark. It was one of the few times I ever saw Adam at a loss for words.   His expression, on the other hand, spoke volumes. It was ominous as a thundercloud, no less dark or dangerous.

He started to say something, then clamped his jaw tight. Before he could regroup, even get a word out, the woman lobbed the next grenade in my direction.

"And I gather, *you're* the one who finally managed to nail the guy's hide to the barn door—? Congratulations...I'm impressed."

From her tone and the look she gave me, condolences would have more appropriate.   That particular missile finally got results.

"Carey," Adam said stiffly,   "I'd like you to meet Eve Brennerman. Eve, this is—"

"One of the statistics,"   Carey said. "Carey Biesen, local divorcee—stuck with running the only no-tell motel in the county."

Adam added a terse translation. "That Best Western on the Aurelius-Xenaphon line? Carey's. If a tourist lands in town—it's either head her way or the highway."

The two were talking past me. For once in my life, I resolved not to stand there and dodge the flak.

"You've done a lot with the place, Carey," I told her, keeping my tone light. "Still, replacing those annuals out along your frontage with something more...permanent could save you a bundle, long run."

"Perennials...I assume?" Her voice had that hard rip-out-the-beds and pave-it-over-with-green-concrete edge to it. "I do read your columns, Eve. Although what on earth you see in...*plants*? I never *will* understand.   Believe it or not, Adam was once of a...similar skeptical mindset when it came to...digging around in the dirt."

Adam laughed, but there wasn't any humor in it. "Carey always had a flair for the dramatic."

Casually, he laid an arm around my shoulder. I stiffened, pure instinct, at what the gesture implied. Adam gave no sign he noticed.

But Carey did. The woman was already moving on. Still, she couldn't resist one last over-the-shoulder zinger.

"Well, at least I know where to go for the plant stock…won't I?"

My lungs felt like they had imploded. Without a word from me, Adam dropped his arm as if he had come in contact with a hot stove. He had never, ever pulled one of those possessive macho stunts around me before—and to his credit, wasn't comfortable with it now.

"Sorry about that," he muttered. "Carey has always been one to…shoot from the hip. Especially if you cross her."

My laugh came across as what it was—a sudden, nervous release of breath. It wasn't fooling either one of us.

"I gather," I said, "you landed on Carey's…dirt list some time ago?"

He just looked at me, gauging exactly how much detail was called for. I kept my face neutral, let him figure it out. Inside? Now that was a different matter entirely.

"Ten years ago," he said finally. "I was home for a longer-than-usual visit…Mom had been in the hospital. Carey was in between husbands. It made a certain sense at the time."

The color was rising in my cheeks. I had asked for this. Quickly it was becoming apparent that some things are best left unsaid.

"You don't owe me an explanation," I told him.

"No…maybe I don't. But for the record…I want you to know."

"You forget… .I grew up in a small town, too, Adam."

"And I've lived here all my life. This…Carey's little performance, won't be the last time."

Mercifully, his friend Frank had maneuvered into earshot. I was finding it harder and harder to maintain an even keel.

"Do you wanna ring the dinner bell, Groft?" he said in that bullhorn voice of his. "Or should I do the honors?"

Adam shrugged. "Go ahead."

"Listen up," Frank bellowed, waited for the decibel level around him to settle down to a dull roar. "Before we eat and meet, I'd like to see us put our hands together for our host here—Adam Groft, for putting on this great spread!"

The applause was genuine, enthusiastic, punctuated by a few verbal accolades. Adam flashed an awkward grin, then waved the crowd in the direction of the buffet.

"I'd better check out the grill," he said reluctantly. "That kid tending it is probably having heart failure. Will you be—?"

"Do what you have to do...I can fend for myself just fine."

I wasn't trying for sarcasm. But realized, after the fact, it could be taken that way. Judging by Adam's expression, he was ready for all contingencies.

"Seriously," I laughed, trying to make light of the situation. "I'm okay—really. There's a lot riding on this."

In more ways than one, I realized. Quirking an eyebrow, Adam nodded. But he made no move to leave.

"You're sure?"

"Go, already!"

He finally did. But as I foraged at the buffet, more from habit than hunger, I caught him looking my way. Deliberately I sustained the eye contact, managed a quick smile. Adam's expression was set on neutral—intense, unwavering.

A junior high science teacher and his wife had settled down on one of the faux outcroppings alongside the patio. They asked me to join them. I did, grateful for any distraction to keep my wayward imagination from straying back to Carey and her mastery of innuendo.

The woman's timing would have done credit to a seasoned Shakespearean actor. If she had wanted to inflict as much damage as possible on either Adam or me, or whatever she assumed our relationship to be, she couldn't have done a better job of it.

Rule number one in street fighting? Go for the jugular. Or when in doubt, that failing, aim a well-placed round of bird-shot and hope it will suffice.

Adam had told me, up front, that his past was a checkered one by most reasonable definitions. Still, I was beginning to figure out that knowing a situation and realizing the ramifications of it were two very different matters entirely.

It didn't take ESP to read the veiled question in his eyes, even from fifty feet away across a crowded patio. Was I up to it? Was I prepared, if that's what it took, to let thinly veiled tell-all conversations roll off like rain water streaming down the Groft greenhouse windows?

For the life of me, I was glad that I didn't have to confront that one head-on. Not without putting some time and distance between myself and the situation.

My instinct was to fade into the woodwork after supper while Frank, Adam, and the others thrashed out strategies vis-a-vis the proposed off-ramp project. That bit of wishful thinking pretty much died in the first two seconds.

"By now you've all read Eve Brennerman's column," Frank said, as his opener, waving a stack of photocopies for those who hadn't seen it. "Pretty much sums up whose axe is stuck in which stump around here. Point is, is this a big enough issue to send us downstream on the same log—together?"

"Eve hit the nail on the head, as I see it," a burly high school teacher from Xenaphon spoke up. "It's the principle of the thing. Once again, somebody in Lansing has this idea...and we read about it on page one of the *Gazette*. If nothing else, we should be able to agree on that."

"That, and I hope the importance of preserving the community garden," someone else chimed in. "A lot of folks have put a great deal of work into that project."

"You're *local*, Eve...?"

There it was. An older gentleman I recognized as an outspoken long-time environmental guru was checking me out. As in, what gives that woman the right to set herself up as some kind of expert on northern Michigan real estate development?

"North of here," I said. "On Little Traverse Bay. But I summered here in the fifties."

"Then you know what can happen when the bulldozers take over. I'm all for improving the traffic count on Main Street in Xenaphon. But that ought to come in the context of some larger plan—"

A low groan greeted that notion. Most of the protest seemed to originate with the agricultural contingent.

"The county has funded two master plans in the last fifteen years," the farm bureau president objected. "Priorities galore and nothing to show for it...especially no sense of how to balance our ag, tourism and

152

local retail needs and then come up with the money or resources to implement 'em. This time they've got the money to let 'em mess with the off-ramp, chew up more acreage of farm land. Next thing, they'll widen the highway—"

"And the unemployment rate still spikes at double digits because outside contractors don't use local folk—"

"So, let's talk about ways of making this a win-win proposition!" Adam had wandered over into the circle and settled down on a boulder across the patio from mine. "As Frank said, we can butt our heads against this alone—then again, getting our acts together would sure save one hell of a lot of aspirin."

"Lotsa luck!" someone piped up.

An undercurrent of nervous laughter broke the tension. As I said in my column, none of these arguments were new.

"Okay," Adam said slowly. "How about insisting the price tag for ramp repair is to budget project funds to pay for moving the garden? Make 'em guarantee a set-aside in the budget for a trust to buy farmers' development rights to the tune of a million or two. Demand that a portion of the construction go to county-based bidders and that outside contractors employ a certain percentage of local workers. Next? Oh, yeah—win the environmental and tourism vote by annexing fallow and forested land beyond the berm and along the interstate for a native prairie and woodland park. It could be accessed through that dead-end road coming off Ellicott Road."

"Not a poor man's version of a state college arboretum either," the teacher I had been sitting with chimed in. "More of a hands-on kids heritage site…move the old settler's cabin from the city park over there and hold four-season living history classes."

"The big tourism thing nowadays," his fellow educator told us, "is intergenerational Elderhostel type programs—for grandparents and grandkids. You've already got a cross section of the senior citizen contingent out there on that berm already! Market the program as rainy day activities for campers and cottagers. Downtown merchants could piggyback with a Michigan of Yester-year theme for retail expansion."

"Start showing classic films at the library—"

Adam laughed, raised his hands, palms out as if fending off a direct assault. "I hope," he said, "that somebody's taking notes?"

I had never seen Adam in action professionally before and had to admit, he had as much of a knack for dealing with people as he had for problem-solving out on the berm. With Frank and Adam tag-teaming the situation, the discussion arrived at a consensus amazingly fast. We settled on a dozen priorities and a basic subcommittee structure to draft general policy statements and to begin laying the groundwork for a lobbying campaign.

I promised to poll the garden crew about the issue of relocating, provided of course we had help to make the move. The possibilities were exhilarating, or scary, depending on how you looked at it. If forced to predict where all this would end, I wasn't sure what my answer would be.

Chapter Twenty-Two

A rose has thorns only for those who would gather it.
Anonymous

It was getting late and the crowd on Adam's patio was thinning. Only a few hold-outs had cornered him to express their thanks and get in their last few thoughts about the politics of area development. I was tired, not looking forward to a rematch with him over Carey or his status with the female population of the county.

From the safety of distance, I managed to signal Adam my intentions—that I was about to make tracks, followed by that universal cocked-thumb and finger gesture for 'call me'. At that, his forehead tightened in a quizzical frown and he appeared to be starting my way, but ran into a stone wall in the form of Frank determined to debrief the meeting.

I seized on that as my cue to exit. Picking my way cautiously across the darkened lawn, I eased the Taurus into gear, and headed back down the lane toward the highway.

It couldn't have been home more than half an hour when I heard a car door slam in the driveway. Already in my nightgown, as a precaution I grabbed the matching robe before I hurried to investigate, slipping into it as I went along. That was more than enough time for whoever it was to cross the yard and announce their presence with an insistent knocking on the wood of the door frame.

I didn't need the presence of that familiar SUV to recognize the source.   At the sound of my turning the deadbolt and the inner door opening, Adam straightened.   Through the screen door, he threw me a look that for a split-second just froze me in my tracks.

"Is there anything wrong?" I stammered, fumbling to unhook the screen.

"You tell me, Eve?"

With the taut deliberate strides of a sprinter about to take the mark, Adam shot past me into the room and steadied himself against the oaken back of my grandmother's Mission-style chair.   Tension crackled in the dim light like the silent discharge of heat lightning on a stifling summer night.   I clutched the robe tighter around me, feeling suddenly very vulnerable—exposed.   Adam showed no sign whatsoever of explaining his presence there.

"I thought it was a good meeting," I said, the words tumbling over each other in my eagerness to fill the void opening between us. "You were great getting everybody to think outside the box.   We pretty much covered the agenda—"

"Theirs?" he said. "Or…*ours?*"

It was no good pretending I didn't understand what he meant. Or that my leaving the way I did was anything but a thinly disguised excuse to avoid what was coming next.

"I owe you an apology," I said stiffly."You had your hands full with Frank. It was late. I didn't want to start…stirring around in that business about Carey…your family, any of it, when I was so tired.   It seemed best just to—"

"Run like hell in the other direction?"

"That wasn't—"

"Eve, don't you think I deserved at least the common courtesy to say, *Time out… I'm not sure what's going on here—but I'm going to suspend judgment long enough to find out*?"

He hesitated, lowered his voice. "Instead of…just…cutting out like that…?"

Put that way, it made absolute sense. I felt my face grow hot. The living room, normally so large and breezy, suddenly seemed cramped and confining.

"Adam, I didn't mean—"

"Yes. Yes, sweetheart… you did.   I could read it in your face

156

the minute Carey got her claws out. For you that whole nasty little drama was about your—about Joel, all over again. Only the faces had changed, not the script. You didn't confront it then...all those years watching him trash your life. Why would you confront it now...?"

When I could run instead? "I can't...change how I...feel—"

"So much the worse for me...!"

"Adam, I have to be honest—"

"I'm falling in love with you," he said bluntly. "You want honesty? There it is. And trust me...I know about running. I...*ran* from that possibility...loving someone, for a lifetime. No more. I'm not *about* to let either one of us just...*walk away from it now!*"

His mouth tightened into a hard line, Adam started toward me—then came to just as an abrupt a halt. His face was a study in shock and disbelief, not so much at my response but his own culpability for triggering it.

"Eve...oh God, Eve—I've scared you. The very last thing in the world I...."

At that I felt the tears began to flow in earnest, welling up from a place inside myself I never even knew existed. It was a bleak and sunless cavern where only the pale, long-buried shoots of memories twisted painfully toward the light. My shoulders shook with the effort it took to stand up against that tangle of unnamed grief and hurt.

Adam's face swam in and out of focus with the disjointed objectivity of a stop-action lens as he crossed the room. Now bleak, now resolute, his voice was spelling out his intentions even as he acted on them.

"Let me hold you," he said gently. "For the love of God, sweetheart...don't—"

I wasn't in a position to object, any more than Margo could that Saturday in the hospital lobby. My relationship with my late husband Joel had gone unmourned, in life and in death. The nest had emptied without fanfare and I had shed my full-time career without so much as a backward glance.

Yet here, in the most unlikely of circumstances, caught off guard by a relative stranger's almost defiant admission that it mattered how I felt—I finally wept. The tears were for myself, for the guilt and heartache...all of it, as if only now I were acknowledging the magnitude of that loss.

The bizarre over-the-edge-of-the-cliff logic that kicks in a crisis told me I was inundating Adam's shirt front. The aftermath of a full-fledged crying jag also was bound to be most unattractive. All the conclusions were true and all irrelevant. The emotional flood was going to run its course and I was powerless to stop it.

Adam's hands moved gently against my back and half-bare shoulders where the robe had slipped open—the way you calm a child, awkward and tentative, as if afraid to make things worse in the process. His voice, muffled against my hair, settled on a mantra of quiet desperation.

"Eve...sweetheart, please—"

Eventually, something in me heard and responded. On a shuddering sigh, inexplicably as it began, the maelstrom began to subside. The only reminder of the storm's passing was the subtle thundering of a headache at the base of my brain.

"You were right...," Adam was saying dully. "I should have known—"

"No...!"

I steeled myself to say it, before I lost my nerve. "This isn't about you...it's about me. I ran because I was terrified to tell you...that I love you. I ran because I'm afraid to trust what I feel...what I want and need—"

"Eve, I wouldn't hurt you for the world."

I believed him...had to believe it, shuddered inwardly at the prospect of admitting that, and more. There would be no right time, no idyllic moment to lay my self-doubts and insecurities to rest. These were realities no amount of time was going to resolve. I needed to know what I felt, what I was capable of feeling, and there was only one way to do that.

"If I don't find the courage to...trust you—trust myself? I'll never...ever have a chance to be that woman you...*think* you love." I hesitated. "The woman I...*want to be.*"

"Sweetheart, I—"

"I...want you to...make love to me...!"

He was reading my upturned features, making his own an open book in the process. It had been years that anyone had looked at me like that, unambivalent in his need, half-astonished to find it mirrored in my upturned face. His eyes widened, then narrowed again.

158

"Are you…sure?" he said deliberately.

I managed a shaky, "Yes."

The "but" came out in a rush. "Face it…what sixty-two-year-old wouldn't be scared to death, Adam? When a man hasn't made a remotely serious pass at me in years—"

These were the same tanned and powerful hands I had watched so many times from a distance, deftly wielding a tool or repotting delicate plant stock. Only now, they were cradling my face and drawing my mouth toward his own—insistent and yet painfully restrained, anticipating the response that touch would unleash.

On a sigh, my lips parted, inviting him to deepen the kiss. By now his hands had strayed to my hair, the fingers tangling themselves in the tousled strands. I was drowning in the taste of him, and when in response my own arms intuitively wrapped themselves around his waist, I felt the muscles of his body tense as it strained to meet the softness it was encountering.

The robe finally slipped from my shoulders entirely. I felt the breath catch in my throat as his gaze moved slowly down the delicate spaghetti straps to my breasts, now taut against the silken fabric of the nightgown.

"My God, Eve…you really don't know, do you?" he said hoarsely. "How…amazing you are? Or what you do to me—?"

"You've been giving me a…pretty good idea."

That was the most astonishing, wonderful and dizzying part of it—wrinkles and crow's feet and all. He smiled, started to lower his head toward my upturned mouth. With a teasing hand against his rib cage, I didn't give him the chance. It was hard to keep a straight face, but I managed.

"We are not…kids, Adam. Hiding out in the backseat of dad's Chevy."

He had not misread me often. This time he did.

"Age…it always comes back to that—?"

The set of his jaw looked an awful lot like a defense attorney on Court TV heading into a summation. There wasn't time for a comeback.

"You want to know what I see?" he demanded softly. "For starters…I see a woman who absolutely glows. Someone intelligent enough to make me laugh—confident enough not to obsess over every gray hair. Wise enough to slow down on a trail when she knows that trick knee of mine is giving me fits…and tactful enough not to mention it—!"

"Nice—all of that," I said. "But you missed the point."

I read the confusion on his face. He started to say something, stopped.

"This area rug we're standing on, Adam? It's a hundred percent coarse-woven Balkan weave—and under that? hardwood flooring."

"You lost me…."

"A mattress would probably work better. Mine. Upstairs."

I flashed a gotcha-grin. Laughter rumbled in his chest, low and sensual—making it plain exactly where his imagination was taking him. Just to make sure he got the message across, he slanted one last lingering kiss against my mouth.

The master bedroom was at the head of the stairs, furnished as it had always been with the bed, washstand and dresser my grandmother had received as a wedding gift from her husband-to-be in 1912. I had made this my space ever since I moved here, although tonight I suddenly was seeing it in another context entirely. I was not alone.

Adam had eased alongside me on the quilted coverlet, taking in our surroundings. Like an elaborate golden oak pergola overhead, the eight-foot headboard was carved with an intricate garland of leaves and tendrils. Arcs and reliefs on a smaller scale spilled across the drawer fronts. The borders of the antique linens were stamped white-on-white with cabbage roses, and from the night-stand, a faux Tiffany shade cast muted blooms of light against the ivory of the walls.

"Time in a garden," Adam said softly. "You come by all of this honestly, don't you? Your grandmother Brennerman had one *heck* of an imagination."

I smiled, savoring his reaction. "Her favorite book in the Bible was the Song of Solomon," I told him. "I found her underlining in the margin. *Come my beloved, let us go forth into the fields—*"

There was no need for me to cite chapter and verse. With that, Adam kissed me again.

Chapter Twenty-Three

And when your back stops aching and your hands begin to harden....you will find yourself a partner in the Glory of the Garden. Rudyard Kipling.

My body was taking me into foreign terrain, but as a lover Adam Groft knew that emotional lay of the land for what it was. Chick-flicks rarely glorify cellulite. Poets are even more brutal when it comes to flora, fauna and love over sixty. People bloom, people fade—an inevitable, depressing end to the human story.

Where in all that is the fierce poetry of the daisy with its petals as thin as parchment from the rain, still boldly lifting its face toward the sky? How sad it is to dismiss the wild, extravagant gesture of the peony when it showers its petals in surrender to the gusty summer wind.

Fortunately perennial gardeners have a healthier take on things. We mourn and move on. Our persistent deadheading—a terrible misnomer, by the way—assumes that with a reverent pruning back of the spent and weathered, glorious new life can flower again.

Deadheading was becoming my task of choice. I was getting better at it.

Regular morning power walks with Vivian had given my sagging psyche a visible lift. And Adam was right about laughter. It was beginning to put those fine networks of lines around mouth and eyes in a whole new light. My writing was teaching me things about myself I had never imagined.

Still, some scars that life inflict are tougher to mask than others, and willing as the spirit might be, the proverbial flesh is not always so obliging. Even the discreet twenty-watt bulb couldn't hide the awkward moments.

"You're uncomfortable."

It wasn't a question. Through gritted teeth, I managed to respond.

"Muscle spasm—"

"Sorry."

Chuckling softly, Adam shifted alongside me—guessed the cause. Playful but effective, his palms and fingertips went to work along the aching knot of muscles of my thigh.

"Keep that up and we might avoid a hip replacement."

"If it's health risks we're assessing here, Eve—"

"Other risks, maybe. I guess these days…I have to ask."

Adam gave me a pointed look. His eyebrows arched, and then with a straight face, he defused my embarrassment as casually as if he were sharing his Social Security number.

"For the record?" he said. "Cholesterol. Very little of it the good kind. Viagra under the circumstances, probably not a good idea. As for condoms…thank God they have a relatively long shelf life."

We really ought to let Cosmo in on it, I found myself thinking. Whatever other medicinal properties laughter had, it was turning out to be the best aphrodisiac.

Our bodies were warm and alive to one another. Patience did the rest. Still half teasing, Adam's mouth began to explore where his hands had been. This time it was pleasure that was robbing me of speech.

––––––––––––

If Eden is a place, we found it—as simply as our namesakes, those primal lovers in the Garden, stumbling upon the ultimate mystery of human existence. Imprinted forever on my memory was not a long-ago marriage bed or past loveless encounters in the night. It was the earth-rending beauty of the spring garden, of fern fronds uncoiling to the sun, vulnerable yet unafraid.

Spent and heart pounding, I snuggled against Adam's shoulder.

A velvet sheen of moisture glistened on his skin, cool like the night air against the flush of my cheek. I shivered.

In the distance, a train whistle wailed softly—at least two o'clock. It was going to be a short night, and still neither of us showed any sign of doing anything about it.

"It's late."

"Who's complaining?"

Adam laughed. "You will be. It's Saturday. If we aren't out there on the berm, we'll never hear the end of it."

I groaned at the prospect. "I can't move."

"A couple of Ibuprofen should take the edge off."

Somewhere far down the street, a car door slammed setting off complaints from a lone dog. A muffled protest cut off the barking. But the silence had a tenuous edge about it now—reminding us that even in this quiet sanctuary, we were not alone.

"You've got some pretty…formidable neighbors,"Adam said finally. "If you think I should go—"

"Stay."

"Tough…like this."

His tone was neutral. It took me a second to figure it out.

"I'm cutting off your circulation."

"Nice, as problems go. But yes."

Reluctantly, we settled in alongside one another. It was hard to let go—not without telling him what it felt like to be so wonderfully, unexpectedly at peace. Another man had known this same body when it was young and supple, still so open and naive about things like trust and fidelity. That woman no longer existed. And yet here I was.

"Words come hard for me, Adam."

Strange to admit that, I realized, for someone who made their living as a writer. If he saw the irony, he didn't show it.

"Eve…sweetheart, you're too hard on yourself—"

"—and *you*. I haven't cut you much slack from Day One."

Adam drew a harsh breath. "No one would blame you for being skeptical—me included."

"I assume you're referring to what happened with my…with Joel? Ancient history."

"I was thinking more of the Carey's out there…."

"Oh."

I had genuinely forgotten. The silence told me that Adam hadn't.

"So along comes a guy who dodged commitment all his life," he said. "You have no reason at all to believe I'm capable of it now."

"You never promised me anything, Adam."

"I promised never to hurt you. I meant it. If the word 'love' frightens you? I won't use it. God knows, it's a first for me…."

At that, I turned and levered enough distance between us so that I could see his eyes. They were dark and troubled.

"Love means a lot of different things, at different times in our lives," I told him—sorting through the heartache of betrayal, the terrible end to my marriage and the guilt that followed for the truth of what I felt. My voice was shaking with the stress of it, but it had to be done.

"Eve, you don't need to justify—"

"Yes…yes, I do. The 'L-word' may come hard for either one of us. But this much I know. I could have gone to my grave believing I could never…touch another human being again. Or let anyone touch me. Is that love? Is it enough? At one time in my life I'd have said, No."

"And now?"

"I could get hit by a bus tomorrow, Adam. So could you. Nothing, no one can take tonight away from me—not my doubts or demons, not even yours."

I let him pull me close. Our bodies nestled against each other like the proverbial spoons in a drawer, comfortable and content. After a while our breathing steadied and we slept.

Chapter Twenty-Four

As is the gardener so is the garden. Anonymous

I should have noticed that the phone message light was blinking last night, but then I had other things on my mind. My daughter Leslie, it seems, had transmitted a terse warning from her cell phone. It would have explained everything.

Instead, the doorbell did it for her. Leslie's car was at the curb. She was standing on my front stoop, suitcase and granddaughter Emma in hand. About the maternity top she had given me fair warning in her Fourth of July phone call. Dan, her husband, was nowhere in sight.

"I've left him," Leslie said.

It was one of those one-sided conversations that pretty much stifle any intelligent response. The thought occurred, *Holy shit…!* Just as quickly another followed. It was the realization that I had left Adam Groft half-asleep in my bed.

Times like this it helps to go on autopilot. I stood aside and let Leslie and Emma into my living room. My daughter put down the suitcase and in the process her face crumpled around the edges like a plant in the throes of transplant shock. Badly in need of a hug, a strong cup of coffee or a good cry, my motherly instincts told me.

Leslie's hug was fleeting and the coffee I suggested, a necessity but postponable. *First things first.* I had already noticed—as my daughter did a split-second later—something which put her potential crying jag on indefinite hold. It was the faint sound of life exerting itself

165

from somewhere upstairs. *We were not alone.*

"You've got company," she said, uncertain now. "I left a message on your machine—"

"Got home late," I hedged. "Let me throw on some jeans. I'll be right back."

I headed for the staircase. *Speed was most definitely of the essence here.* The flash of a self-portrait I caught passing the hall mirror seemed disembodied, not the radiant, carefully put-together face I remembered looking back at me last night from the frame over the vanity on my usual post-midnight bathroom run. The bedroom door was partly ajar as I had left it, wide enough now to catch sight of Adam—back turned, pulling on his khakis.

"*Problems*…," I said in a strangled whisper.

Adam turned at the sound, bare chested and hair tousled. Miles out front, his expression was running a sprint from confused to alarmed. I fought the urge to laugh. The next ten minutes were likely to be anything but funny.

"My daughter, Leslie," I told him. "And granddaughter Emma."

"But you weren't—?"

"Expecting them? No. I didn't check the phone last night. They called."

"Holy shit!"

"I was thinking the same thing."

His shirt was on half-buttoned—wrong, so that the tails hung down unevenly. He was fixated not on me, but on the doorway behind me. All eyes herself, my granddaughter was standing there thumb in mouth and holding her teddy bear. It was not Gramma who had caught her attention.

"You said a naughty word," she said.

"True," Adam said. "I'm sorry."

"Momma never lets me use the S— word."

"Smart lady, your mom."

"I'm Emma."

"Adam," he told her, intent on coping with the last of the buttons. "Glad to meet you."

"This is my Gramma's house."

I felt caught in a surreal ping-pong match with no end in sight to the volley. Adam still was trying with some difficulty to rectify that

166

button situation. The stress lines between his brows deepened.

"And you've come to visit?"

Emma nodded a cautious assent. "Mom says we might live here, too."

The way things were going, I was superfluous in this unfolding of events. Adam already knew more than I had going into this bizarre exchange.

"But first, I'm going to make us all breakfast," I said.

"Him, too?"

I had to hand it to my granddaughter. Emma was certainly persistent.

"Thanks…but I should be at work by now," Adam told her.

I got the message—as credible an excuse as any to justify a hasty exit. Emma frowned.

"It's Saturday," she said.

We should be heading out to the berm right now. I'd forgotten. So, obviously, had Adam. Fortunately, he was quick on his feet.

"I run a nursery, Emma. Busiest day of the week."

She thought about it. "You take care of babies?"

"Not that kind of nursery, Emma. I grow plants. Lots of them."

"Momma grows stuff, too. Tomatoes, mostly. But sometimes Momma grows babies, too. I hate tomatoes."

Adam chuckled. "I did, too, when I was your age."

A sound from the hall reminded me where we were and that all this had been going on far too long. Leslie's perfunctory knock preceded her appearance in the room, but not enough to matter. One look at her face told me all I needed to know. *By now she had figured out which direction the proverbial weather was coming from.*

Introductions were an adult version of the ones that had just passed between Adam and Emma, though far more restrained considering where we were. The room was getting very crowded. Formalities over, Adam was angling for the front door with a ragged entourage in his wake.

Out of breath, I shot a quick reminder his direction. "The garden crew will be wondering what on earth happened to me—"

"No problem. I was heading over there myself. I'll make your apologies."

He flashed a wan smile. Our mutual discomfort was obvious

167

enough, though not the cause. Departure was both a solution and a problem. Given last night, Adam's exit begged some kind of reassuring contact. That, under the circumstances, was fraught.

I stood on the porch with daughter and Emma watching my every move through the screen door behind me. Thank God, they couldn't see the look that passed between us.

"I'll call you," he said.

"Later."

———————————

At least my daughter held off the inquisition until the sound of Adam's car engine had faded. By then I had fled to the kitchen. In short order and triggered by a conspicuous amount of gratuitous utensil rattling, the pungent aroma of Columbian blend began wafting through the room.

"I'm afraid to ask," Leslie said, "what *that* was all about."

Meaning Adam, of course. I was pretty much wrestling with the same question but for entirely different reasons. The Adam Groft agenda would keep. Leslie and Dan getting a divorce? Their relationship always struck me as more solid than most.

"First tell me about Dan…I gather right now that he's—?"

"In London. On business. As good a time as any to do what I should have done a long time ago—"

"Daddy grows computers," Emma informed me. "Not plants."

This wasn't going to go away. If we were going to get beyond the novelty of Adam Groft's presence in my bedroom at eight in the morning, I was just going to have to plant the idea and let it germinate for a while.

"We're friends—Adam and I," I told my daughter. "Good friends."

"Dating?"

"You could call it that."

An understatement. But then Emma was still standing right there looking at the both of us, trying to make some sense out of this strange verbal tap dancing.

"That man didn't have his shirt on," Emma volunteered. "He

buttoned it wrong—"

"For heaven's sake, Mom—"

"For heaven's sake, Leslie…you and Dan? Calling it quits?"

Whatever Adam and I had been up to in her eyes paled by comparison. There were a limited number of possibilities when a relationship went on the rocks.

"Surely, Les…neither one of you struck me as the type to—"

"Fool around?" Her lips thin and stiff, Leslie cut off speculation. "It's *not* somebody else, if that's what you're thinking. Either one of us. I should be so lucky."

Bored by the whole conversation, Emma had wandered off toward the living room, her toes making scuff noises on the self-stick vinyl of the kitchen tiles. I ducked my head and poured two steaming cups of unleaded, scalding out of the pot.

Leslie was less distractable. "Is *he* married?"

"Adam? No."

"Divorced?"

"No."

Surprisingly, a bachelor in her book was even worse. She looked at me like I'd totally lost it.

"For crying out loud, Mom. Not one of those perpetual commitment-phobes? The guy's got to be pushing—"

"He's sixty-nine," I told her, sounding more defensive than I intended. "Then I'm no spring chicken either, Leslie."

"Exactly the point."

Leslie grabbed the cup I had set out for her on the table, two-fisted, prepared to take a swig of coffee. Just as fast, she grimaced at the heat, set it down again. When she thrust out her chin like that she looked just like Emma.

"Typical," she said. "I come up here with my marriage on the rocks…and here's mom, going at it with this…aging stud muffin. Probably yet another workaholic, pissing away his life and those of everyone around him. Men are all alike. ESPN, work—they'll find any excuse to blow off relationships."

The rising tide of disgust in her voice finally gave me my first clue to what really had prompted this pre-partum crisis. I stifled a smile as I settled down at the kitchen table, waiting for my daughter and the coffee to cool off.

Leslie had staked out a spot over by the kitchen window and was looking out over the yard, her back to me. I could see the tension in her shoulders ease a notch. *Pretty impressive what she found out there*, if I had to say so myself. Where a wilderness had once prevailed, I had dug in tidy rows of pole beans, raised beds of zucchini and peppers, and several short but well-stocked rows of herbs courtesy of stock from Vivian's even more impressive collection.

I let my daughter take it in, sensing in due time she would opt to join me again at the table. The coffee was potent. Leslie sipped at it without visible enthusiasm.

"Nice," she said.

Meaning my handiwork in the back yard, not the brew—badly as she must have needed it after a night on the road. Even putting in the long hours earning her Masters in personnel administration or whatever practitioners were calling it these days, Leslie never seemed to share my passion for high-end forms of caffeine.

"Thanks," I said.

"Greatgramma would be pleased."

"I'd like to think so. Emma says you've got pots out on your patio these days, too?"

"Not like this. But, yes...I've started with two half whiskey barrels and some faux terra cotta pots. Emma likes to dig around in one with her name on it. She sets her little dollhouse toys in it like a landscape designer."

But then, it wasn't horticulture that had brought her here. *Time*, I decided, to try again.

"What does she...Emma make of all this" I said. "Your sudden trip...minus her father?"

"A big vacation. Camping out at Gramma's."

I remembered those four-year-old eyes. They were sizing up Adam as if he were an escaped felon.

"Emma probably knows more than you think," I said. "How did Dan react?"

Leslie shrugged. "Hell, it'll be at least two weeks before he even notices we're gone."

"You didn't tell him?"

"He'll figure it out when he runs out of clean socks."

Her voice quavered, stopped. I always had admired my son-in-law

170

for his sense of fair play when it came to work around the house. For all her bravado, Leslie was not as confident about her course of action as she was trying to make me believe.

"It must be tough," I said. "Another round of diapers, holding down a full-time job, a husband on the road quite a bit...."

"That's part of it...but not all. Not by a long shot."

"Sweetie...I don't understand—"

"If anybody ought to understand about second thoughts—*it's you*, Mom."

My heart sank as I sensed where she was headed. Leslie broke eye contact and her voice lowered to an anguished whisper.

"Why, Mom...? Why, in the name of heaven did you stay with Dad all those years? You knew he was...fooling around, knew he didn't really care about anybody but himself. And still you stayed—long after any sane person would have cut and run."

The sins of the fathers. Apparently, mine were coming home to roost—only *this time* in the context of my daughter's life and marriage. Had I misjudged Leslie's situation that badly?

"Leslie, honey...are you suggesting—? You told me that neither one of you was—I can't...believe that Dan would ever be...." I choked out the word. *"Unfaithful...."*

"With another woman? Of course not. But his work, the guys, just about everything else on the planet—"

"And so you wonder if it's...worth it? Or if thirty years from now you're going to wake up and...know you wasted your life trying to...salvage the unsalvageable?"

Leslie nodded. She looked so vulnerable, so frightened, my heart bled for her.

"Sweetie, I believed then...believe now, that some things between couples are just too broken to fix—and trust me, for way too long? I blamed your father for that. Big time. What has been...*tougher is* to admit...*my role* in all that...."

"What...role, Mom? It wasn't...*you* who—"

I shook my head. "No, sweetie. No excuses. When I first started...dating Adam, I cynically asked him, if he believed in change? I was thinking of your father. But Adam wisely made it a whole lot more personal. Was I talking about your father, about men in general...or myself?"

My daughter seemed about to intervene. I waved her off.

"The truth, Les…? All those years I stayed with your father, I wasn't ready—or willing to change my life, to risk losing everything to protect my own head and heart. Not even if it meant a chance to build an…honest family life for you and your sister."

"You sound like her…like my sister, Gina. All these years, pushing the blame off on you." Anger crackled in Leslie's voice. "Well, I didn't buy it back then…don't buy it now—"

I forced a laugh. "Sweetie, we don't have a monopoly on the old blame-game. It's been around since Adam and Eve. So has sibling rivalry—"

"Not…funny, Mom…!"

"No, it isn't." I looked my daughter straight in the eye. "*I chose* your father—my decision and mine alone. And until I could finally own up to the…tragic shortsightedness of my choice…and find the courage to move on? I was permanently stuck—"

"Like Dan and I…just passing each other like ships in the night—"

"Is that…really what you believe…? That Dan *truly* doesn't care about you or Emma? That you would be better off never having met him?" I paused. "Whatever mistakes your father and I made, two things I never regret. Ever. One is you. The other is Gina."

Leslie started to respond, stopped. "I…know Dan loves us—"

"So, tell him. Tell him how you feel. You might just be surprised how…relieved he is that you care enough to…hit him with the truth."

At that my daughter finally started to cry, great shoulder-heaving sobs that left her nose running and eyes red-rimmed. I let her ride it out. When the flood at last subsidized, the calm was palpable, the storm all but over.

"Stupid, huh?" she said, mopping at the damage from the deluge with a handy dish towel.

I tried not to let my relief show too much. Leslie had never been a whiner. If she needed to let off some steam, she certainly was entitled.

"I've heard of dumber," I said.

"Hormones."

"Whatever." The terrible ache that had settled around my heart began to ease a little. "I'm glad you're here, sweetie."

"Me, too, Mom."

Chapter Twenty-Five

Gramma, why do things always taste better out in the garden than in the kitchen? Emma Brennerman Caldwell

An hour or two of weeding was all it took to exorcize any remaining demons, as far as my daughter was concerned. I hated to blow off the berm but a quick call to Bea's cell phone set things straight. For once the garden could live without me.

Instead, side by side in what had been Greatgramma Eva's vegetable patch Leslie and I, and even occasionally Emma, yanked and cultivated and staked up the unruly collection of farm store plants I had dug in last May. Our shared sense of progress was measurable without calculator or yard stick—a gift that every gardener treasures as a perk of the trade.

No chemicals here. A vigorous brushing against a shirt sleeve was all it took to treat ourselves to the last of the snow pea pods. In the end, we stood together laughing as Emma timidly experimented with the first tart handful of raspberries coming into their own at the edge of the plot. The raspberries were survivors from the previous garden that had flourished in this place.

I thought of Vivian and her herbs and what she had said about letting the garden speak to me. In the occasional moments of silence, broken only by the humming of insects and throbbing heat of the summer sun, I heard the truth of what was growing here. Three generations of us, side by side—Greatgramma Brennerman's flesh and blood.

Time moves on.   The unthinkable becomes possible. Adam called early afternoon and wound up taking the bunch of us out to dinner at Marty's.

If the prospect of making small talk with three very outspoken women worried him, Adam wasn't showing it. And despite her initial scepticism, I could tell this go-around Leslie also was enjoying Adam's company immensely. By now even a total stranger could have figured out that my "friendship" scenario was a shameless euphemism. It no longer seemed to phase her.

The restaurant was noisy, full to the gunwales. All-you-can-eat-fish had moved from a Friday entree to a weekend mainstay of all the local eateries. Leslie and I chose trout. Emma picked dubiously at her well-disguised kid-version, periodically humming choruses of "Fishy, fishy in the brook" to make the point. She hated it.

Funny what sticks in your memory. My daughter used the same childhood rhyme on me on a regular basis during her late-adolescent vegetarian protest against anything aquatic but seaweed. Leave it to Emma, though, to say what no one else had the nerve to even think.

"Are you and my Gramma gonna get married?" she said.

It caught Adam mid-bite. Not surprising, he wound up chewing on the notion a while.

"...have you asked *her* about that?"

"Nope."

Emma shot me a puzzled look. Something must have told her she was barking up the wrong tree. I couldn't even bring myself to look at Adam or my daughter.

"Did you *ask* her?" she persisted.

Adam chuckled. "Do you think I should?"

Emma pondered the notion, her delicate brow knotted into a frown. Leslie looked as embarrassed as I'd ever seen her. What a true gift it is, I thought, to live long enough to produce that level of total mortification in your offspring.

"Dunno," Emma admitted. "Gramma can get pretty steamed, momma says, when you ask dumb questions."

I thought Adam was going to fall off his chair with laughter. Leslie and I were not far behind. I saw heads swivel at tables all around us wondering what on earth could possibly be that funny.

"Give Mr. Groft—and your Gramma a break," Leslie gasped

before the clueless Emma could launch another missile. "Try eating your fish."

Emma worked at a pout but did as ordered. I felt just about as ambivalent about the contents of my plate as she did.

"Would, 'Pass the salt' be okay, Emma?" Adam said. "Or is it likely to send your Grandma tearing out of here?"

It was an in-joke. Adam only half-succeeded at maintaining a straight face. After last night, I was going to put up with my share of running-for-cover jibes. Emma was too preoccupied to comment. Her mother was making a show of separating her fish sticks into manageable hunks. I knew darn well that I hadn't heard the last from Adam on the subject of my granddaughter's fishing expedition either.

Emma ate at least a third of her entree, we passed on dessert, and Adam drove us home again. It was almost dusk by the time Leslie dragged a now-cranky four-year-old off to bed. I stayed behind in the yard, grateful for even those few seconds of privacy before Adam took off himself.

There were side air-bags and the steel frame of the SUV door between us. How much trouble could a guy get in through an open vehicle window?

"Emma's a smart kid," he said. "Wondering whether or not my intentions are…honorable."

I knew darn well what he was talking about. A smile played at the corner of his mouth while he tested my reaction. I tried to look stern not panicked.

"We are *not* going there, Adam."

"Thanks to Sweet Emma?" He chuckled—punctuated it with a wink as he slid the SUV into gear. "We already have."

My daughter looked exhausted. After her wild trip to Xenaphon overnight and the emotional release that followed, I half-expected to find Leslie nodding in a chair in front of the fireplace. Instead, she was down on her knees on the hearth rug, putting together an impressively designed edifice of kindling and logs.

"One log a fire never makes…," she muttered.

"A holdover from scouts? I'm surprised it took, Leslie. You quit after a month."

She just flashed a grin and kept on going. I staked out my spot in one of the wing chairs watching her. A fire would be nice. That was the one spectacular thing about northern Michigan weather and it made all the rain and gray days, the sizzling summer heat bearable. Nights—except for a few scorchers in mid-July—always carried with them the promise of the cooler, more tranquil Fall to come.

Leslie put match to tinder, then sat back on her heels to make sure the flame caught. I took a chance and revisited the business that had brought her here.

"And one spouse a marriage doesn't make either," I said. "I tried that. You know the results. Both of you need to give it everything you've got."

Leslie stood and eased into the wing chair across the hearth rug from mine. She was still worrying over the fire.

"I know...I sound crabby, Mom. But Dan really doesn't seem to be trying very hard to get his boss at Globa-Tech to lay off on the extended road trips. Once little Harry here comes along—"

"It's a boy?"

"Would be nice...one of each. But we'd rather not know. Dan would prefer a girl, strangely enough. Says that a guy grows up and leaves you, but that a girl is daddy's forever."

"I wouldn't know."

That sounded a little too much like a pity-party, but then it just slipped out there. Leslie winced as she caught it and gave me her full attention.

"He didn't mention that girls are notorious for giving their *mothers* one heck of a hard time before they finally come around," she said quickly. "Gina and I weren't any exceptions to that, I'll admit."

"I'm not so sure your sister will ever get past all that—"

"Separation angst?" Leslie shook her head. "Call it what it is. A phase, Mom, nothing personal. I truly believe that. After all she's three years younger than I am. Just give her time."

That was the great thing about perennials, I found myself thinking. You separate them, move them a foot or two, and by next morning they're already straining to bridge the gap, fill in all that empty space between them. People for all their hustle and impatience, don't

176

shift ground nearly as fast.

"I haven't heard from Gina in six months," I said. "Except, of course, for occasional photos of little Anna."

"Not much better than my record," Leslie told me. "I actually offered to play Big Sister and spend part of my vacation relieving Gina on the night shift when baby Justin was born. Got a polite but definite, 'Thanks but no thanks'. Part of it must be that husband of hers. Will doesn't seem to be particularly sociable."

"At least your Dan talks to me on the phone once in a while."

Leslie looked sheepish. "Okay, so maybe I am being too hard on him."

"Just a little."

"And too hard on you, too, Mom…and how you feel or don't feel about Adam. You know, it's really none of my business, Mom, what you choose to do with your free time."

"For the record, I don't honestly think I'm up to marrying again," I told her.

"Does Adam know?"

A pained frown gave her my answer. What I didn't tell her was the way I had run for cover the night of Adam's cook-out meeting about the garden or what it led to—our making love for the first time. Truth was, I don't know what I would do if he chose to push me.

For a while the two of us just sat there comfy and silent—mother and daughter and in moments like this, so much more. The fire worked at taking the chill off the room. Seasoned wood snapped and sighed and gave off its brilliant flame. Just as it was meant to do.

"I wouldn't object, you know," Leslie told me. "If not Adam, than somebody else."

"And your sister?"

"You can't let your kids box you in like that, Mom. Not me. Not Gina. She was too young to understand really what was going on with you and dad. Everybody deserves a warm body to come home to."

"Have you thought maybe all you and Dan need," I said quietly, "is a weekend holed up in a hotel somewhere once in a while, away from Emma and work and the phone—everything? Just rip down the old fencing, remind each other why you loved each other in the first place?"

Leslie laughed. "Touche. As is, Emma can throw up a pretty awesome tangle of barbed wire if she puts her mind to it. I shudder to think what she'll do when she has to share the nest with a new brother or sister."

"You'll figure it out."

Leslie reached down to brace up a chunk of half-burned birch that was threatening to slide sideways on to the hearth rug.   When she straightened, her eyes were brimming with tears.

"I love you, Mom," she said.

Chapter Twenty-Six

Odd as it may appear, a garden does not grow from seed, shoot, bulb, rhizome, or cutting, but from experience, surroundings, and natural conditions. Karel Capek.

It was midnight before I thought about sleep although my daughter had long since joined Emma on the sofa bed in the spare bedroom upstairs. As I wandered through the house clicking off lights, it hit me. My column was due on Monday and I hadn't even started.

The *Perennials in Michigan* text lay open where I had left it next to my laptop on the dining room table. A stick-'em note marked the species I had been researching for the berm:

> Obedient Plant. False Dragonhead. *Physostegia.* **Height:** 1-4' — **Spread:** 12-24' —**Flower color:** pink, purple, white —**Blooms:** mid-summer to fall. A reliable bloomer that can withstand even harsh end-of-the-season weather conditions. Popularly called *dis*obedient because of their invasive lifestyle. These tiny, snapdragon-like flower heads are hummingbird-magnets. The first season, protect fall seedlings from winter cold.

On a scrap of paper taped to the computer case I also had scrawled down several shards of gardening wisdom that I'd picked up along the way, intending eventually to work them in.   One swam into focus for me now: *A weed is but an unloved flower.*   That author was anonymous.

Strange how what we write is shaped by or even shapes what we experience.   It has been said that writers cannibalize their day-to-day existence for truth.   Just as often these days, I found myself whacking away at a topic only to find my little fictions becoming inadvertent scripts for the reality of my day-to-day.

There are worse scenarios by which to pursue my life than what lies ahead for the tough little Physostegia we are about to put out there on the berm.   The love in my life is becoming no less invasive, filling in the space around me, unconditionally from all sides.   Leslie and Emma, Adam, George my boss, the gardening gang every weekend.   The list had become pretty astonishing, when I thought about it.

So then, what was this anxious knot of fear I still allowed to root itself around my heart?   The perennial guide tells me the trick to survival for Physostegia is to weather that first hard winter.   The "end-of-the-season" conditions will more or less take care of themselves.

Unless I choose to dwell upon it, the first long, brutal winter of my life is long since past and gone.   Changes of the season still may send me scurrying for the liniment, but I can define them now for what they are—proud milestones of growth and survival.

I slid on to the chair in front of my laptop and wrote:

```
Words like "risk" and "hope" and
"grace" do not pop up a lot in
horticultural magazines. That is odd,
because you cannot survive in the
gardening business long without them.
    Forget roto-tillers and multi-
purpose weeders. A gardener's
greatest nemesis and strength, the
most imperative tool in a gardener's
shed, is the capacity to risk.
    A gardener cannot even choose a
species to plant or hoe a row without
taking a chance. Experts have rated a
plant's chances of survival for us.
They do it by zones. Nine is the
warmest and most hospitable, one is
close to Ice Age conditions.
```

All that is relative, of course. If you mulch a Zone 6 plant well enough, even in our harsher Zone 4 to 5 climate, it just might survive. Experts might discourage introducing something invasive for fear it might crowd out other plants. But even if the "obedient" plants of this world get out of hand, with a little tending they still can find a niche in the garden. Nothing is perfect. There are no guarantees.

Every gardener quickly learns that for all the planning and planting, ultimately the most powerful forces arrayed against a little community of plants are beyond one's control. A creative gardener can anticipate the marauding of four-footed predators and rapacious crawling things. But weather is its own master and often far more deadly. Even conditions as ethereal as the morning dew can stealthily destroy a garden at its very roots.

Mercifully just when growing conditions seem most hopeless and bleak, grace comes to a garden with equal unpredictability. The rain is gentle and shorter than forecast. That last-ditch decision of the gardener to throw up a snow fence traps the drifts and keeps the sub-zero nights from freezing out the daisies yet again.

Gardening is both life-affirming and humbling. It teaches us to have faith in new life to come and to hold on through the darker days. It grounds us—literally and figuratively—in what really matters as the seasons play out around us.

In a garden we are never alone.

By definition, a garden mimics and models the dynamics of living together as a community. It teaches us to share our space and allow one another the room to bloom in our own time and fashion. On sunny days and dark ones, a garden can shock us out of our complacency when we need such hefty doses of individual and collective soul-searching the most.

I searched the draft for mixed metaphors and obvious grammatical glitches. It was nearly one and the house was still.

Adam had proposed we treat Leslie and Emma to an outing tomorrow to the final day of a nearby Summer Fest famous for its street musicians and hands-on art programs for children. My daughter and granddaughter would be on their way back to Chicago by late afternoon.

The weekend was giving new meaning to burning-the-candle-on-both-ends. This was my second late-nighter in a row. Unless I hit the sack soon, I would never make it through another day out and about with Emma.

I saved my work and steered the laptop through its familiar shut-down drill. Plenty of time between now and Monday to finish the piece on time.

The weekend ended far differently than it began. It was dusk Sunday when Leslie loaded the last of the gear in the trunk ready for the trip home. Adam was helping her. My job was getting little Emma settled in the car seat in back. As I wrestled with the safety restraint, Emma giggled and planted a squishy kiss. I felt the tears tight and salty behind my eyes.

Adam pressed a high-five against the glass of Emma's window before he headed toward the porch, giving my daughter and me those last few precious minutes alone together. Leslie was behind the wheel, making a hug impractical. The question in her eyes made up for it.

"Mom—be honest," she said, "When you look in the

mirror—what do you see?"

For what seemed like a long time, I just looked down at her through the open car window. She had her father's nose—more Irish than Germanic. Leslie's eyes? They were all Brennerman. In them, I saw myself as I might have been those many decades ago when love was still so uncomplicated in my own life.

"I see the girl I used to be," I told her. "And never was."

Leslie's voice quavered. Her hands tightened on the wheel.

"Sometimes, Mom? I feel so…old."

I smiled. "Hang in there, sweetie," I told her gently. "Give it time. It'll pass."

The irony of the words hit me about the same time it registered with my daughter. Leslie started laughing.

"If aging is half as fun for me as it's turning out to be for you, Mom? I'd dye my hair white tomorrow."

Still chuckling to herself, Leslie put the car in gear and maneuvered cautiously out of the driveway. I didn't stop waving until she and Emma were out of sight. Adam, I saw, had stayed behind on the porch, waiting for me.

"You've got a great family," Adam said as I joined him.

Yes. Yes, I did.

"They like you, too," I told him.

He laughed. "After the first few minutes, I wasn't so sure. That Emma is a pistol."

"Surprised?"

"No…it seems to run in the family."

The screen door was within easy reach. Neither one of us had made a move in that direction.

"Could I tempt you with a coffee?" I offered. "Tea? Something stronger?"

A hint of a smile teased at the corner of Adam's mouth. He was not going to make this easy for me.

"You left out the most tempting possibility….," he said.

"Not on the menu. Unfortunately, I still have a column to write if I want to get to bed before midnight."

"Is that an invitation—? Or are you tossing me off your porch?"

"That sure would get the neighbor's attention."

"Well, then this should be relatively tame by comparison."

Coaxing me into his arms, he let his kiss finish what had gone unsaid when Emma walked in on us yesterday. The intimacy between us was real. It was not going away.

"Not fair…," I whispered as I caught my breath.

"Just giving you something to think about."

"You succeeded."

Adam smiled. "Good. Now… if you promise a rain check? I'll drag myself out of here. Protesting all the way, of course."

"Blackmail," I teased.

"You bet!"

His car was parked along the curb, far enough potentially to wreak havoc with my resolve. I told him so, stayed on the porch. Watching him cross that lawn alone was bad enough.

As it turns out, I could have spared us both the aggravation. I read through the sketch of the column I had begun drafting the night before. My focus was nonexistent. After a half hour of editing around on the text, I gave up and closed the file.

Browsing through the folders, I opened my electronic journal. Not knowing quite where I was heading, I poured out the story of Leslie's visit. In the end, the garden was never far away:

I learned a lot about weeding this weekend. Weeding is one of those deja vu realities a gardener has to tackle. It never stops. At least the payoff is a sense of progress. In an out-of-control world, weeding gives a gardener the rare opportunity to take control of life, one problem at a time.

I used to look at weeds as the enemy. That seems to have changed. Weeds, I'm beginning to think, may just be tenacious relics of the past coming back to haunt us.

The minute we broke sod out there on the berm, we were forcing change, intruding on a patch of ground where a whole other world had once co-existed and thrived. Change isn't bad. But we can't be surprised either when weeds decide to fight back.

It's tougher to be hostile about weeds when you put that spin on things. Tonight after the girls left and I was heading back to the house, I had one of those clop-aside-of-the-head experiences. Adam to his credit had hung back, watching us from the porch as Leslie and I said our goodbyes. She left and I was on my way to join him.

A strange time, I found myself thinking, to notice a dandelion poking out of an otherwise tidy patch of groundcover at the base of the front steps. Where had that come from? It was no big deal to reach down and deal with it. I did.

Funny, too what else we can weed out as we go along. I didn't need a mirror to tell me what Adam was thinking as he waited for me there on the porch. But in the past I would have been tempted to overwrite that image of myself with a harsher, more critical one—one stamped by the encroachment of time, magnified by my own insecurities.

I took my hands off the keyboard, remembering my daughter's question about how I look at myself, and how past and present blurred in her asking of it.

What I saw reflected in Adam's smile was something I had never seen there before, or maybe it was just I had never allowed myself to see. I was seeing my future.

185

Chapter Twenty-Seven

Bloom, damn it! Artie the Teamster

With a quick phone call, I begged off on my usual crack-of-dawn Monday hike-athon with Vivian. Tuesday we got back on schedule. Some mornings I managed to crawl the extra half mile to her house to pick her up. This time I got lazy and drove.

As I pulled around the corner, a truck passed me—familiar and very unexpected. Vivian's red-faced presence at the curb in sweats and the tousled look about her confirmed my hasty conclusion. The truck was Artie the Teamster's battered pickup. There could be no simple explanation for his presence on this particular side street at this hour of the morning.

"Artie," Vivian stammered. "He likes to come over for dinner once in a while."

I tried hard not to smile. Apparently, breakfast as well.

"You're a great cook," I said, remembering the macadamia cookies.

"Actually, we started spending time together after we all put up that pergola on the berm."

I noticed that she had avoided the word, "dating". Word travels fast in Xenaphon, yet until Vivian enlightened me about their relationship, I had no clue whatsoever. Snapshot fashion I tried to picture the two of them slipping out of town for a discreet little rendezvous.

"Why, Vivian—that's wonderful…!"

Exercise alone wouldn't account for her brilliant flush—an interesting color with her generous sprinkling of freckles. It only now registered that somewhere in the past weeks, her sedate salt-and-pepper hair seemed to have been transforming itself to a muted copper.

"I wanted to ask what you thought about it...," she said. "Small town and all. But then when you and Adam seemed to be hitting it off? I didn't feel quite so—stupid."

"Nothing stupid about needing a friend," I told her. "Male or otherwise."

"I'm sixty."

"Gotcha beat by two."

"Artie's only fifty-five."

A worried frown settled in as Vivian again studied my reaction. Cradle-robbing given the numbers we were reeling off was hardly an issue.

Our pace quickened—whether Vivian's doing or mine, I wasn't keeping score. A woman in bathrobe and bare feet was letting her dog out. She waved, shut the screen door again. The animal just stood there, watching us pass. His ears were cocked to the side, like an computer enhanced creation in a pet food commercial.

I had never thought about it before, but over the years most of my friendships—all professional, were with men. Strange as it was to slip into a walking-buddy relationship with a woman in the first place was the transformation taking place in the past ten minutes. Adam excepted of course, I hadn't discussed my love life or lack of it since I was in college. That suddenly seemed a very long time ago.

"My fiancé was killed in Korea," Vivian told me.

"Joel—my husband died in an auto accident."

If she noticed I wasn't wearing a wedding ring, she didn't comment. Her question, though, seemed headed in that direction.

"And since then—?" she said.

"Two daughters in high school were enough stress without a man in my life. They're through college now. Married."

"You miss them?"

"The girls...? Sometimes more than others. Joel—my...late-husband? Not really—we were heading for a divorce before he died."

Vivian's pace faltered for a split-second, but it was the only sign that she had heard. I let the situation sink in a while before explaining

187

that our marriage was over a long time before the accident.

"Must have been hard," Vivian said slowly. "People expect you to mourn...and instead—"

"You feel relieved. Guilty."

I took a deep breath and plunged ahead. This was something I had never admitted out loud even to myself, much less anyone else.

"Trust me, Viv...I'm still not...totally past that one. When I first...tried to date, it was always there. Just under the surface."

"And...Adam...?"

I winced. "It just kind of...happened. I wasn't expecting anything...and there it was."

"I never dated really after Fred was gone either," Vivian said. "But then Artie didn't really start out as a date. We were just out there together every weekend...on that berm."

"It makes perfect sense, Viv. Dating is hard for any educated woman in a rural area. The pool is pretty much limited to bachelor farmers or guys on the rebound."

Vivian nodded. "I was barely out of college when Fred died. As a teacher, I sure couldn't date a student."

"I can imagine."

The logistics weren't exactly easy now. After only one overnight with Adam, I couldn't leave my driveway without the curtains moving next door. It was enough to make a guy paranoid for life. I couldn't even imagine what Vivian and Artie had concocted to stay out of the line of fire.

"Anyway," she said. "I wanted you to know."

"I appreciate that." More, in fact, than Vivian imagined.

Transplanted out there on that berm, our little community of gardeners was evolving along with the plants we tended. Margo weathered her beloved Howard's brush with mortality by clucking over him like a mother hen. I couldn't imagine an odder couple on the surface of things than Vivian and the burly Teamster. Shakespeare poetry magnets on the fridge and biker tattoos were pretty radical extremes. And yet, here we all were.

Out on the berm that next weekend, I quietly rejoiced at the subtle transformations. Vivian had gotten a lot gutsier about what she would and would not tackle. Artie must have been working hard on his me-man-you-woman approach to problem solving. When he saw Vivian struggling with a heavy barrow full of mulch, he held off amazingly long now before intervening.

Vivian must have shared our conversation. Artie caught me watching him—read my unspoken approval. He just flashed a halogen grin and went on with the task at hand.

The two of them were not the only ones in a growth spurt. Although we still were avoiding the L— and M-words like the plague, Adam and I were spending every free moment together.

My birthday was August 24th, a milestone that could have been stressful if Adam had chosen to make a big deal of it or imbue it with all kinds of larger romantic significance. Instead, he took me out for dinner after work to an elegant restaurant in downtown Charlevoix along the canal access to Lake Michigan.

His gift was a simple but exquisite lace window hanging he found in a Traverse City gift shop—that, and a recording of Leonard Bernstein's opera, *Candide*. The delicate design on the panel was of a picket fence surrounded by a filmy garden of hollyhocks, roses and wisteria. A simple sculpted lace text stood out against the sky, *Time began in a garden.* The artist had appliqued two fabric butterflies, bright splashes of color against the white-on-white scene.

I mounted the hanging against the kitchen window pane. Through the lace I could see the greens and browns of Gramma Brennerman's garden, the intense blue of the autumn sky and the patches of dusky red on the maples at the back of the yard.

The changing season was transforming the filmy off-white panel into a vibrant millifleurs tapestry. Its message grounded me every time I looked up from turning on the kitchen faucet. Gardening teaches us a lot about time, I wrote in my column for the week:

> As a culture, we tend to want immediate gratification. Gardens do not operate that way.
> Gardening works only when we stop fussing about digital watches and

learn to plant by a calendar in which months and years and even generations become the measure of what has been accomplished. A good gardener develops lots of patience.

Gardening opens the possibility of second chances. On the playing field of life, do-overs are rare. A gardener operates with different rules entirely. Seasons pass in the garden, but mercifully they also return, never the same yet always familiar. Our failures are only final if we give up or if we refuse to learn from our experience. The saga of a gardener is the story of hope.

Aging in our culture also has become something to be avoided at all costs. We pull up roots in a frenzied hunt for perpetual spring or summer. Not so in the garden. Plants stay where they are, deal with what comes.

Fall is as crucial to their world as spring, and winter is not the end but just another beginning. That reassuring cycle of the seasons gives us a powerful respect for every stage of life. Gardens reveal the wisdom that every tomorrow brings with it new possibilities for beauty we never even imagined.

In our fast-moving world, we are strangely ambivalent about change. We both fear and trivialize it—witness our wild quests for the flavor-of-the-month in everything from food to fashion.

Plants are pretty adaptable, too. Most of them can be moved an amazing amount over the years and still survive. A good gardener knows better and will not abuse the fragile connection between change and growth.

190

Balance becomes the thread that holds a healthy garden together. Gardening is about life not lifestyles.

A garden reminds us, too, that we are not alone on the journey. Even in the face of dramatic storms and predators from within and without, a garden handles the challenges as an ecosystem in which everything is dependent upon everything else around it.

Every plant has a role to play in every stage of its life cycle. Past its blooming, the iris still shoots up its tough spiky green foliage to shore up the more fragile coleus blooming alongside it. Dying, the annual nurtures the life to come.

The master gardener takes many individual stories and weaves them together into a wonderful whole, turns isolated episodes into a cohesive narrative. If we are lucky, we come to recognize our own destiny in those precious acres. The story of the garden becomes our own.

I wasn't even thinking about my role on the garden crew when I set up a lunch with Bea Duiksma to talk about the off-ramp meeting that Adam had hosted. For a week we had been playing Day Planner roulette. If she was free, I was tied up, and vice versa. We had planned on talking Saturday, and then Leslie and Emma showed up.

Several days after my birthday, I walked down to the county center to drag her off to Marty's. I noticed in passing that someone had clipped my latest healthy community column and posted it outside her office.

"Hot off the press," Bea said. "Your columns are a real hit

around here."

"I've been getting a lot of mail lately—everything from questions about grubs and meal worms to what plant to buy cousin Dawn for her birthday."

"Do you answer 'em all?"

"Try to. But it's starting to get out of hand."

Bea laughed, shook her head. "I know what you mean. I've been feeling that way about the garden lately. Margo and Howard are getting frailer every day. Even with that irrigation system, maintenance is a tough proposition. Adam may have given us all those plants, but every year that's gonna be an issue. Winter is pretty rugged out there. No windbreaks. Months of sub-zero nights—"

"You're worried we won't be able to keep it up?"

Bea nodded. "Nothing against hard work...but we need more volunteers. We need a long-term plan. The fire department can't keep hauling water out there indefinitely. I'll admit, my initial instincts were to fight the state's intervention—"

"And now?"

"I'm thinking maybe we ought to try to use it instead. Negotiate. The state needs more land to improve the exit. The county owns the adjacent land and we have quite a bit of clout with the county. So we get out of the state's way—provided they move the garden for us and dig a well, maybe lay in piping so we can automate the irrigation."

"Actually, that's why I suggested lunch," I told her. "At that informal get-together at Adam's house...what was it, two weeks ago? Some folks proposed a lot of this and more. Trouble is, they immediately go global with the thing. Educational programs, regular guided tours, concerts on the berm—"

Bea's eyes widened. "You're kidding? We're already stretched too thin now."

"If we partnered with some of these other groups, we'd have more help."

Bea looked unconvinced. "All we wanted to do was perk up that off-ramp. Suddenly we're talking about a theme park here."

I read the undercurrent in her voice. It's tough for any of us to watch our baby growing beyond us. The gardening crew had not sought out this problem—or opportunity, depending on how you look at it. It had found us.

"This whole thing would fold without you, Bea. If you think we should stonewall the state...."

I had hit the tap root. Would she continue to lead the project if the price tag for survival was shared control? In a way, I knew the answer before I sought it. When all was said and done, Bea was the kind who would do whatever it took to make sure we succeeded.

"I have my doubts," she admitted. "But then, what could it hurt to check out the possibilities?"

"You were invited to be a part of that concerned citizens' group," I reminded her gently. "We could really use you there."

"Sorry," Bea shook her head. "Not the meeting type, Eve. I do too much of that 8 to 5 already. You've been representing us. That's enough."

"I won't commit us to anything without your say-so."

For the first time since we started the whole discussion, Bea smiled. "I know that," she said. "We can always dig in our heels if the state highway people don't cooperate. That still leaves the question of volunteers, though."

"True."

"Would you think about using your column to beat the bushes? I've thought of asking you before but didn't want to seem...pushy."

I laughed. "Push away," I told her. "I honestly hadn't thought about that before. I'll see what I can do."

When we started the garden project, it was not with the intention of becoming this closed little club every Saturday morning. After all, Adam had joined us last spring, and a couple of weeks in a row several cottagers had showed up in their Birkenstock clogs, ready to help. They had seen us working away out there from the interstate. Unfortunately we weren't ready for them. There weren't enough tools to go around and ever since we had been scrambling to find a way of getting more.

"Maybe," I said, "we ought to think, too, about...formalizing things a little more."

"As in weekly task lists...stuff like that—?"

"That, too. But I meant incorporate. As a not-for-profit we could ask the county for funds, legitimize donor tax deductions."

Bea frowned. "Isn't that overkill? I mean...there's way too much bureaucratic quagmire around here already. The wonderful thing about the garden, it's always been so...simple. Just get out there and do—"

"True. But things change. I mean look at us…who would have thought a year ago that by now we would have two large beds under cultivation out there?"

"So, who would do the paper work?"

"You—I was hoping anyway. You're the agency staffer. I never worked for a non-profit in my life."

"There's a first time for everything, Eve."

Funny, I found myself thinking, how we tend to pigeonhole people. Up until now I always thought of Bea Duiksma as a kind of driven, self-contained community action type with a gardener's almanac in her back pocket. I left that table considering her a friend.

Chapter Twenty-Eight

Plants that are about to be removed have a habit of suddenly doing better. Unknown

September moved in with its chill nights, the blazing warm reds and yellows of the maples on the hillsides. The Gang-Green—as we were now calling ourselves—had no choice but to operate on the assumption that the garden was staying put. Although the berm advocacy group had been talking with the state for a month now pretty much as Bea and I had anticipated, it was too soon for progress.

Over a period of weeks in September, our little team pruned back and mulched as much of the berm as we could, getting ready for the first frost and winter to follow. Artie and Adam were still debating what to do with Vivian's arbor. Events made the options mute.

I should have suspected something when Adam blew into the newspaper office one Thursday in mid-October, his face dark as a thundercloud. Winding down a phone call with the Xenaphon librarian about running a Coming Events notice in the paper, I tapped my watch and raised two fingers signaling the end was in sight. He didn't return my smile.

"What's up?" I said.

A knot of anxiety was tightening in my chest. When Adam didn't respond, I knew it was serious.

"The berm's been vandalized."

I just looked at him, still not comprehending. What could you do to trash a garden? I soon found out. Whatever havoc I had imagined based on Adam's terse blow-by-blow, what I saw as we parked on the access road and hiked down to the site was far, far worse.

Tire tracks crossed and crisscrossed through both beds leaving deep gouges in the earth. Plants were crushed or uprooted. The arbor had been wrenched loose from its stakes and smashed against the ground. Sections of irrigation pipe and the precarious drip system were ripped out and Artie's makeshift water reservoir had been run over, flattened. There were signs of arson near the shed the guys had built to store our garden tools and supplies, but apparently the vandals had been interrupted. Only a few scorched boards and a discarded kerosene bore witness to the intended target.

Even the tornado last spring had not been as savage in its destruction. Devastating as the damage was, the "why" of it was even tougher to handle. This was not just some random, pre-Halloween mischief or adolescent rage venting itself on a convenient target. This was adult, deliberate and very, very personal.

"Oh, my God," I said. "Who could have—?"

"They don't know. A trucker spotted it this morning, called it in. The sheriff called me out at the nursery about an hour ago. I wanted to tell you myself—but stopped here first on the way...," Adam raked a hand through his hair, drew a harsh, cleansing breath.

"The bastards—those cowardly bastards," he said. "Eve, I'm so sorry...."

Something in his voice and expression told me he had not been totally frank with me. Adam knew more than he was telling.

"You know what this is about, don't you?" I said quietly.

Silence confirmed my suspicions. A muscle worked along the ridge of his jaw and his face darkened. Then the mask came down, abrupt and inscrutable.

"You know we've been trying to lever moving the garden...," he said. "Even tying it to some broader community programming?"

I nodded, still unsure where this was going.

"An MDOT official let leak a counter-threat yesterday. Give up the battling over the berm or the county may find its economic development funds in jeopardy."

"And—?"

"The ultimatum was absolutely confidential. Only a handful of us knew. But somehow remnants of the old union rank and file found out. Had a meeting last night—"

"Artie…he knows those guys. But Artie would never, ever go along with something like that. He would have stopped it."

"If he knew, Eve. They would have left him out of the loop. Sheriff Burnell thinks we may be looking at two or three guys with ATV's and a couple of bottles of Johnny Walker."

"What are we going to do?"

The calendar was working against us on every conceivable front. There had not been a hard frost—yet. But soon enough the ground would be unworkable. With many of the roots in a shut-down mode, some—maybe even many of the plants might be salvageable, but what was the point when the whole site might be moved again by spring?

"We were probably going to take down the arbor anyway," Adam said. "It may be repairable."

I could sense he had his doubts. "And the plants—?" I said.

"Re-leveling the site would be a major deal," he admitted. "Disrupting the spring bulbs could be a problem. It might make more sense to just dig in whatever we can and wait until spring to worry about whether to repair the ruts and replant or just move whatever survives to a new location."

"Bea is going to take this hard, Adam."

She wasn't the only one. The shock was so complete, I hadn't even noticed that my own tears had begun to fall. Adam slung an arm around my shoulder, drew me against him as we surveyed the desolate scene. I forced in deep lungs full of cold air, steadying myself.

"We will get through this," he said.

I shivered, wishing I could share his optimism. Had it only been weeks ago that we were speculating about incorporation and expanding the scope of the garden project?

"Eve…in the plant business, we deal with life and death every day. Grubs and cutworms and storms hit us all the time—we don't take it personally. We just do what it takes to prevail."

"This *was* personal. It's hard to take it any other way."

"Was it? Those guys who did it? …maybe they just saw their world shrinking and tried to fight back the only way they know how."

I knew the truth of what he was saying but the words ran up hard against the iron band wrapping itself around my heart. I found it hard to

197

meet his steady gaze looking down at me.

"I can't begin to—how on earth will we explain this to the others?" I said.

The sadness in his eyes was giving way to something else. His jaw hardened and his voice was raw, determined.

"Let's go home," he said. "We'll do it together."

As it turns out, the vandalism did more to coalesce public opinion than any articles or columns or advocacy meetings had been able to accomplish. The county government called an emergency session for the next evening to discuss the escalating tension over the off-ramp proposal. It seemed like half the county was there.

I went as did the entire Gang-Green and most of the principals who had attended that first strategy meeting at Adam's house earlier in the summer. The rest were people I had never seen except in passing.

Starting it off, Sheriff Brunell gave a grim status report that hinted at multiple arrests. When he finished, the head of the county commission invited comments. Nobody moved. The chairman repeated the invitation.

A hand shot up down the row from where Adam and I were sitting. It was Artie. Bracing himself on the chair back in front of him, he said his piece. His voice was a low rumble...uncertain. Still, there was no mistaking the passion in his words.

"I just wanna say that this garden has gotta continue," he said. "It's the best thing that ever happened to me. It's the best thing that happened to this county in a long time. Folks have a lot of different reasons to worry about this little corner of the state. The garden didn't start any of those problems. It just might help solve 'em."

He drew an audible breath. His forehead puckered in a frown.

"See, I learned a lot about how things work in that garden," he said. "Plants need sun and rain and food, and they try to find 'em in the space where they are living. When those things aren't there, they up and die. Plants don't care who we are when we help them. They don't care if we used to work in the milk plant or drive a truck or shuffle paper over at the courthouse. If we treat 'em right, they just try their darndest to bloom."

The room was so quiet we could have heard a pin drop. Artie was just getting started.

"I think Xenaphon is like that. The state was hoping if they threatened to stop helping our county, that we would just let 'em plow that garden under. Some folks here got scared and thought by trashing the garden, everything would be fine again. They were wrong."

"This is our home," he said. "The garden proves how beautiful it could be here. We could just let it go, take the state money and run. But if we do, we'd be losing a lot more than just a bunch of plants along the side of the road."

Red-faced, Artie stopped—looked around him, blinked. Vivian was looking up at him, her face radiant.

"That's all I wanted to say." With that, Artie sat down.

The chair of the county commission cleared his throat. "I don't think anybody can find fault with a word of that, Artie."

Artie sat stone still, not saying a thing. One of the commissioners took the floor.

"Look…if we were to try to fix things out there—what would it take?"

Bea Duiksma was sitting just ahead of us. She stirred in her seat, then stood to be recognized.

"I've talked with some of the nurseries and landscape people around here, and also the Extension Office," she said. "The beds will probably need to be leveled again…you can't do that without moving everything or at least most of it. Pointless—if the state is going to make us move it again in six months."

"With winter coming, you can't leave it like that."

"Of course not," Bea said. "A priority is to get the uprooted plants dug in wherever we can, prune back the damaged ones. The arbor is going to need major repairs before putting it in storage. The irrigation system may not be repairable. We were hoping that the state would agree to put in a well so the fire department didn't have to fill up the reservoir all the time."

"You don't have a lot of people helping out there to do all that."

"No. We don't. Some strong backs would help."

The chair of the county commission whispered to one of commissioners—a woman—sitting next to him at the head table. When

199

he straightened, his mouth had set in a determined line.

"We'll have a crew out there tomorrow. The county maintenance department will take a look at that—what did you call it…?"

"Arbor," Bea said. "It's—it was that wood and lattice structure in the middle of the berm."

"Commissioner Jane Lyons, here, is gonna make a motion."

The woman stood, then laid out a series of steps that would pretty much accomplish everything Bea had outlined. There was more. The motion proposed that the county officially take a stand, supporting the request that the state help subsidize the garden relocation and future maintenance as a price tag for any work on the interstate off-ramp.

The package got a quick second, and when no discussion was forthcoming, the motion carried. The vote for passage was unanimous.

Before the chair could call for other business, I found myself standing, waiting to be recognized. Adam and I were sitting together. He shifted in his seat, looked up at me—clearly wondering where this was going. So did I.

"There has been discussion among the gardeners that we incorporate as a not-for-profit. That it might help with funding and long-term support for the garden," I said. "How would the county feel about that?"

Slowly the commissioners weighed in on the subject. There were some reservations—speculation about whether the county itself should assume responsibility for the project.

As the discussion wound down, Adam stood, thanked the Chair for his leadership. He wasn't through.

"I wasn't part of the group from the beginning," he said, "so I can't pretend to speak for anyone but myself. If you make it a county project, you solve the manpower problem. Still, Artie hit the nail on the head. That garden is a wonderful tool for community building. There's a pretty diverse core of people already who are committed to make it happen. If anything good comes of the vandalism, it might be to raise awareness of the need to get involved out there."

"Well, if that nonprofit idea is the route to go," one of the commissioners asked, "who would handle the paperwork? File the incorporation papers, write the governance documents?"

"I would."

The words were barely out of my mouth when Bea swiveled

around in her seat. The smile started with her eyes, then lit up her whole face.

"Go for it, Eve," she said.

I was quick to clarify. "Of course, the existing garden committee would have to approve all this."

The commission Chair nodded. "Understood," he said. "I suggest you coordinate with the county parks department for any help you need."

"The county could help in other ways, too," Adam said. "If folks are worried that the state might play politics with our economic development fund? Our state representative happens to be on the MDOT appropriations committee. That seems like a pretty high trump card to me."

Chuckling, the commission Chair agreed. "Point taken. We don't need a motion…but a friendly visit seems to be in order here."

If the state was attempting to swat a mosquito, in fact it had stirred up a hornet's nest. Bea and our little garden gang went into this fight alone. With not just civic leaders but the County Commission itself on our side, the odds of our voices being heard had just gone up considerably.

My after-the-fact anxiety attack about spearheading the Community Garden incorporation project was predictable. It hit me on the walk from the Courthouse to the parking lot. By the time Adam swung his SUV into my driveway, he had managed to jolly me out of the worst of my paranoia and insecurity.

By force of habit, on the way in the door I checked the message light on my phone, anticipating the usual tidbit for the community update column in the *Gazette*. Instead, my boss George's voice played back at me.

Time of message was 7:30 PM. Didn't the man ever go home? Unfortunately, tonight he had decided to spread the wealth.

"Evie…Evie," George scolded. "Too much partying going on over there? Your column isn't in yet for the week. Deadline's

201

tomorrow. Chop-chop, Kiddo."

I looked at my watch and muttered something unprintable. *Ten o'clock.* If anything decent was going to come of this, I had better rough out at least a draft tonight. Then I would still have time to clean up the column before e-mailing it down to the office crack-of-dawn.

Shedding my jacket, I fired up the laptop—now a permanent fixture on the dining room table. I could hear Adam banging around in the kitchen, from the sound of it unloading the dishwasher. The commotion subsided and after a few minutes, I noticed him looking at me from the dining room doorway.

"Are you going to get the lights?" he said.

"I wish. Somehow in all this crisis management, I forgot the column. It's due...past due to be technical about it. I don't dare leave it for morning."

Adam grimaced. "I'm not sure about waiting up 'til you finish."

We had already concluded it would be fool-hardy for him to make a run back to his place tonight. "Go to bed," I told him. "I'll be along when I finish."

By now I had slid onto the chair in front of the computer. A blank screen under these circumstances can be an awful, intimidating thing. The surest way to hit a dry patch writing the column was to put a gun to my head like this. I wasn't making any promises about how long this was going to take.

"You look really tired," I said. "Not that I'm very perky myself. But, Adam, I really do need to rough out the column before I call it a night."

"That bed's going to be pretty cold without you...."

"Warm it up for me."

The keyboard seemed like a jumble of random, disconnected letters. It took a split-second for me to remember whether my right pinky finger lined up on the semi-colon or the quote marks. Out of the corner of my eye, I noticed a new release on Fall insect treatments for iris plants from the Ag Extension service.

Predators in a garden, I wrote, *come in many shapes and sizes.* I was not going to add the obvious. That unfortunately, the worst of those predators—our little garden crew found out the hard way—can be human.

Chapter Twenty-Nine

To take up gardening requires a leap of faith, not a rational decision. Unknown

I had dealt with a lot of proposals in my time at the ad agency. Creating a governance plan for a community garden was not one of them. Neither was the proposal Adam laid on me one early November evening.

We were sitting next to one another at the dining room table. Adam had been keeping me company while I wrote. To pass the time he had been studying a technical manual on irrigation drip systems. That must have been tough—given the stream of consciousness complaining I was doing to myself about the pace of my progress.

"I figure you've had a month now—more, to think about it...," he said. "So, here goes...."

Distracted, I looked up from my laptop. The paragraph I had been drafting about the Board of Directors swam out of focus. But then it hadn't been particularly clear in the first place.

It...? As in the bylaws?

"Impossible." I shook my head. "I just can't do this."

Adam looked startled, confused. And more out of sorts, I thought, than the situation warranted. Granted, my mood wasn't the best. I had been working on this blasted document for two solid weeks without much to show for it.

"Not...exactly the response I—"

Response? "At the risk of sounding incredibly stupid," I said.

"What *are* you talking about?"

"Emma wondered if I'd asked you. Well, I'm asking…."

I just looked at him.

"Emma. Your granddaughter."

The clarification wasn't helping much.

"Eve…I want to marry you."

"What…?"

"Marriage. You. Me."

"Now…? Right this minute…?"

"Today, tomorrow…whenever."

At that, he got down on one knee alongside my chair. Adam took my hands in his.

"Okay…I gambled on low-key and the element of surprise," he said. "It's not working. But I'm not beyond traditional as hell if that would help…salvage this disaster. Eve Brennerman, will you marry me?"

I started to laugh…couldn't help it. As proposals went, this had to be one of the most unorthodox. Adam wasn't smiling.

"That dumb, huh…?"

"N-no." I was having trouble choking out the words. "Maybe not the stuff of bodice-ripping romance novels, the way we're going about this. But no, not dumb…! "

"Would a replay help?"

If the man could still even entertain the thought of repeating his offer after the last couple of minutes? He could handle anything.

"Yes…to marriage. Forget the *down-on-the-knee stuff—*"

"Good. With my knees…? I was starting to worry I'd have to stay down here. That settled…when…?"

We'd already covered that ground, once before. "It's rather late today," I said. "The courthouse closed four hours ago."

Adam's eyes narrowed. "You're…not…kidding…?"

I managed a weak smile. This was not going well at all.

"I think the Community Garden would be a nice spot."

Adam frowned, seemed to be doing some quick calculating. While nothing had been formally resolved with the Department of Transportation, at least the County was now dickering with the State over possible dates for moving the garden next spring. The frost wasn't totally out of the ground until late May, so figuring forward from then?

"Fourth of July weekend?" he said.

"An anniversary of sorts. I like it."

That was just over six months from now. The soul of outward calm, my inner state was anything but.

Adam dropped my hands long enough to reach behind him and retrieve something from the pocket of the sport coat he had draped over the back of his chair. It took a while. I was having trouble breathing. Adam leaned over and set a small jewelry case on the table next to my laptop. The velvet covering was a faded amber and the clasp had begun to tarnish.

"Open it," he said.

I did. Inside was a simple silver band with a row of diamond chips and tiny faceted red stones—garnets or rubies—inset into its surface. The setting was old fashioned. Beautiful.

"Grandmother Groft's," he said. "I took it out of the bank vault a week ago."

The words didn't seem to come. I knew how much this meant to him.

"Adam...I'd be afraid to even *wear* this..."

"It's been worn hard before, Eve. Two of the stones had to be replaced. The jeweler called this afternoon to tell me it was ready—"

Gently I worked the band out of its case and held it between my fingertips. Adam took it from me and slid it on to my left ring finger. His hand lingered as he studied it there. My own was shaking.

"I...love you," I told him.

Adam made eye contact. He was smiling.

"Now...that wasn't so hard, was it?"

I returned the smile. Moisture was beginning to form at the corners of my eyes.

"You have no idea," I told him.

But the strangest part of all? He did.

A week passed, the kind when you have a wonderful but frightening secret that you still aren't ready to share with anyone. Adam was disappointed when I insisted on putting his grandmother's ring back into its case until I had time to share the news with my daughters. But he understood.

For the moment, the case was sitting on the dresser top in Grandmother Brennerman's bedroom. I brushed up against it every time I reached for my car keys or grabbed for my hairbrush. Even in that worn velvet box, the ring was the Dutch Courage I needed to do what I had been avoiding.

Out of the blue one afternoon after work I went up to the bedroom and took out the precious heirloom—mine now. Sliding the ring on my finger, I picked up the phone and called my oldest daughter Leslie. Adam wouldn't be home for another two hours at least.

"Hi, Les…!"

In the background I could hear Emma's voice, mid-temper-tantrum. Leslie sounded flustered.

"Mom…? It's a zoo around here. Can I call you back in about a half hour?"

"Of course."

Truth was, those thirty minutes loomed like an eternity. My anxieties about how my daughters would react to my news were multiplying exponentially. I used the time to skulk down to the kitchen counter and uncork that Merlot left over from dinner last night. I poured myself a generous glass and sat down to wait.

"Sorry about that…Emma just had a melt-down." If anything, Leslie's voice seemed even more tired and distracted. "You wanted to tell me something?"

No sense in beating around the bush. "Adam and I are getting married."

"Adam—?"

For a minute it seemed like we were headed for a repeat of the conversation that he and I had around my dining room table.

"Groft. You and Emma met him that weekend you came out to visit."

"Right." It took my daughter a second to process the connection. "He's the guy that runs the nursery business—?"

"The same."

The words came out in a rush. "Holy smokes, Mom. That's…great. Wonderful. Really."

"When?" That caveat was an afterthought.

"Fourth of July weekend."

"Next year…the one coming up? 2006?"

"I'd like you to be my matron of honor. You and Gina…share it somehow. If Emma's up to it…a flower girl would be nice. A nice little in-joke…."

"Have you talked to her…Gina?"

"Not yet. She wouldn't be home from work yet."

"Wow…," Leslie breathed. "I can't…this is amazing."

"Blame Emma. She was the one who brought the whole thing up."

My daughter laughed. "Sorry about that. She does have a mouth, that girl. Is the news out there…around town in Xenaphon…?"

"Not yet. I wanted to tell you and Gina first."

A loud wail in the distance told me Emma was still on the rampage. And she was getting impatient with her mother for ignoring it.

"It sounds like you'd better go," I offered.

"Thanks, Mom. But listen…I'll call you. Tonight…no, tomorrow. Dan has got some kind of command performance over at the country club tonight. I've got to start getting ready. I look like the wrath of God."

"Go ahead. We'll talk tomorrow."

Emma's crying was getting louder. "And Mom…congrats, really. I'm very happy for you." I heard my daughter fumbling with the receiver. "I love you, Mom."

Then I heard dial tone. *That went well*, I thought.

Outside the kitchen window where I was sitting, phone still in hand, I could see a couple of blue jays squabbling over the leftovers in the bird feeder. I sipped at my wine, caught up in the social dynamics unfolding in the backyard.

It wouldn't be dark for a while. Living at the far end of the Eastern time zone has distinct advantages and disadvantages. In summer, the evenings go on forever. Although in December we grumble about heading off to work at eight o'clock in what seems like the middle of the night, we know at the end of the day we can count once again on that precious light

From the direction of the living room I picked up the sound of the front door opening. It closed again and footsteps began heading my way.

"Eve…!"

"Here. In the kitchen."

Adam's familiar voice was just what I needed to shake me out of my lethargy. I hugged him, fretting that I hadn't given a thought to preparing dinner. Adam loved to cook, but it was my turn. I hadn't even set anything out to defrost.

"So, we eat out," he said. "Or even better…takeout. A romantic evening around the fire?"

Adams hands felt warm and strong clutching mine. As if sensing a change, his thumb had begun to trace the underside of my ring finger. I read surprise in his eyes and genuine pleasure.

"You're wearing it?"

Grandmother Groft's ring. I had forgotten all about it.

"I called Leslie a bit ago."

"And…?"

"She was surprised…distracted. Emma was in one of her moods. But was she okay with it? Yes. More than that, really."

"I'm glad." Adam looked at me hard before asking. "And Gina?"

I shook my head. "I'll wait until the weekend."

"If you show up at work like this…? It'll be all over town in five minutes."

"Less."

"And you're ready to handle it?"

"Yes."

So then, why did my mouth feel dry—like I was sitting out on the berm with thunderclouds piling up overhead? Waiting for the storm to break.

Turns out, I lied…at least about telling Gina. When I showed up for work on Friday, George—ever the observant one—was hot on the story before I had my coat off. Just shedding my gloves had done the trick.

"Atta girl, Evie…!" A low whistle accompanied that pronouncement. "Son-of-a-gun… I knew when those Seniors magazines started running cover articles on sex over sixty, the times—as the song goes—were a changin'!"

"*George—*!"

"So, Adam really did it…that dyed-in-the-wool old bachelor actually popped the question…? Smart man. No doubt here who's getting the best of the deal…!"

208

"Thanks for the vote of confidence, George…I think."

Like my daughter, my boss seemed suddenly obsessed with logistics. Or at least the calendar.

"Have you two set a date yet?"

"Summer. Out on the berm. I was…hoping you might agree to…walk me down the aisle, George. Not that there's an aisle out there…."

He grinned—winked. "We'll come up with something. The pergola should be back out there by then. Do I need to rent a tux…?"

"You think we're nuts…don't you…?"

George must have picked up something in my tone. His face grew serious.

"What I think? Evie…I think you deserve every bit of…happiness there is. Grab it and run."

After that roller-coaster reaction from my boss, the plan to confront Gina with the news on the weekend slid over to the back burner. Despite my bravado, this full disclosure stuff was a heck of a lot tougher than I had anticipated.

The week passed in a blur. Finally, Thursday night, I mustered up the nerve to put a call through to my youngest daughter in Tucson. Adam joined me in the kitchen to lend moral support. My daughter Gina answered on the fourth ring. I had been about to give it up.

"Mom…? Will saw your number pop up on call waiting. It took him a second to get off the other line. Is everything okay?"

Gina sounded out of breath. I wasn't feeling too steady myself.

"Depends on how you look at it," I told her. "A lot has happened in the past couple of months—"

"You're not ill…?"

I caught the tension in her voice. Just spit it out, I told myself.

"Gina…I've met someone."

The silence from the other end of the line seemed as long as the miles and years between us. I took a deep breath and plunged ahead.

"He owns a nursery business outside of town. He's a few years older than I am. We've got a lot in common—we both grew up near here… ."

I was drawing a blank. Just how far should I go with these insights into our mutual characters . . ? For starters, that right now fear of commitment loomed pretty high on both our lists and that for both of us, she was part of the heightened anxiety level.

"He asked me to marry him. I've said, yes."

At that, the silence seemed to intensify. When my daughter's response finally came, it was not what I had expected.

"Does Leslie know?"

I winced. "I just told her, too."

"How did she react?"

"A little surprised, maybe. Pleased for me, I think."

"Has she met him…?"

"Yes. She and Emma came out for a weekend when Dan was on the road for the company."

At least so far Gina wasn't weighing in for or against, I told myself. That was better than rejecting the idea out of hand. Or so I thought, until what followed.

"Mom…I'm flying out. This weekend if I can get an extra day on either end."

Gina's voice sounded calm—too calm. It was like a brittle sheet of ice glazing over a pothole. No one would feel comfortable with what might be lurking underneath.

"That's…great, honey. Adam would…like to meet you…."

"That's his name? Adam?"

"Adam Groft."

"Divorced? Widowed?"

"None of the above."

"I'll call you when I nail down a flight," Gina said.

That was the end of the conversation. Adam had been watching my face through that whole exchange. Quizzical at first, his mood quickly mutated to downright worried…anxious for me.

"Break out the flack jackets…?"

I gingerly replaced the phone on its cradle. "Would you believe, I'm not sure… .?"

"Eve, is there something I ought to know here?"

"Got a week?" I told him.

It's my experience that children find it hard to learn their parents

210

are only human, after all. As teenagers that changes, of course. But then Leslie was at the in-between stage—twelve, the first time she caught her father seriously flirting with another woman.

Leslie's school class was on a day-long discovery trip on Chicago's Museum Row, including the dinosaur exhibit at the Field Museum. What she learned wasn't quite what she or I had expected when I signed her permission slip.

Her dad Joel was at the museum on a sales call, trying to talk the administration into a new motion sensitive faucet system for the rest rooms, guaranteed to save water and reduce mess on the lavatory counter tops. Apparently that wasn't all he was hustling.

Even in a place as populous as Chicago, privacy and anonymity are not a given. When Leslie spotted her dad, he was mid-bite sampling some cheesecake . Trouble was it involved a voluptuous blond who was extending her fork across the table in his direction. The gesture was mundane enough as intimacy goes. Still, Leslie was old enough and smart enough to put two and two together.

I should have suspected something was wrong. At family dinner that night Leslie's behavior was unusually sullen even for a pre-adolescent in the first throes of parent bashing. When Joel castigated her for wolfing down her dessert, Leslie let him have it.

"You're a fine one to talk, Dad. I saw you…packing away more than *your* share of cheesecake at lunch."

Joel laid down his fork. His face was red.

"Now listen here, young lady—"

"I'm through listening to anything you have to say."

What had gotten into her? I sent her to her room to cool off. When I went up an hour later to confront her, Leslie was sitting at her desk doing homework. I could tell she had been crying. With some gentle prodding, the rest came spilling out in a flood of words and tears.

"I was so…mortified," Leslie sobbed. "Daddy was hitting on this woman and the whole class saw it. She…that woman was…gross. A real slut. Why would he…*do* something like that…?"

Brutal as the revelation came about, it was not totally unexpected. The intimacy level in our relationship had been on the wane for years. I wanted to chalk it up to the strains of dealing with pre-teen daughters and a couple of anxiety inducing job changes on Joel's part. But then we Germanic types tend to deal with that kind of barrage of reality by hunkering down and digging in, waiting for the shelling to stop.

"Les," I told her, "your dad has been under a lot of stress...."

"Mom, you should'a...seen 'em."

Leslie's chin jutted out like one of those stone heads carved into the face of Rushmore. She was not exaggerating. That realization was most damning of all.

"I'm sure you just misunderstood...," I lied.

"Mom, I...hate him."

"Hate...who...?"

It was as if someone had sucked all the air out of the room. Gina was standing in the doorway.

"Dad is cheating on mom," Leslie said. "I saw him."

Openmouthed, Gina just stood there looking at both of us. Her arms crossed in front of her and her brow knotted in a frown as she wrestled with what her sister was telling her.

"He wouldn't...do that, Leslie...! You're making it up to be mean—"

"Wanna bet? I saw him."

"Gina, honey...Leslie, I—"

"Forget it, Mom. I know what I saw."

My attempts to defuse the situation were falling on deaf ears. A large tear coursed down Gina's cheek, unchecked.

"Well, then....," she sniffed. "Mom must'a done *something* to piss him off...."

There it was. The battle lines were drawn. Over time, they would only cut deeper and deeper into the fabric of my family. In that split-second I knew—or at least, feared: this was one of those no-win situations from which we might never recover.

For better or worse, in that same split-second? I made a choice. It was safer, I decided, to risk Leslie's anger at my hanging on to my marriage than to risk alienating my younger daughter, maybe forever. Logical, as strategies went—unfortunately, in the end, it backfired.

The more cold and loveless the climate became in my relationship with Joel, the more staunchly Gina clung to her belief that whatever her dad was or was not doing, it was I who had driven him to it. She took his death personally, almost as if that too were my fault. Articles in the newspaper about the accident and blood-alcohol levels, my anxious attempts to fend off lawsuits and Leslie's white-hot rage aimed at her father only made Gina more entrenched in her hostility.

To my dismay, Gina even skipped out on college graduation and chose to elope rather than open the door to family participation in her first adult milestones. Moving half a continent away became a convenient barrier to intimacy with either me or her sister. Her first child, Justin, was now four. Neither Leslie or I had ever seen him except in photos. Only an occasional phone call kept the ties between us alive, however fragile and tenuous.

"So, she wants to come…?" Adam said.

I nodded. "Yes. Although I'm not sure that 'wants' is the operative word here. Feels duty-bound, maybe. Anxious. But not necessarily happy about it."

"She cares about you, Eve."

I had to admit that seemed the case. Though the years had made me cautious, I still wasn't ready to give up hope that someday all that childhood hurt and righteous indignation would dissipate. The problem was that Joel was dead and unable to speak for himself. It seemed left to Gina to carry that torch for him, even if it meant denying the undeniable— that whatever my faults as her mother, her dad too had feet of clay.

"We're not talking hypothetical here," I told him. "Gina plans to fly out here next weekend."

Adam forced a smile as he coaxed me into his arms. Resting my head against his chest, I steadied my heartbeat with his. I felt as much as heard the rumble of his words, putting the best possible spin on the situation.

"Look on the bright side," he said. "We won't have long to find out where things stand."

Chapter Thirty

As obsessions go, I know a lot worse ones than gardening. Overhead in the garden.

I wrote my column that week on plant families. A reader had sent in a question about strategies for making a few perennials go a long way if a gardener is working with a limited budget. It was perfect as topics went, given my mindset.

The good news and bad news about perennials, I wrote, is that they are territorial:

When a gardener is trying to fill as much space with as few plants as possible, the tendency to spread out can be helpful.

Of course, once the plants take hold and start elbowing each other for attention—soil, space, water and nutrients? Then we quickly complain they are 'invasive'.

The plant has not changed. What has changed is the gardener's perspective.

Plants can expand their families in two basic ways: through seeds and by creating new plants from parts of the old ones. Gardeners call that process of spreading out 'propagation'.

Plants that live for only a season—annuals—have to depend on seeds for their families to survive. Perennials stay around longer and that gift of time gives them more choices. They can also spread when pieces of themselves break or split off and form new plants. The new plants are called *off-shoots*.

One of my favorite perennials, the prairie plant bee balm or *monarda*, depends on *rhizomes* to create whole new plant families. The mother plant develops stems under the ground and when they get a certain distance away? Up pops a new baby plant. If the stems reach out above ground, they are called *stolons*. When a new plant shoots up from a stem right at the base of the mother plant it is called a *sucker*. Suckers tend to be very aggressive about choking one another out.

Perennials also use *Bulbs* and *tubers* to create new families. The energetic mother plant creates underground food storage systems that originally stay dormant under the earth but then burst open to become very hearty new plants.

The point is, perennial plant families are a lot like people. If parents hold on too tight, they run the risk of smothering that wonderful new life they are trying to create. Others find it easier to let go but risk leaving their offspring vulnerable to the elements.

A good gardener senses which

plant family will thrive next to
another one so that life in the garden
does not get out of control or
balance. As with human families,
those choices are not always so easy
to make.

I was still editing around on the column when the phone call came
from Gina confirming her flight the next morning. Friday.

The column was as good as it was going to get. I e-mailed it to
my boss down at the *Gazette*…with an apology. I would be skipping out
on yet another marathon session getting the upcoming week's edition of
the paper ready to print.

The closest airport to Xenaphon with a wide choice of flights and
carriers is Grand Rapids—accessible via a confusing network of four-lane
and two-lane highways. I wasn't looking forward to the trip. Adam
offered to come along, but in the end it seemed more prudent to go
alone.

I wasn't looking forward to facing my daughter's potential
censure. But then, the thought of her unloading on Adam was even
worse.

In my nervousness, I arrived at the airport about an hour early.
Pacing the long corridors was therapeutic for muscle tone and the psyche.
What if Gina delivered an ultimatum?

We planned on meeting at baggage claim. The flight must have
been full, judging by the stream of passengers that flowed toward me
from the direction of the security exit. Finally, I saw her. She had a
small carry-on slung over her shoulder and she was scanning the crowd,
looking for me. I waved to get her attention.

Those snapshots from the past four years didn't do her justice.
Tall and lanky, Gina was the epitome of suburban chic in her jeans,
turtleneck and blazer. The resemblance to Joel had always been there,
but I had forgotten how pronounced it truly was. We shared an awkward
hug, collected the luggage and headed for the car. You could have
counted the number of verbal exchanges that passed between us on the
fingers of two hands.

Once in the Taurus, Gina fiddled with her seat belt, avoiding my
gaze. Finally, I took a chance and said it.

"It's really…wonderful to have you here. *A surprise*, I'll

216

admit—"

"After that phone call...? I figured that you'd finally...*lost it*...!" Gina's mouth was stiff. "Anyone in their right mind would get on a plane."

"Fair enough. I realize it's a bit of a shock."

"That's...putting it mildly...!"

Traffic was heavy. Still, I couldn't help but notice the look she aimed in my direction. Anxious, fearful...annoyed—the kind of look a parent flashes when a toddler is heading toward an electrical outlet with a fistful of keys, expecting the worst. Poised to intervene?

"Ironic, isn't it?" I said. "That we actually get to a point in our lives when we can start worrying the heck out of our children."

Gina was not amused. "Some sooner than others, apparently. For crying out loud, Mom—forget the fact that all my life, you've been about as impulsive and...*passionate as*... *a*...*grapefruit*...! And   suddenly, now...you start rambling on about the love of your life...?"

"At my age, you mean...?"

"Time, place...take your pick. Face it, a lot of my friends have...single parents—widowed, divorced, whatever. So, they wind up with a...bed buddy. *Okay*...granted, maybe I could...buy that.... But...*marriage*?"

"This is Xenaphon...not Chicago, Gina. A small town is no place to try to rewrite Hawthorne—"

"So instead you cast yourself as an aging Hester Primm with her Scarlet Letter rushing to the altar with all of Xenaphon at your heels? Mom, get serious...!"

"The point, Gina. I am...serious. And...happy. For the first time in...so long, I can't even remember—"

Gina shifted in the bucket seat alongside me, her body language distant...closing in on itself. Her voice quavered, began again.

"And so...you just expect me...after all that happened with dad—?"

"Gina," I said slowly, choosing each word carefully. "I'm sorry that your dad died. I *regret* that he...that we no longer loved one another. Not the way a couple ought to be in love. Maybe we should have gotten a divorce years before. We didn't. Right or wrong, that was a choice we made. If we hurt you...and your sister in the process? I'm sorry."

"A little late for that...."

"Oh, Gina...I hope not. I truly hope not."

The silence was unbearable. It was Gina who finally broke it. Her voice was low.

"I've always...blamed you for how dad... .."

Probably still did. But I took hope in that past tense, inadvertent as it may have been.

"I know."

"Do you...? Do you really know what a...zoo our home life was? All poor dad seemed to want was a little...*fun* in his life. While you carried on like some...control-freak Super Mom and my sister Leslie tried to make him feel like he was just a...*mega-jerk*—?" Gina's voice was shaking. "Face it...*no wonder dad* ...?"

Her hands were balled into fists in her lap. At least, to her eternal credit, she didn't finish the sentence.

"Dad...*what*, Gina...?" I said softly.

"Why dad...was...*never home*...."

Gina's voice trailed off into a tense silence. It was obvious how tough it still was for my adult daughter to admit even that much—that perhaps the father she had idolized and defended was not so *defensible* after all. I wasn't about to press the matter.

"Love can be a messy business, Gina."

"And so even after all that...*history*, you're going to—?"

"Take a chance that Adam Groft will hurt me...or we'll hurt each other? Life throws us strange curves, Gina. There are no guarantees. I wasn't expecting this. Neither was Adam."

It was suddenly still, that awkward pause when you've both said what's on your mind. You know you're poles apart and nothing at that moment is going to bridge the gap.

"If you're curious...?" I said. "There's a picture of Adam in my wallet."

My bag was lying on the floor between our bucket seats where I'd left it after rummaging around to get the change for the parking attendant at the airport. The wallet was sticking up out of a jumble of receipts, cosmetic items and writing utensils like some battered leather cult object. Gina hesitated, then reached down and retrieved it.

Out of the corner of my eye, I noticed her thumbing past the usual family shots—including her own recent contributions. She stopped at

218

the first unfamiliar face. It was a photo of Adam taken several months ago out in the community garden.

Even a total stranger would have sensed the connection between those eyes and the person holding the camera—*me*. The warmth and love in that smile aimed my way could have melted the polar cap.

"Good looking," Gina said.

She even managed to make that sound like a liability. I put another spin on his credentials entirely.

"One of the most thoughtful, considerate people I've ever met."

"He never married."

"No."

She had already asked me that on the phone…was now revisiting the subject. It occurred to me to wonder how she would have reacted if Adam were widowed or divorced.

"He was engaged, a long time ago," I told her. "It didn't work out. He traveled a lot in his career…tough on family life."

"Like…Dad."

It wasn't a question. My daughter didn't have to add the rest. Was this just a case of history repeating itself? Gina didn't say it, but it was there just under the surface, in her tone, in her body language—everything. I felt the familiar fear of her disapproval rising in me, but held it in check.

A car had been tailgating us for the past few miles, took an opening in the traffic as a chance to dart past us. The driver glanced our way, obviously irritated.

"Besides, Mom, isn't this awfully…*sudden*…?"

"Sudden—?"

"You've known each other…how long?" Gina's tone had started to give me an inkling of how she dealt with her four-year-old. "And am I right…you've already…set a date?"

"We met in April. The plan is to get married next summer."

Gina did the math, at least twice from the length of the silence between us. Then, without comment, she put my wallet with Adam's photo back in my purse and zipped it shut again. Her words were muffled, aimed at the floor mat.

"All those years with Dad…thirty years of Ms. Cool-Contained-Sensible. And in barely a year of meeting some guy…you're headed for the altar—"

"Like a couple of…randy teenagers…is that what you mean?"

"I didn't say that, Mom."

"But you thought it."

Gina straightened in her seat. The look she shot my way bordered on disgusted.

"Obviously, Mom, you've made up your mind. And nothing I say or do is—"

"The point is, Gina…we *aren't* teenagers, are we? Not Adam or I…and not you either, for that matter. At my time in life, you start to realize that…time is precious. So is love. So is family. I love you…more than I can say. You're my daughter and nothing can change that. But I cannot—will not—feel guilty that I love this man. That…is not negotiable."

Her reaction came out in a rush. I could read the pain and uncertainty in her voice.

"God, Mom…what do you…*want from me?* To tell you I think it's…*great? Well, I… just…can't.*"

"You haven't even met him. I understand."

"When Dad died…I was…furious at you—and now…*this*—"

"I know."

Gina's voice had that little girl edge to it. "You're angry…disappointed in me?"

"Sad, maybe," I told her. "That you can't seem to look beyond our failures. Your dad's and mine. But angry…? No."

"What the heck do I…say to him…?"

"To Adam—? All I ask is you give him a chance. Give us a chance. He's a decent man—has his share of faults, of course. But then…so do I."

I already knew her feelings on that subject. Gina shrugged.

"You made it pretty darn clear you don't care…*how* I feel. After all, it's your life—"

Oddly enough, it was what her sister Leslie had told me, more or less, when she first met Adam all those months ago. Only then it was my oldest daughter's way of giving me her blessing.

"We do…care, Gina. *I…care…*more than you know…! Trust me, sweetheart…*you're a parent yourself.* At some point it hits you. No matter how old you get—or your children get, that never changes. It's …*never* just…*your* life anymore."

My hands were white-knuckle-tight on the steering wheel. I couldn't read her reaction. Gina had shifted in her seat so that she was looking out the window.

For some time now, the highway had been easing closer to the Michigan lakeshore. Even on the passenger side, she would be noticing the vegetation-covered waves of sand dunes rolling toward the east away from the water.

"You and Will...?" I said finally. "You're happy?"

Gina laughed. "Who ever knows...? Like most young couples, I guess—never enough time or money."

"I would...imagine your Will is a...great father?"

"He always wanted a son." Gina shrugged. "Then too, Justin is a lot like his daddy. Pretty...low maintenance—"

Not exactly a ringing endorsement. Was there something Gina wasn't telling me?

"I'd love it if you all would come out for the wedding," I said slowly. "Justin could get to know his cousin Emma. She's quite a handful, but smart as a whip."

"It depends on...*when*—"

"I don't expect an answer right this minute," I told her quickly. "Just promise me...you'll ...think about it."

My daughter and her husband Will had met in college—I remembered a hasty introduction one Parents' Weekend. Searching my memory banks for impressions now, I always came up with a football-player build and shock of curly black hair. That, and a lopsided grin.

He was not the kind of husband I would have thought Gina would have chosen. Uncomplicated and unpretentious, Will showed no signs of either her father's calculated charm or my own tense introspection.

"My husband...comes through O'Hare sometimes on business," Gina said. "I've thought about joining him for the weekend, driving up here with the baby. It's tough with my work schedule."

"I'd like that...if you all could make it up to Xenaphon. You'll see...I've done a lot of work on Greatgramma Eva's homestead. After all those years as a rental, it was quite a mess."

"Or you could...fly down—?"

This was the closest to an invitation I'd had from Gina since she moved to Tucson. The hard knot of tension around my heart was beginning to loosen a thread or two.

We stopped for a quick lunch at a rest stop an hour out of Grand Rapids. While still not exactly animated, our conversation came easier now. We skirted the past and the future, settling on the safety of the "nows" of raising an energetic four-year-old.

Outside of Xenaphon, I began pointing out familiar landmarks. I was looking for things Gina would have remembered from her childhood visits here on weekends from Chicago with her sister, her Dad and me.

We passed the exit to the state park where she had dumped a bucket of sand over her head as a two-year-old. It took me weeks to get the grit out of her hair. The Tasty Queen she had loved—had pestered us to frequent—was abandoned now but the vintage seventies Blue Moon Shake sign was yellowed but still legible in the front window.

We were less than three blocks from home. As I turned on to the tree-lined street, Gina suddenly pointed ahead down the roadway. I smiled at the excitement in her voice, so spontaneous compared to that controlled, no-nonsense professional that greeted me at the airport.

"Gram's…right? The house with the big bay of windows on the side?"

"The dining room. I had them all re-caulked a year ago. The job cost a small fortune, but then my heat bills were getting out of hand."

By the time I got the front door unlocked, Gina already had grabbed her gear and was trucking it toward the house. I left the key in the door and hurried to help her.

"I thought I'd put you in the guest room, upstairs. I'm up there, too, in Greatgramma Eve's bedroom."

"Fine, Mom. Whatever works for you."

"We can take everything up now, if you like. So you can get settled."

"Later's okay, too. I want to see the garden."

That bit of nostalgia truly surprised me. I was remembering a sticky summer afternoon twenty-odd years ago with a most uncooperative Gina shelling peas fresh-harvested from her greatgrandmother's vegetable patch. Her complaints ran the gamut from "supermarket veggies are better" to "gardens are hot and boring".

I had to scramble to keep up. Gina had already set down her bags at the foot of the staircase. Together, we walked through the downstairs and out the back door to the garden. On the way past the fireplace, I saw her hesitate for a split-second as she caught the family history laid out in photos on the mantel.

"Will and I've done a lot to the house since I sent you that photo." Gina paused. "We ripped out the lawn…put in desert plants. Native grasses and cactus are lower maintenance and more environmentally friendly. We started creating a dry stream with different kinds of rock to make it look like it's always been there…."

I smiled. "Sounds lovely…."

"Practical. The water bills for that lawn were killing us."

Just when I thought my daughter was letting down her guard, that familiar gate slammed shut again. What was she protecting?

Gina shrugged. "It's a struggle. Keeping down the weeds is half the battle."

"Ditto. I'm planning to experiment with landscapers' cloth next season—a real back-saver. I'm not sure Greatgramma Eva would approve…she preferred watered down sheets of newsprint. Not that I'd don't have plenty of that down at the *Gazette*!"

My daughter laughed. But from the look she shot in my direction, that wasn't where her thoughts were headed.

"So, you plan to…keep on working then?"

"My boss has me writing a gardening column. Actually, I'm thinking of trying for national syndication."

"And Adam…*approves*—?"

Interesting, my daughter's choice of words. One prompted by her diagnosis of what went wrong in my marriage to her father…? Or was this about her own?

There had really been no option for me but to work when I was married to Joel. If Gina had been harboring doubts about whether a woman's professional independence could hurt a relationship, she had not gotten that idea from me.

"Adam's one of my biggest fans," I told her.

"Owning his own business…? I assume he would have enough money to outright…retire if he wanted to."

"It isn't that simple, Gina. Adam never intended to take over the family business…it just sort of turned out that way. When his dad died and left him the nursery, the greenhouses were a mess and the business climate around here not very favorable for a sale."

Gina frowned. "I never thought I'd wind up in advertising either.

223

Not after watching you slog away at it all those years. Funny how things work out—"

I was thinking the same thing. For starters, how badly I had underestimated the insecurity and apparent self-doubt that lurked behind Gina's tough facade all these years. That, and how much alike we were, this daughter of mine and I.

Her face inscrutable, Gina had leaned down and was uprooting a couple of clumps of grass that had strayed over the boundary between garden and lawn. It was a little thing, but something I would have done.

See a job...just do it. I wondered if my daughter even made the connection.

"After those temperatures out in Tucson, it's probably like the Arctic for you out here," I said. "Maybe we ought to head in—?"

"Not on my account." She hesitated. "If you're not too tired, I wouldn't mind driving around a bit...to see where you work, some of the places we used to hang out when we came up here as kids."

It had been a long day, but I agreed readily enough. It had been a long time since Gina showed that much interest in not just what my life was like, but where it butted up against hers. We drove and walked, until after about an hour, we were running out of sights and memories.

"Ready to call it quits, Kiddo? We'll be losing the light soon—"

"Actually...?" Gina hesitated. "I thought maybe we could take a drive out to the nursery."

"Groft's...?"

"Why not?"

"I'm not sure...Adam might be out on a run," I told her. "If a driver calls in sick, he handles the deliveries himself."

"I've got a cell phone...you can call him. We could always hang out and wait."

"Thanks. I've got mine."

Leaning over, with one hand on the wheel and the other in my purse, I fished out the cell phone Adam had given me to make it easier for us to call when we were both out and about. He would know immediately from caller ID that we were still on the road somewhere. I rarely used my cell phone except in emergencies.

"Eve...is everything okay?"

He sounded out of breath.

"I got you off the roof...!"

Adam laughed. "Try under the truck. It's leaking oil like sixty and we've got a delivery to make. I'm going to commandeer Dutch's in another minute here."

"We're on our way over. Gina was excited about seeing the nursery—"

"I'll bet," he said. "Has she got a gun...?"

"A what—? Not in the car."

Gina was looking at me strangely, trying to make sense out of the conversation. Fortunately, she only had my half of it to go on.

"So, what...? You'll be here in about...ten minutes?"

"That's about right."

"Eve...what in the heck am I going to say to her?"

"Funny. That was the reaction I got here too."

Frowning, in a stage whisper, Gina offered to go back to the house. "If now really isn't a good time—"

I waved her off. "We'll be there in a few minutes," I said again, then shut off the cell phone.

At the nursery, Adam was waiting for us on the front stoop. There was only one vehicle in the lot, his...the SUV. Dutch must have taken off to make the delivery they were worrying about. As I pulled the Taurus nose in toward the landscaping timber at the edge of the lot and cut the engine, Adam began walking our way.

I tried to see Adam as Gina would, without benefit of all I had learned about him over the past months. Hard labor in the greenhouse had toughened his already strong frame. There was an explosive edge about the way he carried himself when under stress like this—not someone to be messed with. Even from a distance, I could see the knot of tension between his brows.

It was his eyes, though, that gave a lie to that tough veneer he cultivated. We had come far from that first visit I made to Groft Nurseries. This man cared and felt deeply about things and people. Only these days, he was no longer prepared to let what he loved slip so easily out of his grasp.

By the time he reached us, both Gina and I were out of the car.

Introductions were awkward and brief in the raw December air. The two of them shook hands, and in passing Adam managed a "Hi, sweetheart" and a quick hug for my benefit. My teeth were chattering, not entirely from the cold. Gina's reaction to that discreet moment of intimacy? It was a look that would have frozen water.

"Dutch is making the delivery run," Adam told me. "And the counter gal just went home sick about an hour ago."

"If you want to give Gina the Cook's tour? I'll…mind the store…."

Even as I said it, I felt the fear twisting in my gut. Leaving those two alone right now was as risky as anything I had come up with in recent memory—my relationship with Adam included. Adam called my attention to a hand-scrawled set of instructions next to the cash register explaining the inner workings of the machine. I studied them without comprehending, hoping desperately that I wouldn't have call to use them.

An hour passed. By the time Adam and my Gina emerged again from Greenhouse Four, I was…to put it mildly, a wreck. From the looks on their faces it was patently obvious that whatever went on during their walk-about through the Groft facilities, it was more heated than the air blasting out of the ancient gas furnaces hidden among the greenhouse trusses.

Their body language wasn't much of a clue to what had transpired. Adam was smiling but I could tell by his eyes, he was exhausted…wary. My daughter stood as if rooted in place alongside him. Keeping her distance? I couldn't tell. They were ignoring me entirely.

Gina broke the impasse. "We'll meet you at Mom's, then?"

"Around six. Your mom and I talked about giving you a tour of the Xenaphon nightlife. Starting with Marty's…."

My daughter's laugh was high-pitched, that of a little girl playing at being adult. It was like the two of them were communicating in a language I never heard before, much less understood. Something definitely had happened in that hour—I was sensing the dangerous after-taste. To piece together the truth of it would take two conversations, only one of which I could have on the drive back to Xenaphon with my daughter. But then the unpacking had to start somewhere.

Gina sat silent while I swung the Taurus out onto the roadway. A cloud of snow swirled across the hood. I shivered.

"You're lucky, Mom."

Lucky wasn't the word that came to mind right then. But it was better than a lot of them that had been racing through my brain.

"What in the…what was going on out there in that greenhouse, Gina?"

At first she didn't respond. I started to rephrase the question. She cut me off.

"I was gunning for him. But then, I suppose you know that."

"Did you succeed—?"

"In driving him away? Believe me, when we walked through that first greenhouse door, safely out of earshot…? I thought about it. Big time."

"And—?"

"Adam knew. He called me on it. Right up front, before I could fire a shot."

Gina hesitated. It was the longest count-to-ten moment of my adult life.

Adam, it seems, had stopped halfway down the first hothouse aisle to pinch back an unruly seedling. That done, he turned my daughter's direction. Hemmed in by benches full of plants on either side, and with Adam standing in front of her there was no going forward—only back.

"You could end this right here, right now," Adam told her.

Gina just stood there, staring at him. This was not at all what she had expected.

"Your mother loves you," he said. "If it comes to a contest between you…and me? Frankly, I'll lose. She wouldn't hurt you for the world. If you start stirring around in that old guilt and heartache, your mother will walk out of my life and never look back, if that is what it takes to keep you in hers."

In our little mother-daughter talk, I had made it pretty plain I wasn't going to budge when it came to my feelings for Adam. And here he was conceding the field before they even got started? Pushing things back on her? At that Gina bristled, prepared to fight.

"You've got that one wrong…! Mom has never given a…damn what I—"

"I don't think you believe that, Gina."

"Okay…you want both barrels here? You got 'em. Look at all this—! Any sane person would wonder. Why *you* and my *mother*…?"

They were the questions that I sensed lurking in the darkest places of my heart during the entire trip to Xenaphon from the airport. My daughter couldn't confront me with them. But she confronted Adam. The motive? Adam had already guessed—to drive a wedge between us.

The choice was hers. Apparently Adam again let Gina think about it. When she didn't react one way or the other, my daughter noticed a hint of a smile play at the corner of Adam's mouth. His eyebrow arched.

"It isn't just me, is it?" he said. "You *really* don't believe…anyone could love her, do you…?"

"I'd like to think I know my mother…fairly well."

"Think that if you like," he told her. "My take on it? You really don't know her at all."

Gina felt her mouth go dry. "That's an arrogant—"

"Maybe. Maybe not. But this much I do know. I love your mother because she's honest and vulnerable, a rare combination by the way. After all she's been through, she should be tough as nails…and on some level she is. A survivor, anyway. The question is how she protects herself—? It's never by losing her ability to trust."

"*Trust?* After watching her and my father…now why do I doubt—?"

"And your mother never gives up. Not on you. Not on me. Not on herself."

"She gave up on Dad."

"Did she? Or did he give up on her?"

Gina felt the blood rush to her face. "What right have you…? You didn't even know—"

"I know something about giving up. When I met your mother, I was standing in this very hothouse, trying my darndest to self-destruct… ready to throw away my inheritance with both hands. She wouldn't let me."

"Mom, to the rescue? You can't tell me you haven't had a busload of women in your life before she—"

228

"No. I can't. But you hit on the key word here, Gina."

"Which is?"

"*Before.*"

"So…, suddenly mom pops up with her cellulite and crow's feet and you're ready to write the book on trust and fidelity?"

Gina told me she had seen a man that angry only once before. It was the night around our dining room table in Chicago when her sister Leslie confronted their father about the woman in the museum cafeteria.

She saw Adam pale, flush…prepared to lash out. Then even as my daughter braced herself for the impact, he stopped.

"What's this about, Gina? Really about?" His voice was low. "Your father? Your husband? Or *both*—?"

Gina felt the tears, scalding and bitter, building up behind her eyes. Adam wasn't through.

"Because something…or *someone* has made you unable to trust men…any man," he told her. "I'm just not sure, why or how…?"

A truck was passing us, on a hill. I was fighting the crosswind, trying to stay out of the guy's way. Beside me in the Taurus, Gina grew quiet, processing again what Adam had told her.

I was tempted to intervene, to come to her defense. But the words stuck in my throat.

"Don't," Gina said. "Don't, Mom. Adam…was right. "

Her voice shook. "I look at Will…my husband, day in and day out. He's an attractive man, used to adulation, able to turn on the charm from the first handshake—and much as I love him for it? I'm terrified every single minute that I'll lose him."

"My God, Gina…."

"Oh, I try not to let him see it. If I don't get it under control…that jealousy, that suspicion? Eventually, of course…I'll lose him. I know that. And still, I can't stop myself….."

What had I been thinking? Behind all that little girl trust and blind adoration all those years growing up, stood this woman in the making—my daughter. So afraid, no…terrified that everything she felt and experienced when it came to men was built on quicksand. Adam

229

saw it immediately. It had taken me thirty years.

"Gina," I told her, "if I thought it would help you, I'd—"

"Give him up?" Her eyes were sad. "Adam said you would. I didn't want to believe that either."

A gust of wind buffeted the car. My hands tightened on the wheel. Gina chuckled softly to herself.

"Adam called it like it is. Selfish…projecting my own fears on you."

Hearing his words played back to me like that and the hurt they caused my daughter, it was so tempting to take her side. Once again, Gina wouldn't let me.

"What *would* I accomplish, Mom? Adam asked me that, too. What would happen if I actually succeeded in…forcing you to choose? It would just prove once again that my mistrust—all that conditioned paranoia, is justified. Just drive another nail into the coffin of my marriage…in my relationship with you—in my self-respect."

With that, my daughter began to cry—great choking sobs that robbed her of the power to speak. We were approaching a deserted gas station. I eased the Taurus off onto the gravel apron next to the pumps. The For Sale sign was dangling crooked from a single corner, swaying dangerously in the wind. Even with the windows closed, we could hear the harsh, rhythmic grating of metal against metal.

Awkward with the bucket seats, I clicked off my seat belt, leaned over and held my daughter as if my life depended on it. She let me, but her body was stiff and unyielding. After a while, Gina's sobs quieted and her breathing steadied. The tears stopped.

I levered enough distance to look at her. Gina's eyes were red-rimmed, her nose shiny. She was ten again, this daughter of mine, crying out for truth in the doorway of her sister's bedroom as her world—her ideal of what it meant to be family—collapsed in shards around her. I gave her the only truth I could. Then, and now.

"I love you, Gina."

For a moment, this wasn't about her dad or the terrible ambiguity of mothers and daughters. Her smile was tentative, beautiful.

"I love you, too, Mom."

Chapter Thirty-One

The British playwright Arthur Smith has an interesting formula for successful living. Are you looking for short-term happiness? Get drunk. Long-term happiness? Fall in love. If you want to be happy forever? Try gardening.

Around the table that night in Marty's—Adam, my daughter Gina and I—we pinned down the date for the wedding. A Saturday. The Fourth of July weekend. Gina couldn't help throw in a few jibes about what kind of fireworks we had in mind. Amazing for her. And best of all, I knew now that my family would be there, all of it.

George, my boss, was hanging out as usual at the eatery on Friday nights and eventually joined us, full of good news of his own. The county had received confirmation from the State Department of Transportation that the garden relocation would be completed by mid-June. MDOT's budget would spring for mature plants to replace whatever was lost in the transplanting. Their road crews would help repair and reassemble the pergola.

"I can see it now…watching the two of you up there on the berm tying the knot." George chuckled. "We'll back up traffic at that off-ramp in two directions, from Cadillac to Muskegon. Groft and I in our tuxes and—"

"Leslie and I dragging mom across that field."

Right now, Gina was looking across the table at me. Her eyes were alive with emotions I never thought I'd see there again. Not aimed in my direction anyway. Beside me, Adam sipped at his Sierra Nevada, strangely quiet, considering all that had transpired in the last few hours. Much of it, thankfully, his doing.

"Are you, okay?" I asked him.

"Just tired." A smile flickered at the corner of his mouth. "I think I pulled a muscle in my shoulder crawling around under that damn truck."

Gina and George were single-minded in their quest to organize our lives. With a sheepish grin in Adam's direction, I gave up and let them.

"What are you going to wear, Mom? Or haven't you thought about it?"

"Red. I always thought for second marriages, it would be the most appropriate. Forget the off-whites and ivory. There's nothing like a flaming scarlet to get heads and tongues wagging."

"Move over, Hester Primm. An interesting touch," Gina said. "We could whip up an embroidered A, if you like, for Adam."

We laughed together, our own private little joke, as we remembered her cutting first reactions to my engagement to Adam. All of that seemed so very long ago. My boss George just looked at the two of us like we had lost our minds.

The weekend flew past fueled by memories and giddy plans for the future. My daughters were both a part of them now. It was the happiest time of my life.

Monday, Adam and I drove my daughter Gina back to the airport and kept going ourselves. I hadn't been back to Chicago since I moved to Xenaphon. The plan was to stay for several days while Dutch held down the fort at the nursery. Adam had booked a room in a small hotel near the lakefront. The prospect of three days alone together was heaven.

I had a column due when I got back, but that would keep. Writing can expand to fill the time allotted for it, and I was discovering that the results didn't always correlate with time expended. When I forced myself to sit down on a Thursday night or Friday morning, the results were often as good—better—than spending the whole week fretting over it.

Downtown Chicago was like a winter fairyland. The Christmas decorations were up everywhere. The streets and shop windows were a blaze of light. Adam and I wandered the boutiques along the Miracle Mile, and then over to State Street and Marshall Fields. It felt good to be thinking about wardrobe and gifts for attendants…all the things that go with a wedding. It seemed now like the most natural thing in the world.

My bravado notwithstanding, I picked out a black crepe dress, slim and elegant, for the pre-wedding festivities. My choice for the wedding itself was a subtle champagne satin, with three-quarter sleeves. The dress was understated but stunning.

Adam laughed at my superstitions about seeing me in the dress before the wedding, but he gave in and wandered over the men's department while I tried it on. Still as I stood looking at myself in the three-way dressing room mirror, I imagined him standing behind me sharing the moment, his hands resting against my shoulders. It was not just the dress but myself I was seeing through his eyes.

It felt good. It felt real and honest. Reflected back at me was a woman I had never been before. Amazing, I thought, what a little confidence and a whole lot of love can do. Even at sixty-two.

We hadn't made plans for a honeymoon. Our days in Chicago were that and more. We showed one another the town as we each had experienced it all those years before we knew one other. It was fun to compare notes and laugh about our differences.

Late Wednesday, on a whim, we wandered up to a goldsmith advertised in the Yellow Pages. We have been looking unsuccessfully for matching white gold bands that would stand on their own and yet not compete with the engagement ring that had belonged to Adam's grandmother.

The shop owners—two young women partners, actually—had the perfect solution. They showed us their design for two narrow Celtic etched bands that in Adam's case, would go together to make a single wide band. In the case of mine, the bands would frame either side of the Grandmother Groft's antique engagement ring. It would be simple to inlay several ruby chips at intervals around Adam's wedding band, so that it looked more like mine.

The result was stunning, a perfect marriage of the old and the new We placed the order and were told we could have the finished bands by February, once the holiday rush was safely over.

Tired and giddy with the luxury of that time together, we decided that night to sneak in Chinese to our hotel suite. The sunset was beautiful. Holding on to one another and the railing for dear life, we even braved the wind-swept balcony just as the flaming orange ball of light disappeared behind the skyline. To the east we could see Lake Michigan glittering like a dark and brooding sea between us and home.

It was tough to let the moment go. Thursday morning it started to snow in earnest—dry swirling flakes that melted as quickly as they hit the ground. The ride back home to Xenaphon would be grueling. We talked about work and everything we had to do before the weekend to make up for those three incredible days in the city.

With the holidays less than two weeks away, Adam had his hands full with drop-in customers looking for last-minute gifts. He told me about his plans to spend Friday using a borrowed bucket truck to caulk the few remaining windows on the greenhouse that needed repair. The counter girl was still out sick, so he would talk the high school principal into loaning him a business student to fill in for the day.

We got back to my place just after dark. I could see the fatigue on Adam's face as he eased the car into the driveway. For the last hour or so, the driving snow had intensified the glare of headlights from the oncoming traffic. It was sticking now, a good inch to add to the dusting we had gotten the day Gina arrived.

I suggested a hot bath before dinner, but Adam begged off. Instead, he uncorked a bottle of Cabernet sauvignon while I heated up a container of chili and some garlic bread I had stashed in the freezer several weeks earlier. That and a clean-out-the-fridge salad made for a quick supper. Neither one of us were particularly hungry. I offered to clean up the kitchen, intending to head right for bed afterward. Adam had already gone up.

Then I made the mistake of one last pass through the dining

room, checking doors and clicking off lights. My laptop, the voice of conscience, was sitting mute and dark on the dining room table where I'd left it. The garden column was due tomorrow and I hadn't started it.

Muttering under my breath, I switched on the computer. Pulling out the closest chair, I sat watching the screen and listening as the hard drive ran its familiar sequence. Words had already begun to shape themselves into phrases then sentences in my head.

I was thinking of my daughter and I standing together in my loving re-creation of Greatgramma Brennerman's garden. Gina's face was intent and unthinking as she reached down and plucked out those errant weeds, intuition almost as deep as breathing and sleeping and all the human things we take so incredibly for granted. My fingers were impatient to translate the jumble of thoughts into shapes on the page:

```
Winter   is   a   strange   time   for   a
gardener.        The     ground    is    hard
underfoot.   Blackened   stubble   stands
as   a   sad   reminder   of   the   glorious
summer that came before.
     Poets often use that image of the
garden as a metaphor for death.   But
the true gardener knows that without
that grim and seemingly barren time,
the garden cannot grow.
     It is tempting to want to chop
back   and   clear   away   all   the   dead
stalks   and   stems   that   can   seem   so
depressing to the passerby.   That can
be a fatal mistake.
     Under   that   frozen   ground,   the
tenacious     root     structures     of
perennials are resting, regrouping for
the   glorious   flowering   to   come.
Stalks, leaves and old growth left in
place in the winter garden protects
those underground networks from the
cold and shields them from the wind.
Heat   from   decaying   mulch   warms   the
dirt around the base of the plants.
Nutrients are released into the soil.
     Long     before     the     first     seed
```

catalog shows up in the mail in February, the garden has been doggedly at work healing and renewing and rebuilding itself. Some plants like chrysanthemums even continue through the winter to absorb sun and nutrients through those dead and dry looking stalks from the previous season. If cut back, the plant will die.

Winter can also be an important time to attack diseases or predators. Problems like grubs in iris, are best treated late in Fall so that the poisons or insecticides can work over the winter months when the plant is dormant.

When I walked through my garden this week, a dusting of snow had settled down over the rows like a thin white coverlet. As I stood there, I felt my sadness giving way to a strange sense of excitement.

I stopped, replaying in my head that watershed moment—with Gina there beside me—when I sensed once and for all the power of the memory stored in our very DNA that binds us together as a family. Our lives were coming full circle, mother and daughter and now the fourth generation of Brennerman women counting little Emma, rooted together in this place.

I know that ahead lie spring mornings and hot summer dawns. Ahead lie the first timid green shoots fighting their way above the ground, the budding and flowering, and inevitable falling away.

A childhood friend wrote me from California some years ago about her decision to make her home in a climate where summer is perpetual…or at least where the seasons are less distinct. I asked her what she missed the most

about the Midwest.   The *winter*, she
told me.

Winter,   more   than   any   other
season,   teaches   us   to   love   and
understand   the   rhythm   of   life.   It
helps us appreciate a beauty more real
than the Botox culture around us that
denies aging and the passage of the
seasons in our lives.   Gardeners know
that better than anyone.

I fought for a while over the ending. Finally, I gave up. It might come easier in the morning.

So, I saved my work and shut off the computer, then headed upstairs. Adam had left the small night-stand lamp on for me in the bedroom. He was already sound asleep.

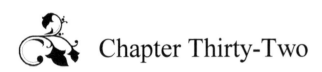 Chapter Thirty-Two

It is not always granted for the sower to see the harvest.
Albert Schweitzer

Breakfast was hurried—oatmeal and hazelnut-laced coffee. Adam wasn't the only one playing catch-up that Friday morning. I owed George some heavy-duty help with putting next week's edition of the *Gazette* to bed.

Adam headed out first in the SUV. I stayed behind to take a last look at my column before e-mailing it to George. If worse came to worse, I could always tinker with it before we locked in the edition for the printer. Once at the newspaper office, the phone rang off the wall all morning. I kept hoping it would be Adam, calling to give a progress report, maybe suggesting we go to lunch. No such luck.

Around ten, I started double-checking the want-ads for errors while my boss played receptionist. The flashing light on my extension came at a particularly bad point in my copy-reading. I snatched at the receiver, prepared to identify myself.

The caller beat me to it.

"Eve…get over to the hospital. Fast."

It took a split-second for the gruff warning to register, a split-second longer to identify their source. It was Dutch. He was breathing hard, obviously distraught.

"H-hospital…?"

"It's Adam—"

My mouth didn't seem to want to shape the name.

"Adam...?"

"The ambulance left two minutes ago—you need to hurry...."

I stood rooted to the spot.

"Dutch...what...?"

"He'd been having...they think it's his heart, Eve."

I hadn't noticed George watching me. Something in my face must have alerted him. Then I remembered. George had been talking to the caller before he buzzed my extension.

"I'll drive, Eve," George said.

My boss had already grabbed my coat and his from the rack inside the door. His keys were in his hand. Taking the phone from me, he finished the conversation.

"Dutch...? We're on our way."

I let myself be led. The wind was howling out of the northwest, kicking up snow devils in the tiny parking lot. George shut the car door on the passenger side behind me, then sprinted around to the driver's door. The lock was frozen.

"Evie...help me out here! Give the door a shove...!"

I complied with some difficulty. Forecasters were already predicting a cold, wet winter. Odd, the banality that surfaces when our lives are falling apart.

"Listen to me, Evie," George said as he jammed his old Subaru into gear. "They probably are going to balk in Intensive Care at letting either one of us in there. Just go...I'll distract them."

"Adam...is he—?"

"It's serious, Evie. Apparently the EMT's were using CPR. Dutch will join us as soon as he can...."

Mentally I was calculating the miles between the Groft Nursery and the hospital emergency room. *Far*, I kept thinking. *Too far.*

George was having problems of his own. The trip was across Xenaphon to the hospital was becoming a nightmare of slow moving traffic punctuated by the only red lights and stop signs anywhere in the county. My boss' knuckles stood out like furrows on the steering wheel. How could a village of under five thousand seem so incredibly difficult to navigate?

The hospital lobby was full of parents with coughing infants and crying toddlers. George propelled me along the gray corridors, double time, all the while snapping out questions to staff in scrubs along the way. None of it was registering, except that Adam wasn't in ICU at all. He was still in the Emergency Room.

A young woman in a pastel nurse's uniform pushed aside the curtain in one of the cubicles enough to exit, on the run, toward the nursing station. What I saw stopped me dead in my tracks. It was the sight of Adam's ashen face surrounded by a jungle of tubes and monitors, and around him, hands and voices feverishly at work. It was then I knew.

"George...he's...gone...."

My boss just looked at me. "Evie, you can't be sure of that."

The tears rolled down my face. George had an arm around me. I don't think I could have stood on my own.

"*Adam—*"

Before George or anyone else could stop me, I used that break in the curtain to reach the bedside. Adam's hand was unresponsive to the touch, unlike the ones that were reaching out to me.

"You can't be in here...," someone told me.

"*Adam.*"

It was the only thing I could think of to say. Words were my livelihood. They flowed out on the page connecting my inner life and the world out there. In that awful moment two syllables were enough.

Adam. Adam.

"Evie...honey, you really have got to leave these people to—"

"Tell me the truth," I heard myself saying.

A man's face swam into focus from the other side of the hospital bed. In bits and pieces I saw the shock of dark hair and wide, troubled eyes under a green surgical cap and the unobtrusive name tag. Dr. Ernst Freund. *Friend*, I recognized the German. I needed the good doctor to be just that. To tell me the truth.

"It's...over, isn't it?"

The doctor's gaze met mine, held. He didn't respond immediately but something must have communicated itself anyway. In slow motion, the frenzied activity around Adam's chest and shoulders stopped.

"I'm very sorry. There's no easy way to tell you this—"

"Oh, God...no...."

I felt like my lungs were shutting down and I couldn't make

240

another sound. For a split-second the room seemed to tilt and then slowly, inexplicably right itself. Something in the soft hiss of the equipment still running in the cubicle momentarily caught the doctor's attention. He nodded to one of the medical team who quickly turned to deal with it.

"There was an organ donor directive on his driver's license. We've tried everything short of…major intervention. If we're going to honor that donor bequest, we are going to have to respond…."

Adam's face was pale and still above the even whiter hospital sheeting. Like the pristine blanket of snow, I thought, spread out over my grandmother's garden. Life goes on. It has to go on. It was what I had written barely hours ago—a lifetime ago.

"Adam—"

George had taken hold of my elbow and was coaxing me back out into the corridor. I wanted to cry out in protest. Adam needed me. I needed to be there. But time seemed be a tide sweeping me past needs and wants.

Ahead loomed the abyss. I let go of Adam's hand and followed where the currents were taking me. What had to be the hospital's organ donor team was already waiting just outside the cubicle.

I didn't, couldn't look back. On this bleak winter morning, for me the miracles were over.

We encountered Dutch in the lobby. His back was turned but I recognized the coat—a red lumberman's jacket he always wore when he and Adam were in the middle of some nasty project. George called out to him. As the old nursery worker turned toward the sound, his face was a study in grief.

Adam never had a chance, he told me. By the time the EMT's got to Groft's, too much time had elapsed. One minute he had been complaining of chest pains and the next he had slumped to the ground outside the greenhouse. At least he hadn't been up on the roof.

Dutch used his jacket as a pillow, tried to keep Adam comfortable. But all that while, waiting for the ambulance, Adam never regained consciousness, never said a word.

"Dutch…I can't…I don't know how to…."

He hugged me, impulsive and awkward. Off to one side, I saw that one of the hospital staff had buttonholed George. The guy looked like an over-anxious twelve-year-old and was carrying a clipboard almost as big as he was. Judging by my boss' frown, George was trying with some difficulty to steer the conversation in my direction.

"They want to know about family," he told me.

"There's a sister. Somewhere…Alaska. They lost touch years ago. Adam never talked about cousins or other relatives. Maybe Dutch knows—"

"Nobody." Dutch shook his head. "His lawyer—Ellis Fry—went through all this when Adam's dad passed. Ellis has the records."

The hospital representative looked confused "So, then, who do we—?"

"He and Eve here were engaged."

That tough edge crept into my boss' voice whenever someone appeared at the *Gazette* to protest a story. I didn't hear it often.

George wasn't through. "If anybody has a say in what comes next, it's her."

"Eve. There was…we found contact information for an Eve Brennerman in the wallet."

"You're looking at her," Dutch chimed in.

That multiple reference finally triggered another checkmark on the form. The young man with the clipboard now looked at me, expectantly. I felt as lost in the process as he seemed to be.

There was one funeral home in town, Freiberger's. It was housed in one of the few surviving Victorian mansions on the edge of town, complete with huge white columns and a pediment that would have done the Parthenon credit   When Adam talked about his Dad's funeral, his only comment was that he sure didn't want to wind up over there someday like some grand lying-in-state in the capitol rotunda.

"What say we turn the berm into a Memorial Garden?" Adam had teased. "Then legally the state can't mess around with it. I'll volunteer to guarantee at least one urn full of ashes."

I shook off the memory—the wrenching humor and the pain of it. That hapless representative from the hospital in front of me had more boxes to check off. We couldn't stay here.

"Adam was…wouldn't…."

Suddenly, I couldn't seem to control my tenses. Past? Conditional? Adam was dead and no manipulating of syntax was going to bring him back. I began again.

"I know Adam would want cremation. No viewing…none of

that…."

"Freiberger's can be very helpful…arranging that."

The young man with the clipboard made a few more notes and then said the hospital would release the body to the funeral home after all the paperwork was complete.   A sheet of paper was shoved in my direction for a signature. I searched in vain for a pencilled X. Finally the guy took pity on me and pointed.

I signed the form. Under Relationship to the Deceased, I wrote "fiancé". Up until that point I had thought widow was the worst title I ever had to tack next to my name. This one hit rock bottom. There was no word for what I had become.

George started steering me toward the automatic doors leading out of the emergency room reception area. None of us had even taken off our coats. Dutch followed close on our heels. Once at George's car, the two men quickly settled my immediate future. My boss would drive me back to the *Gazette* to pick up my Taurus. Dutch would follow me to make sure I got home in one piece.

I didn't argue. Psychology 101 was basic for journalism majors. I had taken the course, passed with an A. Funny, how you can know the stages of grief—the denial, the anger, the bargaining, the depression, the acceptance. You can even feel the truth of them churning away in your brain. But on a one-foot-in-front-of-the-other fashion, you still feel absolutely nothing at all.

Adam was gone. That was fact. I was alone again. Fact.

Where the reasoning process broke down was right there. I was stuck in a terrible "Now", in which past and future ceased to have any meaning. There were motions to go through. I was steeling myself for the unknown.

Chapter Thirty-Three

Gardeners are rarely control freaks. They know better.
Anonymous

Adam and I had built our world together around life. Death had no place in that equation. The holy of holies for us had been that hillside garden, now buried under a ton of snow. As I tried to come to sense of what Adam would have wanted, I knew we couldn't have a Memorial Service for him out on that berm even if we had wanted to.

At least I managed to settle my Taurus in the driveway without getting stuck. Clambering through the snow to the front door was bone chilling. I was home. The door swung open as I turned the key. It was at that point, teeth clenched to keep from chattering, I simply froze—literally and figuratively on the front steps.

"I'll keep ya company for a while, if you'd like, Ma'am?"

I had forgotten about Dutch. From his truck parked at the curb, he had seen what was going on and reacted. As I turned to connect face and voice, I read the deep well of sorrow in his eyes.

"I'd like that," I told him.

He had never been in my living room before. Where Adam had filled the space with the sheer force and energy of his presence, Dutch seemed frail, shy, intimidated. His high-lace work boots were wet with snow. At my suggestion about coffee, he settled gingerly into one of my grandmother's more solid parlor chairs.

He didn't budge the whole time I was puttering in the kitchen.

Armed with two steaming mugs of instant high-test, I urged him at least to take off his coat. Still visibly ill at ease, he complied. The coffee was too hot to drink, the silence unbearable.

"Tell me about him," I said.

Dutch held the stoneware mug in his hand as if half-afraid he would break it. "You mean Adam...?"

"Everything. From the beginning. The first time you saw him."

"When his Ma brought him home from the hospital? I was out at the lake helping his Dad dig in a couple of new trees. That boy was a week old and yelling at the top of his lungs. He ran before he walked and was always making, building, fixing something. Sundays his folks took him to that little Episcopal Church downtown..."

Dutch chuckled and shook his head. "He must have been about five...the time he crawled around under the pew until he wiggled apart one of those pegged wooden racks for the hymn books. Made a hell of a racket when it fell....."

"We never talked about much of that."

"Private man. It was sad...how what came later...got in the way of all those memories and the...good times."

"His Dad...the business?"

Dutch nodded. "Truth, Ma'am? Adam was better at all that than his Dad. It's just those greenhouses out there weren't big enough for the both of 'em."

"Adam told me."

"Then he must have told ya how much he came to love it. Even with the mess and the debts. You gave him that, Ma'am. Don't ever forget it!"

I felt my face growing hot. "You loved him, too."

The old man's jaw tightened. "A man couldn't of wanted a better son."

"Dutch...what am I going to do....?"

It always came back to that. The past was the past. The future seemed as remote as Mars or the next galaxy. The now loomed in front of me without sense or plan or purpose.

"Ma'am, as I see it...if ya can't change dark waters ahead of ya?" Dutch said slowly. "Ya got three choices. Portage, build a bridge or just wade on through."

Right now that water looked pretty darn cold. I thought of that champagne satin dress hanging in my closet and alongside it, still in the protective plastic sheeting, that little black sheath.

"I've got to tell my daughters," I said.

But to what end? If there were a Memorial Service they would want to come, both of them. It meant a lot to know that. The chapel downtown Dutch was talking about still had a vicar. I'd met him. He ran an ad for the tiny church once a month in the *Gazette*.

But was that what Adam would have wanted? Go talk to the vicar. Mentally I began making a list. Phone calls to my daughters moved to the head of it.

"Would you…could you hang out here and keep me company?" I said. "While I—?"

Dutch nodded. "I can do that," he said.

It took me a while to find the portable phone. Dutch abandoned his coffee long enough to coax a fire to life in the fireplace. I hadn't realized how cold it was in the house. The thermostat was set too low for winter.

My daughter Leslie picked up on the third ring.

"Mom…? Is something wrong?"

"I forgot you have caller ID."

"Aren't you usually still at work? It's Friday…."

Sheer reflex, I looked at my watch. Already one o'clock. It was two hours since our run to the hospital. How fast time moves, I thought, when we least want and expect it to. It hadn't helped that emergency crew or my boss fighting the seconds and minutes across town to the hospital.

"Adam had a heart attack."

Even over the phone lines, I picked up that intake of breath. I heard the question in it.

"He died, Les."

"God, Mom…you…not after all you—?"

"Leslie, Honey, he loved me. I want to crawl in a hole and pull it shut over me. But then I keep coming back to that. He loved me."

Leslie's voice was shaking. "What are you going to…? I'll come out, of course."

"No. Not now. It's Christmas. Think of Emma. Adam wouldn't want us to ruin that for her. Legally, the next weeks are going to be awful. He doesn't have any relatives."

"All the more reason for Gina and I to—"

"What could you do? I'm even asking that myself right now. I've got to make a call to his lawyer. Dutch is over here. He knew Adam's family better than anyone."

"Do you want me to call Gina?"

"No," I told her. "I want to do it."

Maybe not want, but had to. How careless we become about the labels we put on our emotions and intentions. No longer.

The call to Gina was even worse. Through tear-choked half sentences, she poured out her guilt and her sorrow. I wound up comforting her.

Dutch sat through it all like cast in stone watching the fire in the grate. Hands shaking, I finally laid the portable phone down on the end table alongside my chair. The stoneware mug had cooled to the touch and its contents were barely tepid.

"Adam told me ya had great daughters," Dutch said. "Feisty. Come by it honestly."

A smile tugged at the corner of my mouth. "Gina especially gave him one hard time of it."

"He said that. Respected her for it."

"Would you...or should I phone Adam's lawyer?"

"I'm not fond of telephones, Ma'am. But if you want me to—"

I shook my head. "It's all right. But maybe I ought to...he still may be in the office."

"I'm not goin' anywhere," Dutch said. "Take your time."

My impressions of the lawyer Ellis Fry went back to that pow-wow Adam staged on his patio when we were plotting strategies to go to war with the Department of Transportation over the fate of the garden. A wiry, nervous little man on the surface of things, I learned from Adam later that he had graduated near the top of his class from Michigan Law School and was a bulldog when it came to handling civil cases.

"It's urgent," I told the receptionist. "He'd want to know. It's about his friend, Adam Groft."

After only a brief sojourn on hold, Ellis himself came on the line. "Adam—?"

"It's Eve Brennerman. I'm Adam's...you met me at that MDOT brainstorming session out at Adam's cottage. Adam and I...were engaged to be married in July."

Were. Ellis picked up on it immediately.

"Something's happened…."

It was not a question. But then if anyone would have known about Adam's health issues, it would have been his lawyer.

"Adam died about four hours ago," I told him. "Heart attack. I'm here with Dutch. He says you handled all of the problems when Adam inherited his dad's business? That there doesn't seem to be any family…?"

"A sister. Estranged."

"I had to sign-off on some forms at the hospital. You may need to follow up. Freiberger's has been contacted."

"Ms. Brennerman, did Adam tell you that he wanted to make you executor of his estate? He intended to. I drew up the papers about a month ago. He also wrote a new will."

"I had no idea."

Ellis let the notion sink in before he reacted. "We should talk…soon. Tomorrow, if you'd like. I'm in the office by eight."

"I'll be there. Thank you."

That way, I could go hunt down the vicar at nine. Ellis was also thinking ahead.

"Do you have a key…to the house, Ms. Brennerman? I think Adam said you did."

"Yes."

"You and Dutch might want to head out there tonight. Check out his desk…see if he was working on any updates or anything else I ought to know about. It could make tomorrow easier."

"We'll do that. Thanks."

Dutch looked up at me. He must have caught the shift in our conversation. I shut off the phone and laid it once again on the end table.

"Ellis suggests I go out to the cottage. And check to make sure Adam didn't leave anything legal behind—in progress, that the lawyer ought to know about."

"Makes sense. Ya want me to drive, Ma'am?"

It was such a simple question, but something in it made me listen intently. Adam was dead. I was alone—doing what I always had done or thought I had done without him. *Coping.*

Deep inside I felt the stirring of a grief so profound it frightened me. And then even as I forced back the sting of tears, I heard another

248

question. *Adam's.* Had I learned enough to let myself be loved as people were prepared, even needed to love me?

"You'd have to go way out of your way to bring me back here—"

"No problem. The truck has four-wheel drive and two hundred pounds of cement in the back end. That road out by the lake can be treacherous."

Since it snowed, Adam never let me drive the road in the Taurus. Uncomfortable as it made me to be so dependent, I knew Dutch was right. More to the point, so was Adam. It was a small thing to let Dutch take over…but for me, in this moment of my life, it was earth-shaking. I was letting go.

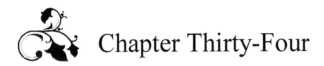 # Chapter Thirty-Four

God gave us memories that we may have roses in December. J.M. Barrie

By the time Dutch and I pulled into the driveway at the palatial Groft cottage, the sun had already set—a cold yellow ball of light slipping down behind the dark stands of trees. The sky was a sullen gray and the snow stood in drifts around the back door, up to my knees. In another hour it would be dark. I turned the key in my hand and tried to work the lock.

"Let me, Ma'am…?"

Gently Dutch took the unfamiliar key out of my hand. Adam usually had opened the lock whenever we were there together. Within seconds the door swung open.

"I'll get the lights," Dutch said.

I stepped inside, glad to get out of the wind. Even with the down in my parka, I felt myself shaking at the chill in the air.

"Ma'am, ya gotta get into something warmer."

Dutch was looking at my feet. It was only then I realized that I hadn't changed my shoes from work. They were my favorite wedge sandals with the thick waffle soles, great for standing at the counter taking Classified Ads but totally out of place in a couple of feet of snow.

"I'll borrow a pair of Adam's socks," I told him.

I headed up the staircase to the second floor, clutching at the stair rail like a lifeline in a stormy sea. Adam and I had traced the same route so many times before, expectant—needing each other. This was going to be our home, at least part of the year. That was understood. Now every step felt wrong, as if I didn't belong here.

Once inside the door to the master bedroom, the enormity of what lay ahead of me finally hit home. The elegant designer bathroom lay off to the right, mercifully close—all midnight black porcelain and gleaming copper fixtures. I sank to my knees on the meticulously set tiles alongside the commode and was violently, helplessly sick.

When I didn't come back downstairs, it was where Dutch found me, spent and shaking, my forehead resting against the cool rim of the bowl. Coaxing me to look at him, he handed me a towel and gently helped me compose myself. I could hardly stand up.

"You know where he keeps his things? Sweaters...and something besides those wet shoes?"

I nodded. Dutch followed me as I located a familiar gray pullover, then helped me slip it over my head. It hung half-way to my knees. Had Adam been that much taller...? How could I have forgotten that? But it was warm and for now that was enough.

The intention was to sit on the edge of the bed just long enough to pull off my wet trouser socks and replace them with a pair of Adam's. It shouldn't have surprised me, but it did. Dress socks outnumbered white athletic ones in his drawer three to one.

Every piece of clothing I touched, the catch-all Native American basket full of spare change and keys on the night-stand beside me, even the simplest details like brands of the toothpaste and shampoo on the bathroom sink were mute witness to a life that I realized I was only beginning to know and understand. Everything had its story and a connection to Adam Groft that I could only guess at—or envy. This was not the way I intended for our lives to merge.

The words slipped out before I had a chance to process them.
"Dutch...I am so...tired...."

"I know, Ma'am. Why don't you just lie down here a bit and I'll make us some tea?"

He wasn't waiting for my response. Dutch already had snagged the throw from the footboard and was awkwardly holding it out to me. Clutching it against me, I watched as he turned and headed out the door and down the stairs.

Once alone, I curled into a ball on the bed—still clutching at the blanket. So close to the surface for hours now, the tears finally came welling up. They poured out of me—deep aching sobs—until there simply were no more tears left to cry. I cried myself to sleep.

When I woke it was dark I didn't know where I was. Outside the window, moonlight washed over the bare arms of the trees like a luminous tide. The shimmering bands of light reached across the pale carpeting toward the bed and the empty expanse of quilt alongside me.

Adam's bed. Groggy and confused, I sat up and tried to focus. A dark shape moved in the doorway. The word caught in my throat.

"Adam....?"

Silence. Then a familiar voice corrected me.

"Ma'am, it's Dutch. I was starting to worry about you."

"What time is it?"

"Ten o'clock."

I had been sleeping for nearly six hours. Awake now, I swung my legs over the side of the bed. The carpet was thick and warm underfoot. Dutch must have turned up the heat in the cottage.

"You've been waiting up all this time?" I said.

"There's a fire going down there. I've got soup warming on the stove. Ma'am, when was the last time you had anything to eat...?"

"Breakfast."

Dutch turned on the light in the hall outside the bedroom door. Standing now, I walked toward it—surprisingly steady on my feet.

"You need help, Ma'am?"

"No. I'm fine. Hungry...but fine."

Dutch had set up camp in the living room in front of the fireplace. An empty mug was sitting next to one of the wing chairs. As advertised, coals glimmered in the grate. Above us, the portrait of Sara Groft looked out over the room, filling it with her presence.

I settled into the wing chair opposite the one Dutch had staked a claim on. He brought a tray with tea and a mug of soup—out of the can, crackers. It was nice to be fussed over in a rough, masculine sort of way.

"You've done this before."

252

Dutch smiled. "Sara Groft was sick a long time. Jacob was dead by then. Adam's parents moved in here toward the end but still Sara was alone a lot. I came whenever I could."

"You loved her?"

I regretted the question as soon as I asked it. Dutch was silent a long time.

"I never told her."

Some things don't need words. "She knew," I told him. "I'm sure of it."

"I gotta think so."

As the old man stared up at the portrait, his face took on a faraway look. I had seen that look before, captured on that photograph of Adam in my wallet. There was love and sadness, a connection so deep that it defied canvas and photographic paper.

"You miss her."

"Ma'am, it's tempting to hang on to the hurt. Trouble is…then it's hard to remember the love. I was lucky. That greenhouse needed a whole heap of time. And when young Adam came back…he was alone." Dutch shrugged. "There's plenty out there to love if you just look around a little."

I thought of Margo and Howard, Bea, Vivian and Artie out there with me lovingly tending to one another in that garden, and this old man laying bare his soul in front of the portrait of the only woman he ever loved, and even George with his dogged passion for that floundering newspaper of his. *My daughter Gina's words came back to me. "You're lucky, Mom."*

She meant Adam, of course. But the truth of her words was bigger than that. In this room—a shrine to a love affair that never was, I saw living proof of it.

"We're both tired," I said. "I can quickly check out Adam's desk in the morning. The lawyer wants to see me first thing—"

The problem was my car. It was still back in Xenaphon in my driveway. Then it occurred to me. Maybe it was better this way. This old man loved Adam like a son.

"Actually, Dutch," I said, "I was hoping that maybe you'd come along with me. To the lawyer's office."

"Of course. If that's what ya'd like, Ma'am."

"Anyway, it's too late to drive back to Xenaphon. If it's all right, you can take the guest room. I'll stay…where I was."

Dutch nodded. "Too many deer on the road this time of night."

"Let me handle breakfast, though," I told him. "You've done enough. It's my turn."

Dutch smiled. "You're on," he said.

Chapter Thirty-Five

Like life, gardening is not about tallying the wins and losses. Meaning comes in the tilling of the ground, the eternal act of growing. Unknown

I had been through my share of the legal red tape involving wills when my Grandmother died since my brother and I were both heirs. Estranged or not, Adam had a sister. Whatever his estate planning had been, given the circumstances probate was probably a necessity. Formal "readings of the wills" make for good theater only in the movies and television commercials. What I had ahead of me with Ellis Fry was far less glamorous. Thank God, Dutch agreed to come along.

Ellis seemed surprised—pleased—when the two of us showed up for that 8 o'clock appointment next morning. He offered us coffee, and when we declined, he simply handed me the will. I started to read.

Odd, what couples do and don't know about each other. I was shocked to realize I didn't know that Adam's middle name was Friedrich. He used the initial on his business correspondence. For some reason, Frank had been my assumption. I was wrong.

As I scanned the contents of the will, I realized how wrong I was about a lot of things. Based on the state of the greenhouses when I first saw Groft Nurseries, I would have assumed a very shaky net worth. Adam and I had never talked money except in the most general terms. Groft Nurseries were only a tiny fragment of the wealth he had accumulated over a lifetime. Even with the drain on his savings as he

255

renovated the greenhouses, his estate totaled upward of three million.

Adam willed most of it to Dutch and me. Half the net income from the nursery would be used to generate income for the Community Gardens in perpetuity. Dutch and I were appointed to co-manage greenhouse operations and work with the Garden committee to administer the endowment funds. If Dutch preceded me in death, his interest in the properties and cash assets would revert to me.

I told Dutch what I thought the document was saying. Then I looked to Ellis to confirm my take on things.

"Bottom line?" I said. "Adam's intent, then, is for Dutch and me and the Garden Committee to work together to keep the community project going—?"

The lawyer nodded. "That, plus the assurance of financial security for the two of you. You and Dutch."

A muscle worked along the ridge of Dutch's jaw. I put into words what I saw reflected in his scowl.

"I don't feel comfortable taking money…."

"Adam wanted you to have it."

"I don't know anything about running a nursery," I said.

At that Dutch finally reacted. "Neither did he…Ma'am," he chuckled. "Not at first anyway."

I returned the smile, thinking about that first day I walked in to the greenhouse. The image in my head was all that ivy and jungle growth trailing up over the corroding trusses.

"I helped him," Dutch said. "He'd want me to help you."

"Adam also wanted me to give you this," Ellis told me.

The lawyer handed me an envelope, sealed and with a return address from the Groft Nursery. Inside I found a single sheet of white bond. The tight lines of print took a while to snap into focus. It began, *My dearest Eve*.

> You once told me how hard it is, after all that happened in your life, to believe that love lasts forever. The very fact that you are reading this, means that our time together was far shorter than I would have hoped. I can only hope as you read this, I had the chance to tell you again how completely and truly you were loved. Nothing, not even death, can change the truth of that, my

love.

Your real and steadying presence in my life has brought me more happiness than most men ever know in a lifetime. That gift was all the more precious, because I had long since ceased to believe that love as we shared it was possible for me. Just the thought of saying, Goodbye is the hardest thing I have ever done. And so, despite everything that has happened to separate us, I will not—cannot do it. Like that ancient namesake of mine, that first flawed and finite Adam, love and life for me began in a garden. Only forget the part about angels and flaming swords. I want it to continue there.

By now my lawyer will have told you the conditions of my will. This is my lasting gift to you—the only way I have left to me to persuade you that the love between us can transcend age and time and death. In my heart, I cannot leave you. I must trust that you will see and know that, in every inch of ground that slips between your fingers, every seed you sow and every perennial you transplant.

Dearest Eve, make our garden grow. You are not alone. I love you now and always.

He was quoting the final lines from *Candide* and the commitment to make our garden grow. The scrawl at the end said simply, *Adam*.

The flashback to our first morning together out on the berm was as intense as it was unexpected. The earth smelled warm and sweet. I was aware of every aching thrust of our shovels and the sweat glistening against our skin. Our lives were connecting even in that moment, long before we knew it, in powerful ways that would change us both forever.

Time had become my enemy and my friend. I couldn't shake the image of my first reluctant drive out to Groft Nurseries and the sight of Adam standing in that greenhouse doorway, at a watershed in his life—and mine. We didn't understand that then. Just as I didn't understand…until this very second, that memories can change lives as well as preserve them. This time, as I remembered the moment, Adam was smiling.

Dutch was right. It is impossible to mourn something like that.

Regrets and grief ultimately have no place in that scenario. Our relationship began with life and goes on with it.

Adam. The lettering blurred as I stared at the sheet of linen bond in my hands. I didn't need to see the words any longer to tell me what to do. That truth was rooted deeper and more permanently inside me than any printed page could ever hope to be.

Outside the lawyer's office, of course, the air was still frigid and the snowbanks were easily three-feet deep. You could have rolled a bowling ball down the Main Street of Xenaphon and not hit a thing. In the distance, I heard the high-pitched wail of the town volunteer fire department siren. It rose to a frantic peak, then fell off again.

My heart was thudding in my chest at the sound. Alongside me, Dutch too was listening. Somewhere out there, people were responding. Not knowing the outcome, but then of course, we never do.

"We can do this, Ma'am," he said. "If that's what you're wondering."

I hadn't noticed it before. But sometime in the last days or weeks, my status had changed from "Miss" or "Missy" to "Ma'am". It was part of the old man's code of ethics, of honor, of simple selfless devotion to those he loved.

"Don't you think it's time you called me Eve?"

Dutch thought about it—his eyes crinkled with laughter. "Adam and Eve," he said. "I always got a kick out of that."

"So did I."

Chapter Thirty-Six

Who loves a garden still his Eden keeps. Amos Bronson
Alcott, 1868

After we left the lawyer's office, Dutch and I drove together to
the chapel. The vicar's car wasn't next door at the parsonage, but the
heavy red door to the sanctuary was unlocked. We went in together. It
was so cold you could see your breath. With the dark woodwork and
narrow windows, it took a while for our eyes to adjust.

Following Dutch's lead, I settled alongside him in a pew near the
front on the left. The window over the altar was of Christ standing at the
seaside, hand outstretched in invitation. Above us on the left side wall, in
stained glass, was an artist's rendition of Mary sitting in the middle of a
sea of lilies in front of the empty tomb. Opposite it—obviously
intentional—was the theme of Adam and Eve in the garden. I didn't need
the brass plate to tell me who the donor was.

"Sara's idea," Dutch said. "She even did the sketches herself. Ya
can imagine what folks around here thought about two naked folk
cavorting in here every Sunday, even if it is from the Bible."

It suddenly occurred to me that when Dutch singled out this
particular pew, it was no accident. In a small church like this, everyone
had their spot on Sunday morning—an unwritten seating chart that
usually went back generations. I ran my hand along the seasoned wood
of the hymnal rack, remembering the story Dutch told me about Adam

playing here as a boy.

A large-print New Testament was wedged next to the Book of Common Prayer in the rack. When I held it in my hand, the book fell open to a well-creased page. Even with the oversize lettering, someone in shaky pencil had highlighted the place that they were trying to find.

The passage was in the Gospel of John. Chapter 14.

"I didn't know you were a church-going man, Dutch."

Dutch looked sheepish. He stared down at his hands, and for what seemed like a long time, he didn't say anything.

"I just come here once in a while and sit," he said. "Think about things."

I read the words a second time. I *will not leave you comfortless*, they said. *I will come to you.*

"You know," Dutch said, "there's a cemetery out back in the churchyard—one of the oldest in the county."

"Sara's buried there?"

Dutch nodded. "Don't go there though. She wouldn't want me to."

I knew Dutch was right. This was Sara's place—where she had left a piece of her heart. In those gardens and flowers in glass, and the stories behind them.

Dutch wasn't finished. "Can't believe Adam would want you trucking out there to a marble tombstone either."

"I've been thinking about that," I said. "Maybe…when the weather gets better…if we had a little service here in the chapel? The girls could come and afterward… we could all go out and weed on the berm. You and I, later—just the two of us…could take his ashes up to Lake Michigan…."

I closed my eyes, overwhelmed by the memory of that Fourth of July watching the sunset over Little Traverse Bay together. What was it Adam said? *If I die tomorrow…you could bury me here. In this time, this moment…I'm a happy man.* There are worse eulogies. There are far worse times to write them.

"You're right, Dutch. He would want me to remember us the way we were that first night together. That Fourth of July…surrounded by the sunset, those deep…unfathomable waters…."

Dutch smiled. "You ought to know…Adam came back to work after that weekend a changed man. Nobody—nothing can take that away

260

from either one of you. Ever."

I felt the tears stinging behind my eyes, but forced them back. The milestones fit. The Fourth of July. Our wedding date. It is what Adam would have wanted.

When Dutch drove me home, Vivian and Artie were waiting for me. It hit me with a jolt of awareness, how very much I had missed them since we had put the garden to bed for the season. They were sitting together in his truck with the motor running alongside the curb. Dutch had pulled his truck into the driveway behind my Taurus. By the time I got out, Vivian was already halfway across the lawn in my direction.

"Eve…honey, we've been so worried about you."

Vivian pulled me into an awkward embrace—rare for her to initiate that kind of overt affection. I could tell she had been crying.

"Dutch and I were out at the cottage last night," I told her. "Making sure things were okay out there."

"Eve…I'm so very, very sorry. Artie heard the emergency call on the scanner. Then later George called—"

"It could have been much, much worse."

Artie had joined us. I had never seen him more unsure of himself. For once this tough, honest bear of a man was speechless.

"Artie, thanks for coming," I told him. "Adam really respected you."

The burly Teamster clapped me on the shoulder. "You just gotta tell us what you need, Kiddo. Anything. We're here."

"I appreciate that."

Even with the reinforcements to my wardrobe I had scrounged from Adam's closet, it was brutally cold in that driveway. Vivian noticed it first.

"You're freezing to death out here," she said.

"Would you like to come in for a bit?"

"We didn't want to intrude—"

"Dutch has been with me since yesterday. He's got to get over to the nursery and make sure the counter girl has been showing up. This is the peak of the Christmas sales rush out there."

Artie, bless him, took charge. "I'll head over there with Dutch," he said. "Viv, you stay and keep Eve company."

And so it began. One by one, I let the garden crew grieve with me in their own way. And one by one, I told them about the meeting with Ellis Fry and helped them to understand what Adam's gift of an endowment for the garden would mean. In the end, the impact for all of us was simple. It meant continuity. It meant hope.

Despite admonishing my daughters to stay at home with their families for Christmas, they came anyway—both of them, with their full entourage including granddaughter Emma's new gerbil—and took charge of the family celebration. They unearthed the presents I had been squirreling away in the attic, wrapped and labeled them for me. They baked, cleaned the house and roasted a Bird. It was wonderful.

Early on Christmas Eve, with Dutch and my other gardening friends in attendance, I hosted a brunch I had not lifted a finger to prepare. When totally out of character my taciturn son-in-law Will proposed a toast to Adam, I was grateful my girls were at my side. Our glasses touched, first Leslie's and then Gina's—message sent...message received. My family was—would be here for me. All of it.

At midnight mass in the stone chapel where Adam had worshiped as a boy and where Dutch and I had mourned together, I took in the flicker of the candlelight and heady scent of the flowers on the altar, grateful for so many things. The flowers were from the greenhouse, in Adam's memory, delicate white roses spilling out of their vases like the snow cascading outside the Eden window.

I shivered. Leslie noticed.

"Are you...cold, Mom...?"

"Just...remembering," I said.

Gina's voice quavered. "Mom, you...know that we love you."

That was the best part of all. I did.

Chapter Thirty-Seven

Gardens are about life. They are about seasons. They teach us about faith and patience. They teach us about flowering, about aging with grace. They teach us to accept the rhythm of things. They teach us about love. Life in a garden isn't about easy. It is about real. Eve Brennerman, "Time in a Garden", *Xenaphon Weekly Gazette*, April 2005.

It has been months since Dutch's frantic call from the nursery. When I walk into the quiet of my living room, Adam's presence still follows me from room to room. The sense of time can hang heavily in the silence. And in such moments, something inside me still cries out—a sharp, agonizing awareness of the solitude.

My boss George hadn't been pressuring me about going back to work but gradually I did. The columns at first were soulless things full of talk about fertilizer and spring planting. Gradually, that is changing. Adam's story and mine, and the adventures of our beloved garden crew, are close to the surface as I write—like the still-frozen berm as the spring sun begins to penetrate deep into that hard ground, warming that rich earth, readying it for the growing season to come.

Two days ago the state actually began moving the garden out on the berm and when it is a little warmer, is pledged to install a new irrigation system to replace Adam and Artie's triumph of duct-tape-and-bailing-wire engineering that had been damaged by the vandals last Fall.

Bea and I are taking turns going out there to supervise. I am thinking about mining that experience for a couple of columns about transplanting—about living with change.

For a long time too the laptop's presence on the dining room table was a joyless reminder of deadlines to come. Tonight? There seems no sense in delaying the inevitable. Another column is due on Friday.

On autopilot, I click on the computer and wait for the screen to run its familiar sequence of checks and counterchecks. By the time I pull out the chair and sit, the menu has fixed itself on the screen. Accessing the word processing program, I call up a blank page and sit staring at it.

The column will keep. Instead I type in a title, center it. TIME IN A GARDEN, it reads. Single-spaced and double indented, I add my favorite garden quote, taped to the keyboard of my laptop:

> *Life began in a garden. We spend our lives trying to return.* Unknown

Then, curving my fingers over the familiar keypad, the words begin to flow. With them flow the tears that still well up from the dark places in my heart, often when I least expect it. Every life has a story just waiting to be told. This is mine. It is only in the telling—the sharing—that our lives become truly human.

We all do battle with stony ground and unseasonable dry spells over the years, I write.

> At sixty-two, I've had my share. To survive, we learn to root out our share of quack grass, turn over spadefuls of spent and decimated ground and plant again. Though we may not call ourselves gardeners, it is the human experience.

About the Author

With Bachelor and Master's degrees in literature from the University of Wisconsin in Madison, author Mary Agria has spent her career writing in and about rural life and communities. Through experience as a college chaplain, director of economic development agencies in Michigan and Pennsylvania, and researcher for the Center for Theology and Land at the University of Dubuque in Iowa, Ms. Agria has come to appreciate in rural life a powerful microcosm of the human search for community. She coauthored *Rural Congregational Handbook: A Guide for Good Shepherds* [Abingdon Press] as well as writing numerous books on community building and labor force issues. Her syndicated column, *Winning the Rat Race*, ran for 20 years in newspapers around the country and a book by that title [Wm. C. Brown, Publishers] was used as a college textbook.

Ms. Agria is proud mother of four daughters and a growing crew of grandchildren. With husband John, a retired university president and professional photographer, Ms. Agria travels extensively from India to Peru, learning about ancient cultures, music and religion. She gardens enthusiastically both at her Long Island, New York home and on a community garden crew while summering in the Methodist chautauqua at Bay View, Michigan where she writes a weekly newsletter column, "Notes from the Garden". Ms. Agria is currently working on a novel set in western Pennsylvania, *Vox Humana,* about the life of a rural church musician and polishing another, *A Community of Scholars*, about politics and intrigue at a struggling liberal arts college.

Editors say of her novels: *The writing is...engaging and the plots and characters intriguing. You have a way of creating community in your novels that [readers will] find very appealing.*

Visit the author online at www.northforknaturals.com

A preview of upcoming novels by author Mary A. Agria...

VOX HUMANA

Still reeling from forced-retirement, job counselor Char Benninger impulsively moves from Philadelphia back to her roots in Hope, a tiny village in western Pennsylvania...full of questions about what to do with the rest of her life. She finds unexpected challenges as organist at a struggling rural church, but even more in her relationship with the priest of the tiny Episcopal parish she has decided to serve. A desperation venture to save the economically at-risk community—by creating a liturgical weaving studio in the church undercroft—helps set Char on a journey that will shake her assumptions about life and love to their very foundations.

Named for a stop on pipe organs that imitates the sound of the human voice, *Vox Humana* is a life affirming story about music, weaving, and community...the compelling search for what we are called to do with our time and gifts.

from the Prologue...

If we are lucky or persistent or both, there are moments in our lives when who we are and what we do—our inner and our external lives—come together. In such moments, we catch a profound glimpse of why we exist and where our lives are headed. *Finding our voice*, vocal coaches and writing instructors sometimes describe it.

As for the rest of the time? Fortunately, it is not our mistakes that define us, but our ability to strike that first terrifying note and then move on.

In my job as a career counselor for 30 years, I tried to make sense of that regroup-and-go-on process for thousands of clients worn down by unemployment or a lack of purpose in their working lives. Strange, how unsettling it can be to be forced by circumstances to take one's own advice.

. . . *Be careful what you wish for*, the thought occurred to me. We all what-if about that far-off day when we can shuck off the constraints of eight-to-five living and have all the time in the world to live and be as we choose. Fiction had become fact.

I was retired. I was free. I was on my own. And I had never been more terrified of anything in my life.

A COMMUNITY OF SCHOLARS

Professor A.J. Ferinelli has devoted his life to academe, as a scholar and teacher of political science at a small liberal arts college in central Pennsylvania. Grieving over the death of his young wife and unborn son, he shuts himself off from everything but his students, as he clings to his untested faith in the integrity of the scholarly life. When a young woman faculty member comes to him—in desperation—for advice and support, A.J. finds himself thrust into an anything-but-civilized world of intrigue, violence and betrayal that threaten not only his assumptions about the academic community but the future of Bolland College itself.

from Chapter One

A woman—in jeans and a blazer, briefcase in hand—had taken up vigil in the corridor outside A.J. Ferinelli's basement office in the Academic Center. It wasn't an everyday occurrence at seven o'clock on a Thursday morning in October. But certainly an improvement, A.J. decided, over coming across the night janitor finishing his rounds.

The woman's back was turned, her dark hair in an intriguing twist at the nape of her neck. She didn't hear him coming. They had installed new carpet over the tile flooring of the building a month ago.

"Looking for someone—?"

She swung around in his direction. It was a trifle too quick, anxious.

"Professor Ferinelli...? we talked—at the faculty meeting a couple of months ago. The schedule on the door says you come in early on Thursdays."

A stack of essay exams tucked under one arm made it hard to maneuver, but A.J. managed to shift his briefcase and keys so he could shake her hand.

Her grasp matched her eye contact, straightforward. What A.J. read in her face told him whatever brought her here at the crack of dawn? It was not to discuss class scheduling.

Visit the author online at www.northforknaturals.com